The Butterfly Hunter and the King

and other stories

by

Niko Zinovii

Zinovii Art Studio

Santa Monica, California

chrysos
argyros
chalkos

Published by: Zinovii Art Studio
Santa Monica, California
www.zinoviiartstudio.com

ISBN: 978-0-9860685-6-0   (trade paperback)
ISBN: 978-0-9860685-7-7   (ebook: ePub)
ISBN: 978-0-9860685-8-4   (ebook: mobi)
LCCN: 2019905348

First Edition, 2019
Printed in the United States of America

The Butterfly Hunter and the King
and other stories

Dedication

To those who imagine

Contents

Opening Note from the Author   1

Stories

The Butterfly Hunter and the King   3
A tale of a young man who, searching for something
missing from his past, travels to a remote Fijian isle,
where he encounters something ancient and unknown
to the outside world.

                                                              47

The Million Eyes of Nobo Savu
A tale about a psychiatrist who believes he has a rational
explanation for UFOs, only to learn otherwise.

Hollow Boat
A tale set in Japan in 1803, featuring a poor bamboo   93
cutter who, along with the fishermen of his village,
encounters a mysterious castaway.

The Psychonauts
A tale about a man who has committed a crime so   107
offensive to humankind he is sentenced to imprisonment
for a thousand years.

To Rise Again
A tale of a man who falls in love with a deceased woman   151
and what happens as they journey together into the
unknown.

Down, Down, Down   173
A tale about a man who takes his bathyscaphe into the
depths of the sea to discover the secret of Japan's
Atlantis.

Dancing with Sirkka
A tale about a young man who is struggling to uncover   225
the point of existence, and experiences love and
witnesses a most astonishing event along the way.

Ending Note from the Author   268

Opening Note from the Author

Contained in this book are seven tales of speculative fiction that this author wrote from August 2017 to April 2019. They are presented chronologically in the order in which they were written. They can be read in any order.

The title of this book, *The Butterfly Hunter and the King*, is the title of the first story contained within.

Niko Zinovii
Santa Monica, CA
30 April 2019

Niko Zinovii

The Butterfly Hunter and the King

~1~

Egon Bruck, a slender, young Austrian, cut the outboard engine of his small rowboat a half-mile out from the remote and uninhabited island of Tuvuca. The sun had just begun to rise, and he could see the silhouette of the island, quite pronounced, in the offing, rising to approximately eight hundred feet above sea level.

Egon excitedly checked his instruments: latitude -17° 40' 16" S, longitude -178° 49' 17" W. *Yes, yes.* It was indeed Tuvuca. He had successfully traversed the distance of twenty-seven nautical miles over the predawn hours, having left the neighboring island of Lakeba, of Fiji's eastern Lau Group, shortly after 3:30 a.m., traveling at a steady nine knots.

Turning himself about, Egon popped his craft's short oars into place and began to row, taking slow, steady strokes. As he did so, he smiled to himself, for he had done it. He had defied the Fijian government's decades-old decree forbidding any visitation of Tuvuca. He even laughed as he thought of how Fijian officials had recently gone as far as to spread a rumor that a lion was loose on the island, to keep away the curious.

There had once been a small, traditional village on Tuvuca, but plans to work the island's untapped phosphate deposits never materialized, and little by little the islanders had left, seeking work in Suva. Shortly after the last of the inhabitants had sailed off, the island had been deemed restricted. No official reason had ever been given as to why. Egon suspected it was to protect the island's valuable timber.

As the sun rose still higher, the sea sparkled around Egon with a beautiful turquoise translucence. A lone seagull flapped by, soaring aloft, rising upward into the heavens. Egon thought of how, from up high, the vast archipelago that was Fiji must have resembled green champagne bubbles afloat upon the deep blue Pacific.

He glanced over his shoulder to view Tuvuca, glimpsing its volcanic peaks, its lush, intense, densely wooded forests of sandalwood and teak. He had planned this excursion for months. Ever since being sent to Lakeba on assignment, to take inventory of that island's outstanding hardwoods. This unauthorized side trip would give him the chance to dream, to play, to shut out for a time the demands of the present.

Egon sunk one oar deep and held it there for a moment, correcting his course of travel, aiming his boat toward the narrow and shallow passage in the reef that was one of the few entrances into the island's protected lagoon, into which no large or deep-keeled vessels could enter.

Egon then stopped rowing and spun about to fully face Tuvuca, allowing the swift current to take him in. Reef-rimmed, partly volcanic, partly coral limestone, Tuvuca was breathtaking. Over five square miles of Miocene-age beauty, covered by nearly a hundred different species of trees.

As Egon went over the side, splashing down into the warm waist-deep water, to pull his boat to the shore, he heard something quite unexpected. He stiffened and stopped. It had sounded like the distant roar of... a lion... He waited, motionless. But the sound did not repeat itself. There was a crash of a far-off wave on the reef. It rumbled noisily, almost like a growl, the growl of a wave. Slowly, Egon nodded. *Yes*, he told himself, *it must have, it had to have been a wave…*

~2~

Egon strained as he pulled his small craft across a stretch of wet, white sand and then a few dozen yards up a freshwater stream that was flowing out of the coastal forest of coconuts trees. There, he securely tied the boat to a large rock, where it was completely out of sight from the sea. He even tossed a number of fallen palm fronds over it for good measure, hiding it completely.

"That should do it," Egon said to himself, cheerfully. Slipping on his backpack, he assembled his netted pole and walked up the gentle slope of the island. Passing a number of dark seaside grottos, he felt rather like an adventurer. And for a moment, just a moment, he fancied himself a modern-day Alfred Russel Wallace. It made him smile.

Reaching level ground, he stopped beneath a canopy of coconuts and stood there, looking at himself. Dressed all in white—hat, shirt, shorts, socks, shoes—and carrying his two-foot-deep white net, attached to its six-foot-long white pole, he realized that he must have been quite a romantic and comedic sight. The stereotypical fantasy image of a young European, blonde-haired and blue-eyed butterfly hunter, appearing more adolescent than adult. Yes, it was a rare hobby for a twenty-seven-year-old: butterfly hunter. He understood full well that he was living out an unlikely fantasy. But he embraced it, fully. This was his fantasy, his escape.

Egon pulled out his map and scrutinized it, planning his route. He would for now make his way through the coastal forest, enjoying the shade offered by its low canopy, traversing the uplifted and exposed weathered limestone that lay beneath it. Slowly, he would make his way inland, into the hilly interior and the forests of the volcanic uplands, to Tuvuca's one freshwater lake. Egon found himself smiling as he recalled how according to legend, the lake's fish had been dropped into it by a Tongan deity flying high over the island, on her way to visit her lover.

Egon took a compass heading, north by northeast, put away his map, and headed inland. He soon entered a spectacular bamboo forest, where there was a *splash!* and a *splat!* as a passing light, tropical rain started to fall, to pitter-patter. This caused Egon to look up, and when he did so he experienced the unexpected ethereal sight of the gently swaying, towering bamboo. The forest, like a cathedral grown by nature, thrilled Egon's soul, instilling in him a religious-like sense of awe, a sense of beauty that was intensified by his realistic recognition of life's temporality—his eyes dropping to the ground, he looked for and saw the young bamboo shoots pushing up through the decaying stalks of fallen giants claimed by time.

~3~

As Egon hiked farther inland, he entered the island's secondary forest, which was less rocky and had a greater canopy height. He observed the different trees in absolute delight, identifying each species as he passed it: *Alphitonia zizyphoides, Dysoxylum richii, Pleiogynium timorense,* and *Melicope cucullata. Annona muricata, Barringtonia edulis, Cocos nucifera, Mangifera indica, Pometia pinnata,* and *Bischofia javanica.* The overall richness of the number of species was amazing. Here there were plant and tree species undisturbed by the outside world, isolated for tens of thousands of years.

Egon noticed *Alangium vitiense, Cryptocarya hornei,* and *Maniltoa floribunda* species regenerating in the understory. The forest had apparently been disturbed by a cyclone, he surmised, likely not more than one year ago.

No tree stumps, he observed, and nodded in approval. The government's rumor of a lion seemed to have been working quite effectively in keeping illegal loggers off the island.

Egon then laughed at himself, realizing how immediately transfixed he had become by the trees. But he could not help it. He was an arboriculturist by profession, a tree surgeon who specialized in diagnosis and treatment, in the pruning, study, and cataloguing of individual trees, and he truly loved his work. But he loved his new hobby even more.

He smiled fondly as he thought back to one year ago, when he had begun educating himself on the order Lepidoptera (butterflies and moths). He treasured all those satisfying hours spent hidden away in the Bishop Museum, in Honolulu, going through old bulletins that recorded the findings of early fauna and flora expeditions to various south Pacific islands. At a young age, he had come to realize that the more he explored, the less he felt he knew, and the more he wanted to know. And so he had embraced the idea that education was not something one could ever finish. This had become his rule to live by.

Butterfly eggs... Egon stopped and reverently examined the tiny, beautiful yellow pinheads that lay clustered together atop a broad, green fern. Slowly, silently, with anticipation, he looked about. He peered at the surrounding wildflowers, beneath leaves and branches, hoping to spot a butterfly at rest, drinking nectar, or roosting. Perhaps he would spy a double-spotted line blue, a butterfly of the family Lycaenidae, of the species *Nacaduba biocellata.* The males, blue with narrow black margins, were particularly attractive. No... Nothing... Not yet.

Shrugging lightheartedly, Egon continued his inland trek.

~4~

The mixed pinewoods thinned, and Egon used his binoculars to briefly survey the verdant, jungle-clad mountainside that lay ahead. He took the opportunity to sip from his canteen. He then sat upon an old log, took off his right boot, and removed a pebble from within it. It felt good to have his foot set free from the boot, so he removed the other.

Stretching out his legs, he relaxed and made himself comfortable. There were nearly one thousand species of butterfly in Fiji. And he had yet to see one... But it was still quite early in the day. Butterflies usually made their appearance shortly before noon.

Egon thought of pulling out his guidebook, *The Butterfly and I,* but he decided not to. The forest before him was too beautiful: tropical flowers blossoming everywhere, bending in the soft South Sea breeze, indifferent to the outside world.

Egon felt the coolness of a passing cloud, high overhead, and its pleasant comfort pulled him into a meditative state, which set his perception utterly free to wander. Looking up, he noticed the daytime moon, faint and powdery, silent. For all of man's history, Luna had hung there overhead, so remote, like tiny, isolated Tuvuca.

It was then, at that serene moment, that the roar permeated the air over Tuvuca. It was a raw, rough, vibratory growl, coming from seemingly nowhere, and then suddenly it was everywhere, like thunder birthed in a storm. It was something that stretched and sheered the very air as it moved through it.

Egon leapt to his feet, standing absolutely rigid, wide eyed. As the sound subsided and vanished, his mind struggled to analyze it. This had been no wave crashing on a reef. It was something that seemed to come from deep within... the body of something. Yet it did not sound entirely natural, so forceful was it, so loud, so utterly different than anything he had ever heard... *Could it have been artificially produced?* he wondered.

Although it had shaken the island, or seemed to, Egon guessed it had originated miles away.

And there was something else... strange and paradoxical. The leonine roar, though mighty enough to have been meant for the distant moon, carried upon it, within it, a hint of weakness and... pain?

In his mind, Egon pictured giant golden paws, and the shaggy mane of a lion...

No. Egon shook his head. *There is no lion on this island. It's something else...*

~5~

Egon entered the island's mid-successional forest, which was rocky and of shorter canopy height, filled with shade-tolerant plant species, abundant in birds. It was lovely, yet Egon's carefree smile was absent, his countenance most serious, wary.

Suddenly, emerging brightly, beautifully, from the bushes floated a butterfly. It was pearl gray in color, radiating to burnt orange along the periphery of its wings. A set of false eyes, yellow with black pupils, decorated its hindwings.

Deudorix epijarbas, Egon found himself immediately identifying the species in his mind. *A cornelian.*

Come to me, little butterfly, Egon's thoughts whispered as he silently readied his net. To catch a butterfly in flight was difficult. He knew this from experience. The trick was to follow it, wait for it to land. Sneak up on it, slowly, from behind. And Egon did just this.

As he crept up on the resting butterfly, he found himself marveling at how well camouflaged it was. If he had not seen it in flight, he likely would not have noticed it at rest, where it had landed.

Egon swept his net forward, but he missed. And the butterfly was aloft again, flapping to the left, to the right, up and down, all around.

Egon went chasing after it, strategically waving his pole around, full of youthful enthusiasm. He realized that he must have appeared charmingly theatrical, but he did not care. He was a butterfly hunter.

He swept the net forward quickly, immediately collapsing and folding it over so that the butterfly within could not escape. "Ah-ha!"

Bringing the net to the forest floor, kneeling beside it, Egon softly flattened it so that it forced the butterfly's wings to close, to fold together.

Reaching into the net, he then gently took hold of the butterfly by the thorax and abdomen. He was careful not to squeeze—even though the time-old technique was to squeeze until the butterfly stopped struggling, until the butterfly was dead, a small act of violence in the name of science.

Instead, Egon, with his other hand, removed a small digital scanner from his pack and, holding the device a few inches distant, panned it over his catch from a few important angles, positioning the butterfly with extreme care. He next optically measured its wingspan: thirty millimeters.

When he was done, he observed the butterfly closely, marveling at its delicate, exquisite beauty. He then stroked it once, softly, affectionately, and let it go. As it flapped away, Egon felt himself imbued with the air of mystery and romance that was the natural world. He breathed it in, appreciating being alive, celebrating in his heart the beauty of the day. Knowing that life was brief. Content that he had not caused the little butterfly's life to be any shorter than it would otherwise have been.

But slowly, Egon's moment of serenity dissolved, until he thought only of the unusual roar that had torn through the air. The sound that had shaken the island so terribly. Putting his scanner away, he looked about warily.

… I think it came from the north…

Yet Egon proceeded on his original course, north by northeast.

~6~

Egon found himself paying little attention to the species of trees. With a heightened alertness, he listened intently, his eyes searching the jungle as he walked.

For some odd reason, he found himself recalling how a colleague of his had once asked him why he went to the trouble of hunting butterflies when he could simply collect caterpillars instead and watch them develop into butterflies. His friend did not understand the difference between being a collector and a hunter.

And Egon suddenly wondered if a different type of hunter might be stalking him at that very moment, a lion concealed somewhere within the forest…

Egon pushed the foliage before him aside and jumped back, startled. For directly in front of him—moments ago hidden by the jungle—was a lone totem pole. It was very old and large, made of a resilient hardwood. It must have stood nine feet in height. There were seven heads carved upon it, each stacked atop another, all gods of ancient Polynesia, gods of the wind and sea. Except for the head sitting at the very top of the pole. It looked rather like a lion… A broad-snouted, maneless lion with tiny eyes and small triangular ears, one of them half broken away.

The longer Egon looked at the carved lion's head, the less it looked to him like a lion and the stranger it seemed.

11

He wondered if this was perhaps because it was so zoomorphic in style. Or maybe because it was not meant to be a lion at all, but something else entirely…

As Egon wondered about it, drums abruptly sounded out from somewhere within the forest nearby. The unexpectedness of the drums gave Egon quite a fright, and it took him several moments to compose himself. When his critical thinking finally returned, he listened carefully.

The drums were loud. Close by. The sound was all wood, heavy wooden clubs beating upon big, hollowed-out logs, Egon guessed. The drumming seemed ceremonial in cadence, its rhythm mimicking the spoken intonations of the South Seas, likely a Polynesian tongue. *Polynesian, like the deities carved on the totem pole. Why not Melanesian? Why not Fijian? These are Fijian waters…*

The sound must have carried over the expanse of the entire island. It was almost hypnotic, the way it altered between high and low, those jungle drums.

Who else can be on this island? Egon wondered. After all, Tuvuca was officially off limits to everyone.

Overcome by curiosity, he altered his course to follow the sound of the drums.

~7~

Egon considered turning back when he encountered the vertical spears, their points embedded deeply into the earth, their long shafts topped by old skulls of what seemed to be wild boar… surely a warning not to trespass further. But he was now so close.

Tiptoeing past the skulls, Egon crept up to and knelt beside a huge, fallen *Pisonia* tree, concealing himself behind it, leaning into its soft, weak wood, which was rapidly decaying into the forest floor. He could feel his heart beating excitedly—for in a secret jungle recess, a mere twenty yards before him, lay the source of the mysterious drumming.

Slowly, ever so slowly, Egon peeked over the top of the fallen *Pisonia*. There were half a dozen natives in a small clearing. All were bare-footed, bare-chested males. Two were beating clubs upon hollowed-out logs, as Egon had surmised. Of the remaining four, two were quite lean, young, in their mid-teens, boys; the other two were middle aged, authoritative in bearing.

They were all taller than Fijians, and with markedly lighter skin. They lacked the Negroid features and wavy hair of the Melanesians. And their clothing: all but one of them wore the distinctive *ta'ovala,* a pandanus-leaf mat worn wrapped about the waist, secured by a cord of coconut fiber. They were Tongans.

Egon could see the great courage in their hearts carried openly upon their faces. So unlike the Fijians he had encountered on Lakeba, who, although happy, held in their eyes a distant look of hopelessness, a lack of vision.

Tongans on the forbidden Fijian isle of Tuvuca? Egon could not understand it. The isles of Tonga lay over four hundred nautical miles distant. But then Egon remembered once reading how the southeast trade winds had made it easy in the past for Tongan warlords to sail to Fiji's Lau Islands and exert their hegemony there.

The sixth native, Egon came to notice, wore a *lavalava,* a solid-colored sarong hanging to the knee. He was a Samoan.

Five Tongans and a Samoan…

Egon slowly began to pick out additional details that had at first escaped his notice. The middle-aged Tongan had a magnificent split whale's tooth dangling about his neck. This was of exceptional significance. This man was likely a divine chieftain. Half of the short-leaf pandanus strips worn by him were decorative, painted either dull yellowy brown or crimson red.

The traditional skirts of the drummers were unpainted, old and torn, signifying the fact that these men were commoners, of low rank in Tonga's highly stratified society.

The *ta'ovala* worn by the two boys were identical, plain and cut short, like a war skirt, hanging to mid-thigh. Despite the intense, complex face paint worn by the two boys, Egon could see that they were brothers. *Fraternal twins*, he guessed. Egon also noticed the family resemblance between the brothers and the chief. They were his sons.

The drummers began to chant, and the two boys took their positions, lying face down upon long sheets of dark *masikuvui* cloth.

The Samoan uttered sacred words and raised half a coconut shell, filled with a sooty black liquid: the pigment of candlenut.

And Egon suddenly understood what he was observing. The Samoan was a *tufuga,* from Samoa. Only a non-Tongan could perform *tatatau* services in certain sacred Tongan ceremonies. This Samoan was a *tufuga tatatau*. Ta: To strike. *Tatau:* Repeatedly. *Tatatau:* To strike repeatedly.

The boys were to endure the painful rite that would visibly mark their cultural identity. This was the time-old ritual by which these adolescents would become Tongan men.

But why here? Why on Tuvuca? So far from Tonga? Egon still could not make any sense of it.

The Samoan picked up a long handle of bone attached to a small adze-like instrument, pointed by a shark's tooth. Dipping the tooth into the coconut shell, he began to tap the sooty pigment into one of the boy's skin, and the tattooing began.

The Samoan started a chant of his own, in Samoan. Egon wondered what the words meant, for he had not a clue. If he had spoken Samoan, he would have understood that the

Samoan, the *tufuga tatatau,* was invoking the spirit of the land breeze to cool the pain of his subjects. The Samoan next called out to the boys' ancestors, to help guide them through this rite of passage.

The rhythm of the tapping soon mirrored the beating of the drums. The chanting, the drumming, the cadence of the tattooing, it all became trancelike—so much so that Egon completely lost himself in the ceremony, so deeply did it cast its South Seas spell over him.

It was the unexpected, thunderous roar that abruptly yanked Egon back to reality. As before, it was a sound that tore through the air, shredding it, booming, echoing, suddenly everywhere although it came from a distance.

So startled was Egon that he actually, once again, leapt to his feet. And he stood there rigid, motionless, until the uncanny roar faded and vanished. It took several utterly silent moments—no drums, no chanting—before Egon felt their stares.

Egon saw that the Tongans and the Samoan did not appear at all surprised by the tremendous roar from the mountains. But they were surprised to see him. Very surprised.

"Mālō... 'etau... lava." Egon did his best to say hello in Tongan, struggling to remember the phrase. And he forced a smile. It usually went a long way in the South Pacific.

But Egon felt himself shiver as he witnessed the drummers slowly picking up spurred clubs, the weapons of foot soldiers.

The chieftain growled some order, and the two boys spun about, picking up long, narrow tubes of bamboo. This puzzled Egon, until he saw the Tongans bring the tubes to their lips and blow fiercely.

The first dart whistled past Egon, the feathers along its shaft brushing his right ear. The second dart, bone tipped, struck him in the shoulder, painfully. Instinctively, he quickly swatted at it, knocking it loose from his body. It dropped to the forest floor, now blood stained, its wrinkled feathers shining iridescently in the sunlight.

Oh God. Egon's thoughts raced as he realized that the blow dart was likely laced with some incapacitating drug or deadly poison. *Why?*

And Egon ran off, feeling that his life depended on it. Rather than running to the south, to the lagoon and his boat, he instinctively ran eastward, deeper into the jungle, seeking the safety of the trees. It was not long before he heard the two young Tongans, fast and agile, bounding through the foliage as they gave chase. Egon, the butterfly hunter, had suddenly become the hunted.

~8~

Egon quickly reasoned that his only chance to evade his pursuers was to do the unexpected. And so he turned about and began racing back toward them. He ran as fast as he could, covering as much ground as was possible in the precious seconds that he had. Just when he saw the jungle foliage parting before him, he dove for cover behind the upturned roots of a fallen tree.

The young Tongans ran straight past him, intent on catching up to their fleeing quarry—a man whom they had last seen running for his life. A man who they assumed must still be twenty to thirty seconds ahead of them.

Egon held his breath as he waited for the young Tongans to disappear from sight, which they did quickly, being fleet of foot.

It was as Egon rose that he felt the first terrible effects of the drug that had been darted into him. His eyes ached, his vision blurred, his heart thumped, and his balance faltered. *Oh no...*

Egon forcibly turned himself about, to face north, and he ran off as best he could, arms outstretched, unsteady, wobbling on his feet. Several times he crashed to the ground, but each time he pushed himself upright and kept going. He was unsure if there was a poison circulating within him, about to kill him, or if something milder was about to render him unconscious. If it was poison, he would soon be dead. If it was not, he knew that he must now put as much distance between himself and the Tongans as he possibly could. And so he ran, half blind, his left arm dropping, hanging paralyzed at his side, all pins and needles.

The forest began to whirl about Egon in his blurred, drugged vision, like a pinwheel all the shades of green, dotted by splotches of intense color. *Tropical flowers?*

Slowly, the colors took on an odd, unsettling, sharp texture. And he felt an aversion to the vegetation. Yellows became radiant, like undulating waves of searing heat, reds darkened to deep, contorted purples, and blues blackened to lonely, funereal splotches of darkness.

Egon lost all sense of direction as he forced himself onward. For all he knew, he was accidentally doubling back to the Tongan's sacred clearing. He suddenly barked out a laugh at the thought of this. *The effects of the drug?* He then shushed himself, quite sternly, and fought off an uncontrollable urge to giggle. And then to cry, out of stark fear, as he suddenly felt convinced that he was being pursued by some ill-defined, unfathomable thing of horror. *Tuvuca's lion?*

In his head Egon suddenly heard the drums beating again, loud, angry. The sound permeated the jungle. Was the drumming real? Or was it an auditory hallucination brought on by the blow dart?

Egon's legs went numb and felt weighty, uncoordinated, and he floundered feebly, but he forced himself onward. For he dimly understood somewhere in his brain that if the dart had been tipped by poison, he would have been dead by now. But he was not. The dart must have been meant to merely incapacitate him, to enable his capture. Something he knew he must not allow.

Egon's sense of time began to falter, to become terribly warped, to slip helplessly away from him. As he ran, in his stupor, it seemed as if entire days were passing rather than minutes. He felt himself freefalling through time… He shivered with terror and cried out in horror.

Slowly, ever so slowly, he realized that he was no longer running but crawling. *How long have I been crawling? For a thousand years? Tired… so tired…*

The isle of Tuvuca blurred and the world dropped away, the present tumbling into the past. Egon experienced a jarring, distorted sense of self and a flood of mental anguish. Somehow he was once again that eight-year-old boy crawling from the wreckage of the automobile accident that had tragically claimed the lives of his parents, leaving him an orphan.

Wracked by unutterable pain and exhaustion, Egon's mind and body screamed out in agony, and he finally surrendered completely to the drug, his world going instantly black.

~9~

Tock. Tock. Spring water dripping upon mossy rocks.

Egon slowly regained consciousness to find himself deep in tropical woodland, lying prostrate, one arm tucked beneath him, the other stretched out in front of him. He sat up and removed his backpack, shaking his one arm to bring feeling back into it. *I'm alive…*

He listened. *No drums…*

He noticed that the forest floor beneath him was a deep red. He was somewhere on one of Tuvuca's interior volcanic slopes, although the forest here was level. All around him were figs and fallen leaves—leathery and glossy green. He looked up to see that he was sitting beneath a magnificent, leafy banyan tree, its many prop roots, as thick as trunks, spreading out laterally through the forest.

Ficus prolixa. Egon unintentionally identified the species of banyan in his mind, out of habit.

He noted the position of the sun. It was late in the day. Five or six hours must have passed since he fled the tattooing ritual. He looked at his watch—*yes, 4:20.* The sun would set in about an hour and a half.

He was about to reach for his compass within his pack when he noticed the natural spring behind him, trickling into a tiny pool. He shuffled over to it, cupped his hands, and drank from it. He then proceeded to refill his canteen as he sat there beneath the banyan tree, his legs weary, his mind weary.

Slowly, his vision focused past the spring. As his eyes absorbed what lay before him, so did his mind. At first, he did not understand what he was seeing, so unexpected a sight it was. It took his intellect many seconds to accept what his vision was displaying to him.

Not more than a dozen paces distant was the mouth of a great cave. And before that cave, aloof and silent like a Buddha, lying upon a gathering of leafless twigs, a melon oddly clutched tightly to its chest, was Tuvuca's "lion."

Egon nearly died of fright. Silent seconds ticked by. Egon's instincts were screaming for him to flee, but his shocked mind held him rooted, absolutely transfixed.

The lion wagged its long tail, toying with a small butterfly. Only this was not a lion at all. It was the size of a lion, roughly the shape of a lion, but it was not really an animal… It seemed something carved from wood, yet it was somehow alive.

In look, it was the lion of the ancient totem pole that Egon had encountered: a lion-man-beast hydride. Broad-snouted, maneless, tiny eyes, small triangular ears, one of them half broken away…

It grinned at Egon intelligently, with a face wrinkled by untold years of time. Egon trembled. This lion, this creature, was unlike anything he had ever imagined. It seemed something that stood in the gulf that lay between plant and man and animal, an impossible thing from some parallel universe. Yet it was here, on Tuvuca, right before him.

"Toro voleka." The lion's deep, fibrous voice was like two great trees gnashing together to produce sounds and words.

It can talk…

It sounded Fijian, the language, but Egon had no idea what the words meant. But the lion's voice was male—of that, Egon had no doubt.

The lion's small eyes regarded Egon, looking him up and down. Moments ticked by. Egon felt himself bowing his head obeisantly, so overwhelmed was he by what he intuitively sensed in this impossible joining of manlike intellect to animal strength and instinct to treelike resilience. For Egon felt convinced that this lion, possessing the qualities of all, surpassed all.

As Egon stared at the lion, he found himself in awe of the incredible creature. It truly appeared as if it were composed of wood, tawny golden wood—he could even see what appeared to be the grain of the wood. The texture was quite handsome, the mixture of its grain patterns unique as it combined both straight and cross-grain forms, the cross grain showing extreme spiraling and artistic diagonal deviations. On the lion's torso, in its trunk wood, beneath its arms, were dark circular knots, around which the rest of the wood fibers flowed. The lion looked so utterly unnatural, yet simultaneously like a thing of nature.

"Toe ofi ange." The lion growled its words, coarse, woodily, irritated.

Now Tongan? Egon guessed. *Something that looks as much tree as it does animal is attempting to communicate with me?*

"… I don't understand," Egon responded, his voice trembling a bit.

"English!" the lion bellowed.

"Yes." Egon nodded, frightened yet fascinated. "English."

"Come closer," the lion ordered, this time saying it in English.

"… No," Egon answered.

"Why?"

"Because…" Egon explained, "In my mind, I can see my footprints leading to you… but none leading away…"

The lion once again regarded Egon, staring at him in silence for a long moment. "The powerful are not to be trusted?" the lion finally rumbled angrily, affronted.

Egon nodded, slowly, admitting it.

"I will do you no harm, white one." The lion's voice dropped low.

Egon sat there stone faced, wondering if he should attempt to run off.

"I am old and weak…" the lion beseeched Egon. "Lonely…"

Egon found himself touched by the sadness and frustration he sensed in the lion's voice. He decided to trust it. He rose and slowly walked over to the creature, standing before it.

And the lion rose, mightily, for a split second standing upon its hindquarters like a great man-beast, towering over Egon. Almost immediately it pounced forward. Its huge paws—each a foot wide—smacked forcefully upon Egon's shoulders. The enormous weight of the lion instantly sent

Egon hurtling backward, crashing to the forest floor. It was as if a great tree had fallen upon him.

Egon gasped to breathe. The weight and power of the lion were absolutely terrifying. Pinned, helpless, Egon watched in horror as the great beast reared back its head and roared.

Like booming thunder, the ear-shattering roar was instantly everywhere, tearing through the atmosphere, shredding the very air. For Egon, it felt as if all the miles of sky above him suddenly collapsed as a downpour of tangible sound, intent on pelting the life out of him.

It took forever for the roar to subside and vanish. When it did, Egon found his ears ringing, momentarily deafened. Although he could not hear his own words, he found himself speaking them nevertheless.

"Please…" he begged the lion as he watched a mighty paw lift up high, preparing to strike him dead. "Forgive me… for having doubted… your words…"

The lion hesitated and lowered its wide head, its tiny eyes looking deep into Egon's.

"… Please…" Egon pleaded again. "I'll find some way… to return your mercy…"

Slowly, the lion dropped its threatening paw and slumped back, weak, exhausted, setting Egon free. Silent, it pawed its melon toward itself and began to eat it, rind and all.

Egon sat up, gasping, struggling to catch his breath. He was about to scamper off, but he noticed the lion's pensive countenance. Slowly, the lion turned to him. Egon could see the nearby mountains reflected majestically in the creature's eyes.

"I once knew power greater than storms," the lion said to Egon wistfully. "I was like a great wind that could fell the largest tree. I was a king. But now… I only know the weakness of old age. The pain of it."

"The pain of it?" Egon asked.

"I'm without an end," the lion explained, its voice mournful, distressed. "I never learned how to die. Everyone's journey through this world is not the same. Whatever mine is, I cannot understand it. I only know that I have grown old and feeble, my hide weather beaten. Can you understand the pain of one who was once so powerful, now unable to protect himself?"

Egon thought about it. "No. I don't believe I can. I've never been powerful."

Egon noticed a number of odd lacerations scarring the lion's shoulders and upper arms. "What are those?"

"My pain," the lion growled woodily. "I was as good as I was great! Generous! Forgiving! But those who have forgotten past favors now kick me in my weakness. And I suffer the base insult... They cut me and run away, calling it bravery."

"... The Tongans?" Egon guessed.

The lion let loose a loud growl, but then fell silent, fatigued.

"What are you?" Egon could not help but ask the lion. "Where are you from?"

"A good question," the lion admitted, calming. "And it deserves an answer. But I have none. I do not know. I know I did not swim here. I would have sunk like a stone."

"What do you remember?" Egon probed. "What's your earliest memory?"

And Egon sat there captivated as the lion lowered its great head in thought. "I remember... looking up and seeing the moon. I was dropped from the moon."

... Or from beyond the moon? Egon's thoughts rumbled. *From somewhere where plants are more like animals?* And Egon thought about how different this creature of living wood truly was. *Life is made up of infinite possibilities...*

"I was dropped from a great bird," the lion went on, "into the hands of a holy man who raised me as his own. But this is legend. I do not remember this. I only remember... a feeling."

"What feeling?"

And Egon saw the sadness of a child pall the lion's face.

"Being abandoned," the lion made it clear.

Abandonment... Egon knew this feeling intimately. It was a feeling that had haunted his heart for so long, since the loss of his parents. He too felt abandoned, even though it had not been his parents' intent. Could a similar accident have happened to this lion creature? Could an exploratory spacecraft from some distant world have crashed here on Earth, long ago, with this lion, a cub then, the sole survivor?

"Why are you on my island?" the lion asked Egon.

"Tuvuca is your island?"

"I am its king."

"But to be a king without a people..." Egon thought of how the islanders of Tuvuca's small village had all departed many years ago.

"For all my youth," the lion responded, its voice achingly forlorn, "I was alone on Tuvuca. Running, playing. Happy. When dark ones of your kind, the *Kai Vanua,* first came to my island, I hated them. But slowly, I grew to love them. And now, without them... it is lonely... But where my subjects went, I could not follow. I am rooted to this land. I have been king here from the time when the sea was low, when Tuvuca stretched for many days to the south... I remember how large Tuvuca once was. I remember that."

"When the sea was low..." Egon realized almost immediately that this could only mean during Earth's last glacial period, when so much more of the planet's water had been locked up in ice. When Tuvuca had been physically joined to

Lakeba and other nearby Lau islands, due to the drop in sea level. *This lion has been on Tuvuca since the Ice Age?*

Egon searched his memory. The last glacial period had ended over eleven thousand years ago…

In shock, Egon looked at the lion anew. Could this strange creature be thousands of years old? He then half smiled as he remembered Earth's bristlecone pine, *Pinus longaeva.* There was one in the White Mountains of California that was over five thousand years old. And bristlecone pines elsewhere nearly as old… There was an olive tree in Portugal well over three thousand years old, displaying longevity similar to the *Sequoiadendron giganteum,* the giant sequoia. *Trees don't grow old the same way animals do…*

Egon recalled that Earth's last glacial period began roughly a hundred and ten thousand years ago, continuing, interspersed by warm interglacial periods, until the last of the ice melted. It was as Egon thought of the ice that he stood up, stunned.

"I—I recognize you," Egon mumbled numbly to the lion. "I know what you are. You're like the Ulmer sculpture. You're a Löwenmensch. A lion-man."

And Egon explained to the lion its remarkable resemblance to the oldest known figurative sculpture in the world, which dated back to over thirty-five thousand years ago: a lion-headed figurine, carved from the tusk of a woolly mammoth. The sculpture was zoomorphic, with human characteristics, a maneless Löwenmensch: a lion-man. The carving had been unearthed in southwest Germany, and a second, similar figurine had been found nearby. At the time when these sculptures had been carved, Europe, like the rest of the world, had been deep in a glacial period of the Quaternary Ice Age.

Egon speculated aloud, his imagination racing. He proposed that extraterrestrial lion-headed "gods" from a far-distant solar system might have been routinely visiting Earth during the Pleistocene, surveying the planet on a global scale. In Europe, humankind's Cro-Magnon ancestors may have seen these aliens and sculpted the Löwenmensch figurine in their likeness. Perhaps these Ice Age visitors had even interacted with early humans…

But these ancient astronauts had then stopped journeying to Earth. *Why?* Had there been war on their home planet? A terrible plague? Did their sun go nova? Perhaps an asteroid or a comet collided with their world, causing their extinction… Or did they freely choose not to return to Earth? Maybe Earth was too cold for them, back then, during an Ice Age. Or did the Löwenmänner—lion men—grow old as a race and tire of exploring? Egon felt sad that he would never know the true answer to this puzzling question.

Slowly, Egon was pulled out of his speculations by the weight of the lion's stare.

"I am a Löwenmensch?" the lion asked, lonely and miserable.

Egon nodded. "The only remaining Löwenmensch."

"I was left behind?"

"It appears so…" Egon answered gently.

"Then I must try to finally die…" the Löwenmensch stated in a subdued, dignified manner. "Not far from here lies *Nai Thimbathimba.* It is a sacred jumping-off place, facing the sea. To the west lies *Nai Thombothombo,* our land of the souls. At Nai Thimbathimba, beside a *ngingia* tree, there is a great canoe that I carved from hardwood. A chiefly canoe. Inferior softwood will not carry one into eternity."

"To the west," Egon said hesitantly, slowly and respectfully, "across the Koro Sea, lie only a few small islands like Tuvuca, and then, a great distance away, Fiji's huge, heavily populated Viti Levu... I don't think it would be wise for you to journey there..."

As Egon said his words, he realized that the Fijian government's edict banning any visitation to Tuvuca was to protect the Löwenmensch, whom the Fijians likely believed to be an old *thing* surviving from their past, a god, something sacred, important to protect, and to keep secret. So Tuvuca had been made into a sort of restricted preserve—one now being furtively trespassed upon by the Tongans.

"Drums!" the Löwenmensch growled.

Egon felt himself tremble as he remembered being darted and pursued. He listened. The drumming that had commenced sounded quite near, perhaps not more than a quarter of a mile distant, somewhere to the south...

The Löwenmensch rose and, walking on all fours, catlike, headed off, moving west.

"You—you're going to Nai Thimba..." Egon asked.

"Nai Thimba**thimba**," the Löwenmensch's voice rumbled, woodily.

Egon yearned to know more about this incredible alien creature. Simultaneously, he had no desire to encounter the Tongan intruders again. He found himself picking up his backpack and skipping after the Löwenmensch. "May I accompany you?"

"... If you wish."

~10~

As Egon followed the Löwenmensch westward toward the setting sun, they left a rocky, pure pinewood forest and entered bushy, verdant, tropical jungle. Egon paid little attention to the manifold plant and tree species surrounding them, so focused was he on the alien lion. He watched in amazement as the lion picked and ate wild fruit as they walked.

He asked the Löwenmensch about its diet and was surprised to learn that the creature was a vegetarian, subsisting primarily on fruits, in addition to leaves, seeds, and the stems and shoots of bamboo. Egon thought how its diet, despite its predatory, leonine appearance, was akin to that of a gorilla crossed with a panda bear's. But it made sense, given that the Löwenmensch must have originated from a far-distant planet whose sentient life appeared to be as much plant as animal.

Egon marveled at the dexterity of the Löwenmensch's front paws as it fed itself. Its palms could fold vertically in half, completely. There was no need for an opposable thumb, for the four digits of each of its paws were themselves fully opposable to each other, due to the great width of the paw and the incredible flexibility of the palm. Egon imagined the paws of this alien's bold ancestors, thirty-five thousand years ago, effortlessly manipulating the intricate controls of wondrous interstellar spacecraft.

"You have no claws…" Egon observed.

"The greatest pleasure can result in the greatest misery," the Löwenmensch responded, its deep voice tinged by heartache. "When I was young and strong, I was led astray by passion. I felt love for the daughter of a *turaga i taukei*. This was long ago. I do not remember her name… I remember pretending wisdom, telling her about an eclipse, of which I knew nothing.

"The chieftain set the condition: my claws must be clipped. I was strong, but passion had tamed me. Love had mastered me. I agreed…

"That night, many of that *mataqali* tried to club me to death. Even without my claws, I killed more than I could count. I killed their *turaga i taukei,* and his *tokatoka*. I taught them fear that night. All the *yavusa!* I made myself their king that night."

Egon could hear the pain reverberating in the Löwenmensch's voice. Alone on this Earth, it had attempted to live amongst the Fijians. With love in its heart, it had willingly sacrificed to become one of them—only to be brutally rejected, and to learn most painfully that one should exercise caution against being led astray by passion.

A king truly set apart from its people, utterly alone, and with an empty heart.

Egon found himself curiously glancing beneath the lion's hindquarters, where an Earth mammal's sex organs would be— in the case of a real lion, a barbed penis. In the Löwenmensch's genital area, there was a flat, heavily grained, triangular platelet. Intercourse with a human female would have been impossible. Impregnation a fantasy. This was a being with a completely different, unearthly evolutionary history. Yet it had still felt the need to love. *Is love universal in the cosmos?*

"The drums have stopped," Egon remarked.

The Löwenmensch snarled, ill tempered, as it continued westward, toward Tuvuca's jumping-off place, Nai Thimbathimba.

~11~

Egon smiled, surprised, as he followed the Löwenmensch across a small field where one, two, three—at least a dozen differently colored butterflies flapped about them, settling upon ferns and low bushes, preparing to roost for the coming night. Egon heard himself excitedly identifying the varieties in his mind: *A long-tailed blue!—Lampides boeticus. A meadow argus—Junonia villida. A yellow admiral!—ah, ah, Vanessa itea, yes. A lemon emigrant... Catopsilia pomona.* He found himself thinking of his net, but he remembered that he had left it back near that fallen *Pisonia* tree, where he had first observed the Tongans.

The island suddenly dimmed, and Egon's elation disappeared, replaced by fear. He had forgotten how fast the sun set in the tropics. He found himself glancing about, caught off guard. Already all that remained were waning rays of light, reflecting otherworldly off the clouds and land. Egon imagined the sound of Tongan blow darts. He shivered and stepped closer to the Löwenmensch, sensing security in being near such a powerful creature—even if the lion had described itself as *old and weak*.

And in that odd South Sea twilight, Egon glimpsed something he had not noticed before: brown, discolored spots, like water stains, dappling the left side of the lion's wide back. Between these spots were a number of sunken cankers, within which there seemed to be growing… spores? It reminded Egon of a fungal disease caused by a plant pathogen that he had once studied.

The babbling of water pulled Egon's attention forward, to a wide stream that flowed across their path. Egon knelt with a cupped hand to scoop up a mouthful of water. He was quite surprised when the Löwenmensch picked him up and forcefully threw him into the stream.

"Learn your manners," the lion growled. "I drink first."

And the Löwenmensch lowered its great head and began lapping up water with its huge wooden tongue.

Egon slowly pulled himself out of the stream. Standing on its other side, he began to wring the water from his clothing, grumbling to himself.

"Companionship with the mighty is never trustworthy," the lion admitted to Egon after it finished drinking, almost as if the words were meant as an apology. As if the lion recognized its brash nature as something that it was incapable of rising above. "Why are you on my island?"

"Because… I'm a hunter," Egon answered with an edge to his voice, disgruntled.

"A hunter? A hunter of what? You have no gun. No spear. No knife."

"Of…" Egon hesitated to admit it. "Of butterflies."

The Löwenmensch's face expressed surprise, then bewilderment, and then absolute amusement. Its tiny eyes squeezed tightly closed, and it laughed loudly, heartily, with a tremendous, tonal fluttering sound emanating woodily from deep within its mighty chest, like birch trees rubbing against each other in a great wind.

"It's not funny," Egon mumbled, most seriously.

But the lion kept laughing for some time.

Is laughter also universal in the cosmos? Egon wondered, offended yet intellectually stimulated by the implications of what he was observing.

When the lion's laughter finally ended, it grew serious, even angry, and asked, "Why do you kill butterflies? To all living things life is equally dear!"

"I don't kill them," Egon defended himself. "I scan them, photograph and record their characteristics, their beauty. For science. I then release them…"

The Löwenmensch shook its great head and then focused most thoughtfully across the stream at Egon. "You are no hunter, white one… Catching butterflies is not what is important to you. You are looking for something else…"

"Yes… I guess I am," Egon admitted, realizing at that moment the truth of the lion's direct words, recognizing the keen, insightful intellect of the alien.

"What?"

"Something of me that I lost long ago," Egon answered enigmatically. *My boyhood.* "Something I suspect you lost as well…"

"What did I lose?" the lion demanded impetuously.

As Egon opened his mouth to answer, he heard the loud *thud* and saw the look of shock and confusion on the lion's face.

The Löwenmensch snarled and wobbled on its paws as it slowly and deliberately turned around. As it did so, Egon saw the throwing axe sticking out of its upper back.

"The Tongans!" Egon exclaimed.

Behind the lion stood the two youngest Tongans, their bare chests painted warrior red. They were holding between themselves a great net. Farther back stood the drummers, clubs in hand, and behind these men their chieftain.

Rearing back its head, the alien lion roared out, sending punishing shock waves of sound tearing through the air in all directions. The sonic assault was massive and devastating. It seemed to shake the world.

Egon dropped to his knees, cupping his hands over his ears, squeezing his head as if his very life depended upon somehow blocking out the sound. His equilibrium disturbed, he fell over onto his side as he watched the young Tongans, their legs freshly tattooed, racing toward the Löwenmensch and casting their huge net over the creature.

How can the Tongans find the coordination to attack? Egon's thoughts raced. *Did they stuff their ears full of wax? Did they drink some native potion to dull their sense of hearing?*

The mighty, defensive roar ended abruptly, and the lion collapsed, weak, exhausted, struggling within the net. Before the Löwenmensch could free itself, the Tongan drummers raced forward and clubbed stakes through the periphery of the netting, securing it tightly to the forest floor, pinning the lion helplessly within it.

The scene eerily reminded Egon of how he had captured his first butterfly on Tuvuca, by collapsing his net, bringing it to the forest floor, flattening it to secure the butterfly.

Egon immediately felt the urge to help the Löwenmensch. But what could he do? There were five Tongans, armed, and there he stood defenseless. *What can I do?* He struggled with it. He knew that at any moment the Tongans would be turning their attention to him. He thought of the blow darts. And he forced himself to run off, his legs carrying him away quickly but rather unwillingly.

~12~

After running for a half a mile, Egon stopped, spun about, and froze, looking back in the direction from which he had come. He listened intently. There was only the stillness and the silence of the night that had descended upon Tuvuca after sunset.

Egon noticed a tall, leafy *Pouteria grayana* tree beside him. He removed his backpack, wrapped his arms and legs about the tree's slender trunk, and shimmied his way up to its lowest outstretched branch, from which he then climbed upward, branch to branch, to the tree's crown.

High above the forest floor, he peered eastward, back toward the bubbling stream, where he had abandoned his companion. He could not see the stream in the darkness, but there was a growing fire there. The Tongans, having secured their prey, were apparently making camp for the night.

Why are the Tongans doing this? Egon wondered, guilt ridden. Did the Tongans plan to kill the Löwenmensch? Were they planning on taking the alien back to Tonga? For what purpose?

Or was this part of a ritual test of manhood? Exclusively reserved for the sons of a chieftain. To face the Löwenmensch. Was that why the Samoan *tufuga tatatau* was now absent? Had his tattooing role in what was unfolding ended?

Egon remembered the scars on the lion's shoulders. And the ancient Polynesian totem pole... How long had the Tongans been journeying to Tuvuca? For years? Decades? Hundreds of years? ... Thousands of years?

... Was this possibly a game of catch and release, played by the Tongans? Like the game he himself played with his butterflies... Did his butterflies, at their moment of capture, feel the fear that the Löwenmensch must surely now be experiencing? If the Löwenmensch could feel fear... Egon imagined the sheer elation that his butterflies must feel upon their release. He had felt it, when the lion had earlier released him. He then remembered the promise that he had made: *"I'll find some way to return your mercy."* And he knew that he must go back to help the Löwenmensch.

~13~

Egon crawled upon his belly as he approached the flickering firelight of the Tongan's camp. He could hear the crackling of the fire, the subtle wavering of its flames, and the Tongans speaking amongst themselves in their native tongue. But above all, he heard the Löwenmensch barking in Tongan, making what Egon guessed were vengeful threats and curses at the Tongans. Egon did not sense any fear in the lion's voice, only anger. And he found himself drawing courage from this.

Strengthened, Egon crept farther forward, doing his best to do so silently. And in his soul he felt the excitement of the living, the clear awareness of danger, of the reality of life and death under the cloak of night. For a moment he fancied himself a great cat, stalking forward in the darkness. He was suddenly a boy living out a fantasy. And he felt descending upon himself an uncanny brotherhood with the Löwenmensch. It felt real. And empowering. He was a hunter.

Egon was soon close enough to see the Tongans. They were sitting together cross-legged on the far side of the fire, opposite the net that held the Löwenmensch pinned captive.

The Polynesians were passing halves of coconut shells between them, clapping before and after drinking from the shells, drinking down the contents in one sip. The drummers were refilling the shells from a small barrel. Based on the Tongans' inebriated movements, Egon guessed that the barrel contained bush beer, an extremely alcoholic concoction that dated back to premissionary days, made from fermented bananas.

The beer... Egon felt a clever idea form in his mind. He squinted in the darkness, looking over the Tongans' possessions. *There...* Egon saw, lying beside two long, narrow tubes of bamboo, an assortment of blow darts.

The Tongan chief, the man wearing the prestigious whale's tooth about his neck, yelled something at the noisy Löwenmensch.

The lion roared in response, but the sonic shock waves of its defensive cry were weak, less than a third their earlier strength. The roar was sufficiently distracting, however, to allow Egon to act. As the island wobbled under the sonic assault, Egon shuffled in closer and reached a probing hand out from the concealing foliage.

The roar subsided as Egon pulled his arm back into the cover of the bushes, his hand carefully clenching half a dozen of the Tongans' drugged darts.

Rising, the chieftain picked up a long, stripped-down, slender branch lying beside him, strode over to the netted Löwenmensch, and began to cruelly whip the lion as a barbarian might discipline an uncooperative horse.

For a moment Egon just watched the lashing with passionate pity, but then he launched into action. For this second distraction provided him with the opportunity to drop the darts into the Tongans' barrel of beer, where they would sink to the bottom and infuse into the beer the powerful drug that they were tipped with.

35

The Löwenmensch finally grew silent, the great beast submitting, lying motionless, succumbing to the humiliation of the lashing. Witnessing this, Egon felt his heart and soul grow enraged. The justified fury empowered him with even greater courage.

As the chief returned to the other Tongans, and as the Tongans recommenced their drinking, Egon crawled, silently, ever so silently, around the periphery of the camp, making his way to the Löwenmensch.

Reaching the far side of the net, Egon opened his pocketknife and began to work on the thick netting. His knife was small, and the cutting went slowly.

Egon was looking at the Löwenmensch when the lion shifted beneath the net, turning its great head, making eye contact. Egon saw the shock in the lion's eyes, and then the silent appreciation.

Without sound, Egon mouthed the words: *I'll find some way to return your mercy.*

And there, on Tuvuca, that night, beneath the stars, a once-strong king and a small, fragile human suddenly found little difference between themselves. They were one.

Egon crawled into the net to enlarge the hole he had cut, to make it big enough for the Löwenmensch to escape out of. As he did so, he could not help but smile and shake his head. For suddenly he was the mouse in Aesop's fable "The Lion and the Mouse." *No act of kindness is ever wasted. Mercy brings its rewards. There is no being so great that it cannot have empathy for a lesser. There is no being so small that it cannot help a greater.*

Egon heard a ruckus erupting from the Tongans. The drugged beer was having its effect. As a punishment, he hoped that the Tongans would find themselves mentally trapped in endless time, as he had so terrifyingly experienced.

Captive in time, falling through time, to relive the most painful parts of their past lives. *That would be justice.*

Egon put his pocketknife away, but the Löwenmensch was too weak to make its escape. Egon moved deeper into the net and whispered to the lion, "Little friends may prove to be great friends."

And Egon took one of the lion's great paws and pulled, helping his abandoned companion to escape.

~14~

It took half the night for Egon to help the Löwenmensch to Nai Thimbathimba, which was little more than a small sandy cove shadowed by moonlight and palm fronds, looking out over Tuvuca's wide western lagoon.

There, beside a *ngingia* tree, Egon found the lion's great chiefly canoe, carved from hardwood. It was against this canoe that Egon sat the Löwenmensch. Weak, the creature leaned sideways, embracing its canoe, resting its great head against it.

"Thank you, white one," the lion said softly, genuinely.

"Egon. My name is Egon."

"Thank you… Egon…"

"Do you have a name?" Egon asked.

For the longest moment, there was only the sound of the eternal surf, peacefully washing against the timeless shore. And then the Löwenmensch answered.

"Kalou."

"King Kalou?" Egon asked softly, respectfully, as he heard his inner voice whispering, with appreciation for its remote South Sea intonation, the words: *King Kalou of Tuvuca.*

"No… Now… only Kalou." The Löwenmensch pined, its bold and barefaced spirit broken.

A gentle breeze caressed the two of them, palm fronds fluttered high above, and moonlight danced over the lion.

37

In that moonlight, Egon once again noticed the odd brown spots on Kalou's back. He examined the discoloration more closely. It was a fungal disease, he was sure of it. He had seen it before on fruit trees, studied it in the laboratory. It was caused by a particularly virulent pathogen, one that often reduced strong trees to rotted waste in mere days.

"How long have you had these spots?" Egon asked.

"Many of your lifetimes… Since I became old."

"Kalou," Egon said, "I don't think you're weak because you're old—but because you're ill. Trees die from disease, and environmental factors. Not from old age. When a tree becomes old, it has difficulty protecting its exterior. It can't fight off pathogens as it did when it was younger. Woody plants attempt to heal themselves by sealing off the damage from the rest of the plant. Isolating the infection. I believe this is what I'm seeing on your back."

"I am not a plant!" the Löwenmensch growled, recovering some if its brash spiritedness.

"No, but you are remarkably like a tree. Do you trust me?"

"What?"

"Kalou, do you trust me?"

Kalou looked deep into Egon's eyes, into his soul.

"Yes, I trust you, Egon."

Egon removed his backpack and fumbled within it, pulling out a small hand axe, a sampling hammer, a number of wood chisels of different sizes, and a variety of small canisters.

"The way your body has isolated the fungi," Egon explained, "I believe I can remove the infected tissue. I don't know if it will be painful to you, but I believe if I do this it will cure you."

Egon went on to explain that he was a tree surgeon by profession, an arboriculturist who was specially trained in diagnosis and treatment. In pruning. He had been awarded his Pruning and Care of Trees certificate by the prestigious French Ministry of Agriculture and had earned his MS degree in tree management in the United Kingdom.

He informed Kalou that he wanted to carefully cut away all the infected "wood" from its back and then apply a heavy coating of a broad-spectrum biofungicide.

In response, Kalou simply leaned farther onto the canoe, turning its broad back to Egon.

Egon selected a particular chisel, picked up his hammer, and began to cautiously trim away the infected wood from King Kalou's back.

Egon marveled at how stoic the Löwenmensch was, enduring the surgical removal of so much tissue. Egon did surmise that the level of pain was likely much lower than what an Earth animal would experience if its flesh was cut into, but still, he knew that there was pain—and he was reminded of this every so often when Kalou would flinch.

As Egon worked into the night, he once again wondered about this incredible alien being. He thought about Kalou's fantastic roar and likened it to the defensive spray of a skunk, or the tactile armor of a porcupine—only in the case of the Löwenmensch, it was an assault of sound on the sense of hearing, rather than smell or touch.

He thought of how his companion was a vegetarian, yet so kingly and fierce. He thought of how handsome and powerful and unusual a creature the Löwenmensch was, existing somewhere between plant and animal—and with human-level intellect. Or higher?

Once again, Egon thought of the Löwenmänner as a race and of how these lion men had visited Earth during the last Ice Age. He wondered what had urged them across the vast distances of dark, interstellar space at the dawn of man's prehistory. He wondered if they would ever one day return? He hoped so.

Perhaps one day, man of Earth might become as courageous as the Löwenmänner and also travel to the stars… Maybe human astronauts would even one far future day find the home planet of the lion men, if it still existed…

Egon wondered, if the Löwenmänner planet did still exist, what it was like. Was it ringed like Saturn? How many moons did it have, if any at all? What color was its sky?

As Egon's thoughts wound down, so did the surgery. He had carefully cut through the equivalent of a transparent, living bark layer, and then trimmed away infected tissue from what would have been the cambium and sapwood layers of a tree. He had not needed to cut down into the heartwood layer. This was a good sign. Also promising was the fact that he had noticed what reminded him of wood rays infused throughout what he would have identified as the counterpart of a tree's secondary wood.

After all the infected wood-like tissue was removed, Egon painted the entire wound with a biofungicide from his backpack. He waited for the fungicide to dry, and then he repeated this action twice more.

Exhausted, Egon and Kalou fell asleep together, side by side, against the king's great chiefly canoe.

~15~

Egon awoke to a question.

"What did I lose?" Kalou asked.

Egon opened his eyes to see Kalou standing over him, on all fours. In the early-morning sunlight, the king appeared like a great golden lion from another dimension. Kalou's countenance was imbued with renewed vitality, untamed prowess, and unsurpassed confidence.

"Your claws…" Egon remarked. "They—they're growing back."

"Yes." Kalou's great, fibrous voice boomed with power. "I am no longer old. I am young again. Strong again. Thank you… Egon."

Egon nodded, appreciatively.

"What did I lose?" Kalou asked again.

"Your boyhood," Egon answered. "When you were accidentally abandoned by your parents…"

Kalou snarled, struggling with it. "What is memory but a wind that blows through the mind. I have my island again. My strength again! You gave me back my youth. My *boyhood*. I will never forget you… Egon."

And Kalou turned to leave, great power rippling across its frame, its huge paws digging deep into the sand as it moved.

"Wait," Egon said. "Where are you going?"

"To *play* with the Tongans!" came Kalou's answer, and the Löwenmensch ran up the hillside, disappearing into the jungle, heading east.

~16~

Egon paddled Kalou's chiefly canoe slowly, carefully navigating around the coral heads within the reef as he headed south to where he had hidden his motored boat. He believed that Kalou would not mind his borrowing the canoe, especially as the lion had abandoned its plans to journey to Nai Thombothombo, the land of the souls.

From the lagoon, Egon admired Tuvuca's volcanic peaks and its lush, densely wooded forests as he began to say goodbye to the island in his mind.

He had chosen to abandon his butterfly pole and net, having left it in the jungle near that fallen *Pisonia* tree. He would not be chasing butterflies ever again. He would never again play

41

such a game of catch and release. Besides, he had had his boyhood, last night, when he crawled into the Tongan camp. The sheer adventure of it, combined with his coming to the aid of the King of Tuvuca, had filled what was missing in his life, what he had long ago lost. For a little while, he had been a boy again, a boy on a South Seas adventure with a magical lion.

Suddenly there was a tremendous roar over Tuvuca, the strength of which had not been heard for many human lifetimes. It was a raw, vibratory growl of unimaginable might, from a power greater than storms. Like a great wind, it seemed to come from nowhere, yet suddenly it was everywhere, its awesome power echoing over and shaking the whole of the island. Trees swayed and bent. The sand trembled. Shock waves rippled across the water of the lagoon.

There was a *lion* loose on Tuvuca.

Fijian Words and Identifying Notations

• Fijian language and social organization:

Turaga i taukei – The prominent chief of a Vanua
Vanua – Several tribes of a particular land, composed of
        a group of *Yavusa*
Yavusa – A tribe of several clans
Mataqali – A clan of families
Tokatoka – A family unit

• "Education isn't something you can finish."
—Isaac Asimov

• "The more I explore the less I know,
  but the more I want to know."
—Nomi Prins

A Note from the Author

This author hopes the reader appreciated this modest South Seas fable-like tale. It was inspired by:

1) This author's appreciation of the Paleolithic's *der Löwenmensch* sculpture: The Lion-man of Hohlenstein-Stadel

2) Aesop's fable: "The Lion and the Mouse"

Niko Zinovii
Santa Monica, California
18 August 2017

The Butterfly Hunter and the King

Niko Zinovii

The Million Eyes of Nobo Savu

~1~

Dr. Claude Arnoux, fortyish, suave, French-born, sat quietly beside an empty first-class passenger seat, studiously reading the latest issue of the *Journal of Psychiatric Research*. There was a bump of air turbulence and he glanced out the plane's window. The sky was exceptionally clear, vibrantly blue, the sun at zenith.

"Excuse me," Claude called to a stewardess, charming, debonair, his deep, accented voice silken. "Was the captain able to radio ahead?"

The stewardess signaled that she would check, and she went to do so. And Claude sat there gallantly, patiently, the epitome of the dapper Frenchman, impeccable of manner and dress.

The stewardess smiled as she returned. "The private plane is confirmed. Apparently it's all been arranged."

"Thank you," Claude responded, his resonate voice filled with warmth and presence. "And how long until we reach Bali?"

"Oh, about an hour and a half."

Claude nodded appreciatively and turned back to the window. He then smiled to himself as he amusedly recalled the last time he had flown over the Pacific, less than one year ago. As his flight had left Brisbane, he had glanced toward the setting sun. To his astonishment, he had found himself witnessing a string of brilliant silver discs, elliptical in shape, flip-flopping

47

slowly across the horizon, exhibiting curious oscillating movements. "Good heavens, flying saucers!" he had exclaimed, causing quite a stir.

But as his jet had advanced farther toward the saucers, Claude had come to see that the silver ellipses were in fact only seagulls catching the rays of the setting sun. At the time he had felt astounded. He still did. For he had been born by the sea, he had lived by the sea all his life. He lived by the sea now. He had seen seagulls a million times. But only once in his life had he ever witnessed such an optical phenomenon. Apparently, under certain conditions of illumination from a low sun, seagulls and other birds were capable of casting an absolutely convincing impression of metallic saucers oscillating across the sky.

At the time, he had genuinely believed he had been having an actual UFO sighting. The experience should have made him all the more skeptical on the subject of unidentified flying objects, prejudicing him into dismissing it entirely. But instead it only made him all the more curious, for the phenomenon challenged him as a psychiatrist and psychoanalyst. Were flying saucers real or mere illusory fantasy products of the human mind?

Over the past year, since experiencing his seagull illusion, Claude had read everything he could find on UFOs. He had researched the subject thoroughly. And in culmination, he had volunteered to present his conclusions last week, in New York, at the annual conference held by Civilian Saucer Intelligence, a reputable independent research group. He had not done this with a light heart. For in doing so, he put his hard-won professional reputation for reliable scientific judgment and truthfulness on the line. But he had come to a certain conclusion that he felt was sound, and he wanted to share it.

But was it also due to ego? Claude asked himself. *Yes, yes it was.* He admitted it to himself with a shrug. The conference had indeed been but another opportunity to step once again into the spotlight, to grab the spotlight. *And why not? Why deny myself?* For in Claude's view, such moments represented the colorful pleasantry of life's rich experience, something to be sought out and embraced.

Claude smiled, and he felt his ego inflate satisfyingly as he recalled his presence at the conference:

"And so, in conclusion, we must ask ourselves: are UFOs real material phenomena of an unknown nature, flashing about freely through our troposphere and stratosphere, presumably coming from outer space?

"Descriptions of the phenomena suggest signs of intelligent guidance—implying that UFOs are piloted. Yet these seemingly weightless objects don't behave in accordance with the laws of physics. In fact, they don't behave like material bodies at all but instead like weightless thoughts, like objects out of a fantasy. For the reported accelerations, speeds, and angles of turn are so tremendous that no earthly being piloting such craft could ever hope to survive doing so.

"These weightless objects are clearly impossible. Yet they are ubiquitous. Reports of UFOs have come from every corner of the globe. They have been reported *everywhere*, yet the phenomena display no recognizable connection to our planet, or its inhabitants.

"And yet the impossible is continually reported as being seen. *Things are seen, but it isn't known what.* In such a case, is it in any way possible to form a correct idea on these objects? Can one affirm or deny their existence? Is it possible to determine even the approximate nature of the observations, without an empirical basis sufficient to permit conclusions to be drawn?"

Claude, remembering his words, recalled how he had paused, rather dramatically, after asking that question. He had practiced the pause while rehearsing his speech. In retrospect, he believed the pause had been quite effective, as it seemed to have heightened the audience's focus on him before he had continued.

"Yes, I believe so. For the common element in the equation is man. Man is the witness. It is man that is *everywhere*, seeing UFOs ubiquitously. I believe this must be a human phenomenon.

"No, I don't believe the available evidence indicates that we are being spied upon by nonhuman intelligent beings of extraterrestrial origin. No, this can best be understood as a psychic phenomenon, common to all mankind, based essentially on a shared, omnipresent emotional foundation. Yes, I believe UFOs are a psychic product.

"We see something, there's a mistake in observation, and our brain reflects back what had previously lain hidden in the unconscious. Projection by unconscious extrapolation, the unrecognizable transformed by the mind into a weightless thought, a fantasy—the subject's psychic assumptions invading the conscious mind with illusion and vision.

"What is the psychic cause for the projection, the common underlying motive? It may involve our evolved propensity to need to interpret the unknown. Perhaps it's partly due to our collective modern myth of claims of things being seen in the skies. But in truth, I do not know, but there must be a universal trigger. I am certain of it. In time, I believe science will provide us with the answer... as to what that universal trigger is.

"This is my conclusion on the subject of UFOs. My belief. Thank you."

Claude, remembering his ending statement, also remembered the dead silence that had followed, the shaking of heads, the frowns of skepticism and disbelief from the audience. It was a different reaction than he had hoped for, far from satisfying, but not entirely unexpected, given those in attendance.

The worldwide media coverage that followed was much more accepting, portraying his expert opinion as welcomed, clear-headed, and scientific. And more, his statement was received as reassuring, in the sense that it announced that man was not under the scrutiny of strange advanced beings from afar, but alone and in control of his present and future. *Is the security of it what so appeals to me?* Claude wondered.

"You look a million miles away," a soft, angelic voice interrupted his thoughts.

"Oh, not that far off." Claude smiled lovingly to his willowy, flaxen-haired wife, who was gently seating herself beside him. "More like ten thousand."

"New York?"

He nodded, making meaningful eye contact with her in a manner that personified European romance. He appeared very much the dashing, polished lover, yet his countenance simultaneously displayed the firm strength and ego of an authoritative man of action.

"Because of the dreams?" she asked tenderly.

Again he nodded. "Yes, because of the dreams. Judith, if you don't mind, may I see your notes on the last dream?"

She gracefully reached down into the handbag at her feet and provided him with a small notebook.

He flipped forward several pages, stopped, lowered his chin most seriously, and began to read, silently, soberly. The handwriting in the book was his wife's, documenting the dream that he had had the night before last, which he had dictated his memory of to her:

"I was walking along the Left Bank of the Seine, in Paris, it was late in the afternoon. Spring. The sun felt warm. The air smelled sweet, like flowers. There were people everywhere, enjoying the day. Suddenly the National Alert Signal wailed. But this time it wasn't a test. Everyone ran off, disappearing into the city.

"I was the only one left outside, standing there by the river... The siren stopped. And then... There was a bright flicker of light, and I looked up. I saw a pulsating flying saucer, lens shaped, glittering, metallic, falling from the sky like a stray drop of rain after a storm. I just stood there, dumbfounded.

"*An interplanetary machine?* I wondered as I watched it slowly stop, soundlessly, to just hang there, directly over Notre-Dame, absolutely weightless. It then cautiously circled the cathedral, in an odd, inquisitive manner, before it darted off—absolutely silent—in a random zigzagging manner as if hoping to haphazardly discover some new interesting object.

"I couldn't make any sense of its movements. Its flight was so... it didn't appear to be based on any logical pattern. Its behavior instead seemed based on pure whim. I found myself refusing to believe that unknown beings, spies from outer space, were inside the thing, carrying out a survey of our Earth.

"It was then that the saucer noticed me... and it came straight toward me, its curiosity aroused. I told myself that I shouldn't run off like the others, that I should stand right there to get a good look at the thing, to learn what it really was. But as it approached, I felt the distinct impression of being scrutinized, and I turned my back to it... And my dream ended."

Claude slowly folded the notebook closed. Normally, he could see so clearly into his own mind, he knew himself very well, nothing of his own thoughts was normally concealed from him. But there was something hidden in these dreams that he had been having. He was sure of it. His subconscious was actually concealing something from his conscious mind. *What? Why?* He could not guess. But it appeared obvious that it had something to do with his staid conclusions on UFOs—with the speech he had delivered to the Civilian Saucer Intelligence group. *Am I subconsciously doubting my own conclusions? If so, why?*

~2~

The small private plane transporting Claude and his wife had been delayed for many long hours before leaving Bali's Ngurah Rai International Airport. From there, it motored eastward, languidly moving away from the evening's setting sun and out toward Nobo Savu, a remote, privately owned island lying in the backwater of the Banda Sea.

"There it is," Claude announced rather quietly, tired.

And his wife joined him in looking out the window to see for the first time, from up high, the rather mysterious island of Nobo Savu. Mysterious in that it was unusual for the island to ever receive visitors. But this was a most unusual case.

"It's so attractive," Judith noted.

Claude felt the fatigue born from travel momentarily leaving him as he too appreciated the remarkable natural beauty of the sight below.

Rising majestically from the tropical depths, Nobo Savu spread itself out upon the surface of the sea like a lovely opened flower, its center rising up rather dramatically to three worn peaks, the remnants of extinct volcanoes. So pleasantly alluring was the sight that it stirred something in Claude, and he wondered if what he sensed was similar to what a lost seagull or a far-traveling albatross might feel upon sighting such an inviting landfall.

~3~

The plane landed with a bump and a skid upon the short, paved airstrip that ran along the island's verdant, low west coast.

The hatch opened automatically and Claude, ever the gentleman, motioned for his wife to disembark before him. He had not expected to hear her gasp, and when she did it startled him. He quickly moved forward to her side, placing a protective arm around her. And then he gasped too.

For all about them, crawling over the runway, everywhere, were hundreds upon hundreds of bright red land crabs. And they were big, their shells almost half a foot across. The eerie clicking of the mineralized chitin tipping the thousands of crab legs sent a shiver up Claude's spine.

"A crab migration?" Claude guessed as he noticed that the crabs were creeping out of the surrounding forest and making their way across the runway, toward the sea. Their plane, upon landing, must have unavoidably crushed many dozens of the crabs.

Claude heard a shuffle behind them, and he turned to find their pilot emerging from the aircraft, carrying their luggage. Tall and thin, gaunt in the face, the man looked rather like a gentle poet, so sensitively intelligent were his eyes.

"The crabs," the pilot explained unhurriedly, his low, gentle voice a mirror of his pensive visage, "their migration is triggered by the annual rains that mark the beginning of the wet season. Each year at this time, a half a million crabs all simultaneously make their way to the sea, to spawn. I understand it's been happening this way for the past forty-five million years or so."

"Remarkable," Claude commented. He then looked to his wife, reassuring her, although he himself still felt a bit unnerved: "It's nothing to be alarmed about. Just an unexpected… natural wonder."

"One can almost feel it," Judith remarked philosophically as she slowly gathered herself, "the rhythm of nature, how strongly it beats. How it moves the crabs."

"Yes... It's rather amazing," the pilot responded slowly, evenly, intellectually appreciating her sentiment. He then smiled softly as he led them over to a nearby jeep. "Careful where you step."

~4~

The pilot drove for perhaps a hundred yards and then stopped before a small aircraft hangar. Claude was quite surprised to see a dozen or so men there, working in the twilight, unloading crates from a small truck. He was surprised because all of the men were dwarfs, not one of them over four feet tall. All were perfectly proportioned with similarly prominent foreheads and depressed nasal bridges, Semitic in look, and despite their truncular obesity they all appeared extraordinarily healthy, and happy.

Claude glanced to their pilot, wondering if an explanation might be offered for the dwarfs—so unexpected and unusual a sight they were—but none was given.

"Our humble receiving and reception station." The pilot motioned to the hangar as he guided Claude and his wife inside, where the owner of the island, Walter Sinclair, approached them immediately.

Sinclair was exactly what Claude had expected from the media accounts he had read about the man, being tall and broad shouldered, with a courtly, sturdy, and wise bearing. There was an unexpected easygoing charm to the man, and his strong, reassuring voice put one immediately at ease. He was also a perfect gentleman, and Claude, although meeting Sinclair for the first time, could not help but feel that he shared with this man a long and comfortable past. He seemed an old friend, a man of approximately the same age, a man whose career had also similarly been a long glow of steady achievement.

Perhaps it was this comfort that drew out an immediate appreciation in Claude for his host, for Claude sensed in Sinclair that although the man seemed to come from a world that had ended long ago, he was someone who lived for future dreams and not in memories of the past. This confused Claude.

"Excuse me," Claude said to Sinclair, after introductions had been made, "I don't mean to be so forward, but…"

"But?" Sinclair prompted.

"You were an accomplished engineer," Claude continued, puzzled, "at the top of your game. Sought after by the entire world. And yet you retired early from your profession, to live in seclusion out here on Nobo Savu, an island so remote and inconsequential few even know it exists."

Sinclair smiled urbanely, unruffled, and turned to Claude's wife.

"Mrs. Arnoux," Sinclair began.

"Judith, please," she insisted gently.

"Judith," Sinclair continued, good-natured, "how do you explain your husband's tendency to jump to a conclusion without knowing all the associated facts?"

"What?" Claude asked with an amiable smile, appreciating the directness of the genuine interaction.

"I'll show you tomorrow," Sinclair explained, "how I'm anything but retired. But before Thomas drives you off to the accommodations I've had prepared for you, I need to ask you: how can a UFO be a psychic product?"

"Down to business so quickly?" Claude asked warmly, polite but surprised.

"I realize you must be tired," Sinclair apologized, "but… I need to understand your answer. It's important to me."

"And you can't wait?" Claude smiled.

"And I can't wait." Sinclair smiled back.

Claude nodded, shifted his stance, and allowed his thoughts to focus and settle meaningfully on the subject. "The very thought of a UFO provokes like nothing else conscious and unconscious fantasies. This is the psychic component, the psychic aspect. When someone witnesses something that they cannot immediately identify, an unidentified aerial phenomenon for example, in that instant the brain is confronted with a seemingly insolvable enigma.

"In the mind, in the subconscious, the brain is fully aware of the flying saucer mythology that is so prevalent in today's society. Grasping for an answer, the human mind creates a psychic interpretation, a psychic product."

Sinclair, hand on chin, critically considered the explanation. "So a psychic interpretation is based on something physically real?"

Claude recalled the seagull illusion that he had experienced last year. "Yes, it can be. But it may not be necessary that something actual exists for the vision to arise. Let me explain. Take, for example, ghosts. Some people claim to see apparitions. But that doesn't mean that the dead have returned to haunt the living. No, I believe it's all in the eye of the beholder. I have a theory that I suspect may be true. The human eye is basically a camera. An image of the outer world forms on its sensitive screen, on the retina, and this image is then transmitted to the brain.

"Could this system sometimes work in reverse? Could the brain send images to the eye? Making the eye not only a camera but also something like a television screen. Then seeing would be believing, would it not? Without requiring something physically real to actually be seen. Such a psychic projection might be caused by emotional tension, distress, a sense of danger. Grief. Expectations. Drugs. Perhaps linked to a vital psychic need. I confess, I don't fully understand the triggering mechanism, but this is what I believe."

"Excuse me," the pilot, Thomas, said politely, slowly, calmly, in his distinctive, carefully thought-out manner, "but the possibility of a purely psychological explanation seems illusory, given that a large number of the observations point to actual physical phenomena."

"The psychic projection," Claude explained, "can be triggered or occasioned by an actual physical phenomenon. This would detract nothing from the hypothesis. Many sightings of UFOs have been explained to have had meteorological or other natural phenomena as causes."

"Meteorological phenomena," Thomas countered with the utmost calm, "don't cautiously survey the earth from the air."

Claude felt Sinclair's eyes settle upon him, studying him, as Thomas continued, expounding:

"The fact that UFO sightings have been reported in far greater frequency since the Second World War, and that reliable military personnel have reported objective inspections by unknown craft—lens-shaped, sometimes cylindrical, spherical—of airfields and nuclear installations, suggests aerial reconnaissance by an unknown source… whose attention has been aroused by our discovery and use of fission and fusion bombs. Such a clandestine survey suggests a certain disquiet on the part of a neighbor…"

Claude nodded, quickly gathering his thoughts for a rebuttal, his rich baritone voice suddenly touchy. "Any real study of UFOs must insist on tangible evidence and not be totally dependent on human testimony. There are no close-up photographs that aren't hoaxes, no spectroscopic identifications, no pieces of UFOs that have been reliably acquired.

"Many would love for extraterrestrial beings to visit the Earth. But we can't impose our wishes on nature; we have to discover what nature is teaching. I believe that what nature is teaching us about UFOs is that this is a psychological and not an astronomical phenomenon. UFOs are a psychic product."

Thomas looked at Claude incredulously. "*Things* have been observed that have no visible means of propulsion."

"Weightless fantasy objects," Claude countered, his words delivered with an increasing irritable sharpness, "that show no inclination toward communicating with human beings."

Claude felt his wife squeeze his arm. And he immediately wondered why he suddenly found himself growing so uncharacteristically ill tempered. Was it due to fatigue? Was it the challenge to his hypothesis? Or was it something else?

"I apologize," Claude offered, genuinely. "It was a long flight. I must be more tired than I realized."

Sinclair nodded, apologized himself for broaching the issue so soon upon their arrival, and directed Thomas to take their guests to their accommodations.

"We'll pick this up tomorrow," Sinclair proposed, adding with the utmost gravity: "Tomorrow, I'll take you out to our radar facility. Introduce you to our UFO problem."

~5~

The guest lodging was an uphill, inland drive from the airstrip. The sun had set, and as the island darkened, the shadows cast by Nobo Savu's looming volcanic peaks shrouding the interior plunging it into an early, eerie blackness.

As Thomas drove away, after having shown Claude and his wife about the cottage that had been prepared for them, Claude stepped back outside to look about. They were on a hillside, partway up one of the island's extinct volcanoes. Claude could see the lights of distant dwellings near the area whence they had come, close to the shore. There were only a few lights in the mountains. He found himself trying to draw comfort from the lights, so dark and ominous was the night.

"Would you like to talk about it?" Judith asked, stepping up to his side.

Claude shrugged, and admitted: "I'm unsure of myself. For the first time in my life. It's an odd feeling."

"Uncertainty?"

"Yes," he confessed, his deep, charming voice resonating in the night. "There seems to be some nagging doubt somewhere in my subconscious, about my hypothesis on UFOs."

He saw his wife look at him, wondering.

"No," he assured her, "I don't believe that mankind is being observed and spied upon from outer space."

"Why not?"

And Claude thought about it, critically questioning his own belief. "Because the evidence doesn't point to it. And... perhaps... maybe it's because the thought of it is so unsettling?"

"Go on," Judith prompted.

"If it were true," he thought it out, "mankind would suddenly find itself in the same crippling situation faced by primitive societies of the past, when those peoples were discovered by those much more advanced than they.

"The feeling of control would be painfully wrenched from our minds. And as an old shaman once told me, with tears in his eyes, we would have no dreams anymore..."

"Claude..."

"Yes?"

"There's something I've never told you," she confessed.

"What is it?"

"I saw one once."

"One what?" he asked, truly not understanding.

And she just looked at him.

"A UFO?" he finally responded.

She nodded. "Seeing is indeed believing. I can't help but believe they're out there. What they are, I don't know. But I believe that something is out there. I also believe that to automatically assume that what's out there is the product of an extraterrestrial intelligence—I think that would be a mistake. But… To assume that things that we can't understand are all psychic occurrences—I think that's a mistake also."

"All this time," Claude mumbled in utter disbelief, defeated, his ego wounded, "and you don't believe in me?"

"I believe in *you*," she reassured him. "But I suspect that the things that people see in the sky are a manifestation of a phenomenon that we can't yet explain. That we don't yet understand. That we don't yet have a rational explanation for."

And Claude stood there in silence, struggling with his emotions, with his intellect, feeling let down, painfully deflated, feeble, unsure. It was at that moment that a large crab crossed between them, and they both jumped. It made Claude notice the movement of the surrounding forest floor, which was alive with crawling night shapes. They were far from alone.

He saw his wife shiver, despite the warmth of the tropical night.

"Let's go inside," she said. "It's as if the island is somehow alive… And watching us with a million eyes."

~6~

Is the sea really so alluring, Claude thought to himself as he lay there in bed beside his wife, emotionally weak, listening to the creeping going on outside the cottage, *that these crabs find its siren call so irresistible? Crawling out of the jungle, instinctively traversing mile after mile, distancing themselves from their natural habitat, to enter that utterly different realm of the ocean, to spawn…*

Slowly, ever so slowly, despite the subtle background sound of an uncountable number of creeping crab legs, Claude began to fall asleep.

Soon after all sound faded from his perception, he entered the world of dreams:

Claude was home, working in his vegetable garden, alongside his house by the sea. There was a bright flicker of light, and he looked up. In the sky overhead floated the same lens-shaped saucer from his previous dream. It was shiny, glittering metallic in the bright sunlight.

The interplanetary machine… it's back… Up high, the thing in the sky curiously circled his garden. It then spotted him and began to descend, fluttering as it did so, like a dropping leaf in autumn.

Claude told himself not to turn away this time. He told himself that he needed to get a good look at the thing, to learn what it really was. So he backed up against his garden wall and braced himself, leaning back, looking up at the unknown aerial phenomenon as it slowly dropped lower and lower and lower.

Quite low, it looked utterly different. It seemed rather like a huge ladybug, a flying artificial beetle made of shimmering, spotted metal. But then its coloring changed to a metallic blue-green and iridescent copper. Suddenly, it more resembled a Japanese beetle.

Claude felt his mind flood with concern for his garden, for his vegetables, and he started to wave his arms about madly, yelling frantically at the machine, trying to ward it off.

He awoke in bed to the sound of his own yelling, his arms swinging about.

"A dream," Judith appealed to him, "it's only a dream. It's only a dream."

"Judith…" he said as he regained his senses, calming, catching his breath. "Please… get your notebook. Before I forget the details… Such a ridiculous dream!"

~7~

The next day was an interesting one. Interesting beyond Claude's wildest expectations, beyond what he could ever have imagined. For Sinclair, driven by Thomas, gave Claude and his wife a tour of the island's western lowland and the port town that had recently been built there. It was amazing. Amazing because everything was in miniature, at half scale.

And it had to be so, for the island's inhabitants—outside of Sinclair, his pilot, three doctors, and half a dozen technicians—were all dwarfs, averaging three and a half feet in height. Nobo Savu, uninhabited until just seven years ago, now had a permanent population of 321, of which 310 were Laron syndrome dwarfs—dwarfs who were Jews or descendants of Jews. Most of the dwarfs had been collected from several remote villages in southern Ecuador; others came from Spain, Israel, Egypt, Iraq, and Saudi Arabia. All the world's Semitic Laron dwarfs had been painstakingly collected and assembled here on remote and inconsequential Nobo Savu. *Why?*

Walter Sinclair described his ambitious project on Nobo Savu as being the outcome of innovative thinking and a double coincidence of needs. By this, he meant that his engineering goal was to initiate man's long-overdue colonization and conquest of the sea, using Nobo Savu as an island base. Just as the island's crabs routinely returned to the Banda Sea, Sinclair envisioned this island as a station from which man could likewise return to the realm from which his distant amphibian ancestors had arisen.

But there was a problem. Sinclair had to self-finance the project. For he could interest no venture capitalists in taking part in it. Such money was still being funneled into more traditional and less speculative investments.

Sinclair had calculated that he had only half the sum required for the project he had in mind, a project that would not remain viable if the investment sum were reduced by any amount.

But then Sinclair had done what he did best. He thought outside the box. And the solution presented itself to him. He would produce everything at half scale. But he would need half-scale humans to make this reduction feasible. Fortunately, Sinclair was aware of Laron dwarfs, due to a paper he had once read on the genetic interrelatedness of the dwarfs, who were nearly all Jewish, of Semitic origin, having undergone a diaspora in the past, which had spread them to the lands from which Sinclair had collected them.

The dwarfs, when they had been living in the outside world where buildings, houses, infrastructure, automobiles, and such were all scaled for the normal-sized human, found themselves at significant risk of accidental death due to their small stature. Being three and a half feet tall in the modern world was dangerous. Accidents were in fact the number-one cause of death amongst the Laron dwarfs.

This was at odds with their potential for long life. For extreme health is the norm among these dwarfs. Their diminutive size is caused by a rare genetic defect. This genetic disorder, however, also makes the dwarfs immune to diabetes, heart disease, and Alzheimer's. It likewise protects their DNA against damage that causes cancer. Laron dwarfs are simply not subject to the diseases associated with aging. But they are subject to a high risk of accidental death, when living in a world designed for normal-sized humans.

The double coincidence of needs: Sinclair needed half-scale humans to permit the self-funding of his project. The dispersed communities of Laron dwarfs ideally needed an environment scaled to their size, to reduce the risk of accidental death.

Sinclair pointed out, as they toured the island's hospital, that although the Ecuadorian dwarfs were all of normal IQ, a significant number of the dwarfs from elsewhere suffered mental disabilities, which he was having treated by new genetic procedures at their hospital.

On Nobo Savu, Sinclair had united the world's Laron dwarfs, providing them with a safe community to live in and needed medical treatment. In turn, he was provided with the means to begin the colonization of the sea.

"Enter the sea," Sinclair explained, his refined voice radiating wisdom, "where gravity plays a far less inhibiting role, where one floats almost weightless and physical handicaps melt away. In the sea, where man is master over fish, these beautiful little people become giants, in a new, unpopulated undersea world all their own. They now have dreams."

Claude thought briefly of his discussion last night with his wife, when he had described how he believed that the outcome of humankind being visited by an advanced extraterrestrial civilization would diminish man, as it would take away his ability to dream. Here, on Nobo Savu, Walter Sinclair had united a dispersed people, given them safety, and provided them with a dream to pursue.

"A utopia?" Claude asked, finding it all rather ingenious, and inspiring.

"I would prefer the term *practopia*." Sinclair smiled.

"Please excuse my ignorance," Claude remarked with deep and genuine interest. "But I haven't heard such a term used before. A practopia?"

Sinclair nodded in a stately manner. "Here on Nobo Savu, we're not seeking unreal, idealized perfection. We're not pursuing the best of all possible imagined worlds. But rather a new world that lies within the range of what is realistically attainable. Revolutionary, yes, but practical."

"A practopia," Claude repeated the term aloud, appreciating it.

"You might say we're practicing euthenics," Sinclair added. "Improving the development of a population's internal well-being by improving the external factors of their environment."

"You've started all this on your own." Claude nodded in appreciation, but wondered about the loneliness of it. "No financial backers, no national support, no one outside of Nobo Savu believing in you, even aware of you. No recognition. Doesn't that bother you?"

"No," Sinclair confessed, "not really. Man's entry into the sea is still so young. Our journey is only just beginning. I'm content that here on Nobo Savu we're laying down the first new footsteps that one day will be followed. It's a beginning."

As Thomas drove toward a warehouse stretching along the waterfront, Sinclair pointed to an underwater habitat being assembled in dry dock, explaining how it would be their third permanent undersea station, another, deeper stepping stone in their colonizing of man's next frontier. He also proudly stated that the habitat was being built at half the size and at half the cost of his original plan.

The jeep stopped, and they all disembarked. Claude smiled to his wife as they followed Sinclair and Thomas to a point overlooking the work on the new underwater habitat, which, manufactured as a dozen separate, connecting tubular sections, looked rather like a disassembled bicycle-tire-shaped space station, a proposed design popularized by artwork in the 1950s. Claude wondered if perhaps Sinclair had adopted and modified this old space station wheel design, adapting it for the depths of the sea.

As they stood there, Claude's focus shifted, and he suddenly felt more like an anthropologist in a pygmy village than a visiting psychiatrist, so closely did he find himself visually examining the dwarfs. Their hands and feet were so small, like children's. And so homogeneous they were in look, with their protruding foreheads, collapsed nasal bridges, and sparse hair— dark and a bit curly. And all were obese, some morbidly so. Yet, to Claude's understanding, they were all incredibly healthy.

Claude watched as Laron dwarfs moved in and out of the sea, swimming, diving. Children, too—who were also dwarfs. Laron syndrome apparently had a recessive pattern of inheritance. The Laron population, isolated and breeding only within their own gene pool, would produce only dwarfs.

The obesity of the little people seemed to give them a welcomed buoyancy in the water. As if they were tailor made to be the segment of mankind that was destined to return to the sea. Might they eventually, one day, be considered a new subspecies of man? Claude wondered.

And Claude looked at Sinclair, marveling at the man. Here on Nobo Savu, Sinclair could perhaps feel himself a giant, even a god, amongst his little people. But Claude sensed no such ego at play, only a genuine fatherly concern for the island's population, and a keen practical mind at work in pursuit of a clear and well-thought-out objective.

Sinclair had indeed not retired. He was indeed a man who was living for future dreams and goals that would extend even beyond his own lifetime. This revitalized Claude—no longer did he feel himself the deflated, doubting man of last night. He was once again the eminent Dr. Claude Arnoux, world-renowned psychiatrist, Nobel laureate—the confident, dashing, and dapper Frenchman whom he truly felt he was in his heart of hearts.

By the time they started driving out to the island's radar facility, Claude was pulsating with renewed energy, his ego intact. He was a new man, ready to take on the world—and Thomas too, by vigorously defending and standing by his hypothesis of UFOs being a psychic phenomenon. *Round two coming up.*

~8~

Nobo Savu's radar facility was located on a high hill that overlooked the airstrip to the west while offering a rather dramatic view into the island's mountainous, jungle-clad interior to the east. The station itself was a small, two-story cubical building. Above that building, however, loomed an immense tower that rose perhaps ninety to a hundred feet in height. The lofty structure was topped by a wide, continuously rotating parabolic antenna, which was exposed to the elements, unprotected by a radome.

As Claude gentlemanly followed his wife and the others up the stairs leading to the station, he noticed a large rhinoceros beetle on the nearby foliage. In an instant, the beetle flung open its wing cases and flew away, quite an astonishing sight due to its intimidating size.

Claude could not help but immediately recall his dream from last night, and as he did so he found himself becoming a bit unsettled, his reborn confidence slipping away just a little. *A huge metallic Japanese beetle about to eat away my garden? What on earth can it mean? What is it that lies hidden in my subconscious? What thoughts is my subconscious brave enough to entertain but my conscious mind too circumscribed to face?*

~9~

Claude shook the enigma presented by his dreams out of his thoughts as he entered the station. He was immediately relieved to find that the interior of the small building was accommodating to normal-sized human beings and not scaled to half size.

A rather plain-looking technician, young, thin, greeted them at the door.

"This is Jerome," Sinclair introduced the man. "A new addition to our team. He oversees our surveillance radar. Six nights ago, Jerome detected and tracked something on radar that was invisible to the eye."

"Invisible?" Claude heard himself asking, surprised, seeking clarification.

"Yes," Jerome explained, his voice quite controlled. "The target came in out of the southeast, an odd blip, descending. One object. Inbound. Slow moving.

"There were no known aircraft in the area. So I went upstairs to the visual control room, to obtain a visual sighting. It was night, but because of the target's size, it should have been visible. But there was nothing.

"And yet the visual control room also had this blip. It was stationary at that time, on the screen. I even stepped outside with my binoculars. Still nothing. Even though the object continued to show on the radarscope, until it moved over the center of the island. Where it vanished from the scope. Just disappeared."

"A UFO?" Claude asked.

"I'm the biggest skeptic of UFOs," Jerome responded with a respectful quietness. "But I have no explanation for the incident. So, yes, an unidentified flying object."

"UFOs," Thomas interjected, slowly, carefully choosing each of his words, "have a history of being seen by the eye and not detected on radar. And conversely, of being tracked by radar when invisible to the eye. This fact seems to suggests that UFOs can make themselves invisible at will, when undertaking their clandestine surveys. It suggests the craft must be composed of an unknown substance that allows for visibility one moment and invisibility the next."

This time around, it was Claude who looked at Thomas incredulously. "*Radar* is simply a means for detecting anything that will reflect radio waves of high frequency when they bounce back. Even such things as moisture can give cockeyed results. Radar is sometimes much easier to fool than the eye, sometimes less easy to fool. The reliability of radar is far from encouraging. A radar trace doesn't automatically prove that there is anything hard and solid present."

Claude once again felt Sinclair's eyes studying him, as were the eyes of the others. But it felt good to Claude, being the center of attention. He felt it his natural place to be, and he drew strength from it. He waited for Thomas's reaction.

"Pure psychic projections," Thomas countered somewhat pointedly, "are certainly incapable of throwing back a radar echo. On the other hand, something that possesses a surface, seen or unseen, does throw back such an echo."

Claude felt his wife once again squeeze his arm, cautioning him. This time he glanced at her, gallantly, giving her a reassuring look. Confident, in control, he turned to the radar technician.

"Jerome," Claude asked the young man with silky politesse, "could there have been some sort of technical problem with the radar, an equipment malfunction?"

"Everything was checked thoroughly," Jerome answered matter-of-factly. "Everything had been functioning correctly."

Claude thought for a moment. "Nobo Savu has incredibly high mountains—the peaks must be exposed to trade winds. An unknown radar target can be caused by a temperature inversion, can it not?"

"A temperature inversion," Jerome corrected Claude, "would appear as a single line on a radar screen. Not as a single object. It wasn't atmospheric, or birds, or anything else. It wasn't like any radar target I've ever seen. Its movements were completely different from those of an ordinary aircraft."

"How so?" Claude asked.

Jerome explained: "It would stop. Hover. Reverse its course. Dart off. It wasn't following any recognizable, standard flight path. In fact, it didn't follow any logical pattern. Its movements seemed more based on impulse than reason."

The words struck at Claude's intellect, momentarily paralyzing his thoughts. For they were exactly how he had described the saucer's movements in his dreams. Claude felt his confidence slip, his ego deflate a notch. *Can my hypothesis be wrong? Can my dreams be warning me of this?*

"Dr. Arnoux?" Sinclair prompted Claude, pulling the psychiatrist out of his prolonged silence.

"Were there any corresponding visual sightings?" Claude asked.

"Indeed," Sinclair confirmed. "Two of my little people saw this unidentified flying object that night. And others have reported seeing it each night since."

"You have multiple witnesses?" Claude asked, quite surprised.

"Yes," Sinclair confirmed. "That is our UFO problem. Perfectly normal, reliable people have been seeing *something* that I cannot account for."

Claude's response came out slow and rather automatic, robotic. "Even people who are entirely in full possession of their senses can sometimes see things that don't actually exist."

"That's what I'd like you to determine for me," Sinclair stated. "In this case of my little people. It's the reason why I invited you to Nobo Savu, for your expertise on this matter. I need to know if there can possibly be anything to these sightings. Or if there is something psychologically wrong with my little people."

Claude nodded, his mind partly elsewhere.

"Thomas," Sinclair said, "let's drive out to the first witnesses. Let Dr. Arnoux interview the couple."

~10~

On the drive, Claude sat silently beside his wife, lost in thought. He only half listened to Thomas, who, as he drove, was telling Judith something about UFOs:

"Airplanes, commercial and military, seem to arouse their curiosity. UFOs often fly toward planes at high altitudes, even pursue them on occasion. They also avoid planes, flying away from them. And this phenomenon of UFOs—although sightings have appeared en masse since World War Two, UFOs may have been seen for hundreds of years, perhaps even thousands. This would suggest a long, continued presence on Earth."

As Thomas continued, Claude found himself fortifying his position in his own mind. He reminded himself of the red panda incident that had occurred in Holland a good number of decades ago. A red panda had escaped from the Rotterdam zoo. The zoo informed the media in an effort to alert the populous, in an attempt to recover the rare animal. But just as the newspapers reported the missing panda, the animal was found dead along the railroad tracks near the zoo.

Yet for the next several days, over one hundred people from all over the Netherlands, having read the papers, reported sighting the panda, despite the fact that the animal was already dead. *What were these people seeing? Only what they expected to see... Even though it didn't exist.*

Human expectations. Interpretive filters. Unconscious extrapolation. *If you're expecting to see a panda, you see a panda. If you're expecting to see a UFO...*

~11~

Through the late afternoon and into the evening, Claude interviewed over a dozen Laron dwarfs who, individually and in twos and threes, claimed to have witnessed Nobo Savu's UFO. All reported seeing the object at night, on different days, at different times. All described the UFO similarly, as a distant, round light in the sky, white or possibly blue in color. Soundless. No one claimed to have viewed the UFO for longer than half a minute. Their vague descriptions matched countless reports that Claude had studied and dismissed in his past research. None of the dwarfs reported anything that even remotely matched the unusual movements reported by the radar technician.

All the witnesses presented as truthful, psychologically well balanced, and completely normal. No one seemed to have been hallucinating. Yet in Claude's mind, applying the red panda effect, the reliability, accuracy, and testimony of these eyewitnesses meant very little. The reports could not confirm or deny the existence of an unknown aircraft. It was impossible to determine the true nature of the observations. There was no proof sufficient to permit conclusions to be drawn.

"Could this be a case of industrial espionage?" Claude asked Sinclair, proposing an alternative explanation. "Some corporate competitor sends a helicopter or plane to Nobo Savu, in a covert manner, to spy on your operations here?"

"There have been no reports of any strangers on the island," Sinclair responded. "No reports of any sounds of traditional aircraft."

Claude shrugged wearily.

~12~

Even the jeep sounded tired as it groaned to a halt in front of their last stop for the evening, a small, dome-shaped hut in the interior mountains, not far from the hillside accommodations provided to Claude and his wife.

Inside, Claude was introduced to Paúl Valarezo, thirty-two years of age, three and a half feet in height. Paúl had recently finished his dinner, and he was drinking a glass of a traditional Ecuadorian liquor, *aguardiente*—in English: firewater.

"Paúl," Sinclair stated, "is our most recent witness, having seen something only last night."

To Claude's trained eye, Paúl appeared to be suffering from some internal constitutional inadequacy. This manifested itself in the dwarf's palpable lack of confidence, in his nervous movements, in his inability to hold eye contact.

Claude wondered what it was like to be a dwarf, so diminutive. In some individuals, did it squash the ego? Shrink the spirit?

Crouched over to keep from bumping upon the low ceiling, Claude followed the others' example and took a seat on the floor, the furniture being too small to accommodate a normal-sized adult. Once he was seated, the interior seemed much roomier.

A nervous smile lifted and dropped on Paúl's face as he poured each of his visitors a small glass of firewater.

"I distill it myself," Paúl said in a heavy Ecuadorian accent, his voice and mannerisms displaying an uneasiness. "From the sugarcane we grow in the valley."

Claude took a sip. The drink had a strong molasses aftertaste.

"I wasn't drinking when I saw it," Paúl volunteered, his voice becoming tense. "I was going through the trees, marking them."

"Paúl is out here," Sinclair explained, "identifying mature hardwoods, for our sawmill."

"Oh." Claude nodded.

"I lost track of time," Paúl continued. "Found myself caught in the dark on the way back. The crabs were everywhere.

I just wanted to get back here. I tripped and fell. That's when I saw it. The thing... It was maybe twenty meters from me. Floating there, behind the trees. Glowing. It made all the hair on the back of my neck stand up."

Claude leaned forward. "How did it move?"

Paúl thought for a moment and hesitated before answering. "Like a fish on land. But floating up in the air. Still one moment, then flopping about, but slow. Then still. Changing color. Orange. Then red. Purple. Yellow. Then no color at all. I couldn't see it sometimes. It was so dark last night."

Claude exchanged glances with the others.

"Have you heard this before?" Claude asked Sinclair.

"No, we haven't yet had time to talk to Paúl."

"Could you see an interior structure," Claude asked Paúl, "inside the light? A mechanical craft of some kind?"

"No." Paúl shook his head. Growing unnerved, he took a swig of his *aguardiente*. "It was only the light. The glow. A big glow. Bigger than this hut. Three, maybe four times as big as this hut."

"What happened next?" Sinclair asked.

"The thing," Paúl answered, "it started wobbling through the trees. Moving south. Then back north. Moving back and forth. Circling. Like a dog does before it finds a place to lie down. It was so odd. Then it... it disappeared."

"Was there any exhaust?" Claude asked. "A vapor trail?"

Paúl shook his head.

"Did it make any sound?" Claude asked.

Paúl nodded.

"What kind of sound?" Claude pressed for an answer.

"Like... loud air. Like... forced air. Almost like the bellows that force air to a deep-sea diver."

Claude caught Thomas shooting an intense look to Sinclair.

"What?" Claude reacted.

"When we're outside," Sinclair responded in a quiet voice, with extreme seriousness.

They don't believe him? Claude wondered. And Claude looked back at Paúl, visually examining him again. In Claude's professional judgment, the dwarf, although suffering from low self-esteem—perhaps due to low hormonal levels—and presenting as nervous, frightened, was recounting what he believed to be true and accurate. He was not making this up. And his account was uniquely different than the rather generic UFOs reported by the others on the island. It in fact resembled the more troubling UFO sightings that Claude had researched over the past year. And of notable significance was the fact that Paúl had described something that behaved, in terms of its movements, similarly to what the radar technician had observed on his scope.

"What do you think it was, Paúl?" Claude asked in earnest. Paúl shrugged. He had no idea.

~13~

Outside, Sinclair walked the full distance to the jeep before he turned to face Claude, who uncharacteristically had stepped ahead of his wife to catch up to his host.

"Have you ever heard of the term *USO?*" Sinclair asked. Claude shook his head.

"Thomas." Sinclair prompted his pilot and driver.

"It's an acronym," Thomas responded, "for 'unidentified submerged object.' The many sightings of this oceanic phenomenon, by the various navies of the world, compare to that of the UFO."

"Thomas suspects," Sinclair explained, "that USOs and UFOs are one and the same. The same phenomena traveling through different mediums: air and sea. Thomas suspects that my island has come under the surveillance not of a corporate competitor, but of an alien presence here on Earth that is living in our sea…"

Claude felt himself struck utterly dumbfounded. He immediately felt mentally enervated. *Such a twist!* He found himself looking to his wife, only to find that she was looking to him. He turned his eyes back to Sinclair. But Sinclair just stood there, broad shouldered, courtly, raising a hand to his chin, silently studying Claude, waiting.

Claude nodded, gathering his thoughts. Piecing things together in his mind. Thomas had earlier suggested that mankind's use of nuclear weapons had attracted the attention of an extraterrestrial neighbor. Apparently, he was now suggesting that Sinclair's invasion of the sea had brought about a similar reaction of disquiet in this neighbor. *An aquatic neighbor?*

He replayed Thomas's voice in his mind, from their earlier drive, and he recalled something being said about an alien presence on Earth for hundreds, perhaps thousands of years. *In our seas?* And this underwater neighbor was now carrying out an objective inspection of Nobo Savu? *Sinclair's aim to colonize the sea… Does it represent a territorial threat to this hypothetical sentient undersea inhabitant?*

"I don't believe it," Claude finally declared. "I understand why it's vital to you to determine if your UFO is real or a mere fantasy product of the human mind. But I don't believe this USO hypothesis."

"Why?" Sinclair asked.

And Claude struggled with it. *Is it my ego? Am I fighting being bested by this Thomas? No… all my instincts are telling me there is another explanation. Not Thomas's hypothesis… and maybe… maybe not even my own…*

"What, then?" Thomas added.

Claude glanced to his wife, making eye contact with her, grasping for something. And then it came to him. Drawing upon her expressed insight from last night, he finally found his voice. "Taking into account the essential strangeness of this phenomenon, perhaps we should not expect a rational explanation..."

"Are you indicating," Sinclair asked earnestly, without intending insult, "that you have nothing rational and useful to contribute on this issue?"

Claude thought for a moment, maturely, deeply, calming himself, reminding himself that the essence of an independent mind lies not in what it thinks, but in how it thinks. He carefully considered the facts, his instincts, his dreams, and then responding imperturbably: "Something was seen. And we don't know what it was."

Thomas opened his mouth to speak, but then didn't.

"I'm afraid that's all I can conclude," Claude added. "Now, if you'll excuse me, our cottage is several miles down this road, is it not?"

Sinclair nodded.

"I'll see you later, my dear." Claude kissed his wife lovingly on the cheek and then turned to Thomas. "Please drive my wife back to the cottage. I need a long walk."

And Claude headed off into the dark.

Thomas stepped up to Judith. "Will he be all right?" he asked her.

She nodded. "He needs time alone with his thoughts. When things are different than one had thought, the truth is sometimes a difficult thing to accept."

~14~

Another black night on Nobo Savu, and through it Claude walked, his mind awhirl with disbelieving thoughts. He found himself longing for sleep, but he knew that he must continue his journey deeper into the realm of his own thinking. He needed more satisfying answers.

Claude noticed a dirt road up ahead. It forked off the paved one he was traveling upon. From that intersection emerged one of the island's little people, carrying a flashlight.

"Hello," the dwarf greeted Claude.

"Hello," Claude replied. Claude noticed that the small man was wearing a belted holster containing a large spray can. "Marking trees?" Claude guessed.

"How did you know?"

"I'm psychic." Claude forced a smile, although his rich voice was humorless, filled with discomfort and fatigue.

The two passed each other and Claude stopped before the dirt road. It tunneled into the jungle, into the eerie darkness of the island's interior. Large crimson land crabs were emerging from it, two and three at a time, their many legs clicking creepily upon contact with the main road. The sound unnerved Claude, so unsettling he perceived it to be. Yet, on impulse, he stepped off the safety of the asphalt and onto the wildness of the road that led to he knew not where. Navigating his way around crabs with extreme uneasiness, he soon found himself swallowed entirely by the night.

It was not long before he wished he had a flashlight. And he began questioning his actions. *Am I trying to punish myself, for abandoning my own hypothesis? No...* Claude reasoned that his walking off the main road was more likely a desperate urge to jar himself, so that perhaps his mind would think in a more unorthodox manner. And so he walked on, placing his trust in his instincts.

~15~

How much time had passed Claude did not know. But he knew that he now wanted to turn around and go back. It was at that moment when the land crabs scurried off the road in front of him, fleeing into the surrounding jungle.

"What?"

Claude suddenly felt a tiny prickling sensation tingling across his chest and shoulders, like what one sometimes feels before an electrical storm. But stronger, more pronounced. It sent the hair on the back of his head standing on end. Claude at once remembered Paúl telling how the hair had stood up on the back of his neck—when he noticed the UFO.

Claude looked up and about. Down the road, above the trees, a flying saucer floated into view, undulating, refulgent, glowing white and blue. It was not the interplanetary machine from his dreams. It did not look at all like a machine. Yet it did possess some affinity with the object of his dreams in terms of its size, its movements.

Suddenly, although a good distance away, it seemed to notice Claude, and it tilted toward him, transmuting as it did so, becoming less flat and more round, swollen. Its solid glow pulsed and the light scattered across its surface, which became variegated by repeating bursts of blue and gray against a white, cloud-like surface.

Claude felt his entire world shift off-kilter, so traumatic was his astonishment. It was as if he were suddenly standing at the edge of the world and about to tumble off. He felt waves of pusillanimity sweep over him, and he struggled against them with all his heart, scolding himself.

Don't run away like in your dreams, you coward!

He told himself most sternly that he needed to be brave. That he needed to get a better look at the thing, to learn what it truly was.

But the thing shot straight up into the sky at a great speed. *Oh no...*

Claude watched in despair as it hovered there, so very high above his head that it had become reduced in size to but a point of white light.

Then it turned blue and came dropping back down, rather feebly. It circled Claude curiously, once, twice, and then it became colorless, diaphanous. It was almost impossible to see.

Claude stood there, captivated. Slowly, color returned to the thing. It became speckled by warm yellow blotches as it floated there, like a weightless thought, like an object out of a fantasy.

As it pulsated, like a slowly beating heart, Claude felt himself calming. It was then that he heard its breathing. What Paúl had described as "loud air," "forced air." *It's breathing... My God, it's alive...*

Undulating, the thing glowed red, orange, then purple before it silently floated off, changing form as it moved, quivering like a giant jelly-like mass. Slowly, it dropped behind the top of the trees down the road and disappeared.

Claude went after it, awkwardly setting one foot in front of the other, his movements deliberate but like those of a sleepwalker.

Nothing to feel threatened by... Claude reassured himself. *It's only an unexpected... natural wonder.*

The thing had settled in a clearing, where mature hardwoods had recently been harvested. Dropping to his hands and knees, Claude quietly crawled as close to it as he dared. Less than a stone's throw away, he marveled at its spherical virtual emptiness. It seemed to be composed of bladders of highly tenuous matter surrounding some inner core.

Neither animal nor plant, Claude speculated, allowing his imagination free rein, *but some life-form far beyond our understanding.*

Claude intuitively sensed a lower order of intelligence compared to that of man's. Perhaps something more akin to the great baleen whales of the seas. But something that moved through a gaseous environment, rather than an aqueous one, its shape shifting as needed, as it moved.

Where was it born? Claude wondered as he calmed further. Did it dwell in the upper atmosphere? At the edge of space? Perhaps in outer space itself? Maybe even in the atmospheres of other worlds. Were these Earth's neighbors? Had it perhaps evolved on another world, in Jupiter's clouds, and then migrated to Earth, traveling across airless space? Or was this an indigenous creature, yet unknown to humanity? A floating impossibility that fed on sunlight like a plant.

But why have we never seen you before? Oh... we have. And Claude came to realize that UFOs were alive. They were these unknown life-forms whose diaphanous, membrane-like outer matter likely shone like burnished aluminum when in bright sunlight, while glowing at night, their colors matching their motions, or perhaps their emotions.

And then Claude remembered that the old US Air Force Project Bluebook, when examining UFOs many decades ago, had considered both sensible explanations and highly speculative ones—one such explanation being the proposed life-form hypothesis, which had been rejected on its absurdity. Claude had also intellectually rejected the idea. But it must have stuck somewhere in the back of his mind. Thus, his dreams:

The metallic flying beetles, mechanical yet with a semblance of life. The inquisitive, peculiar behavior of the craft, akin to that of living things. His subconscious was pointing him toward the truth behind the UFO enigma. An outlandish explanation that fit the facts, but an explanation that his staid conscious intellect would never seriously consider. Seemingly weightless objects... Movements suggesting intelligent guidance...

These great things of the sky were the universal trigger that prompted the red panda effect in people's minds. When someone by chance saw one, the human mind interpreted the creature in terms of the modern myth of flying saucers.

And Claude thought of how man's nuclear atmospheric tests must have so greatly threatened these things of the sky. Were they intelligent enough or curious enough to seek out the source of these explosions? Were these Thomas's disquieted surveying neighbors?

Could these creatures also maneuver through the sea? Like giant jellyfish? Were they also Thomas's USOs, or were those something entirely different?

Slowly, Claude came to realize that what he had mistaken for breathing was really the creature pulling in and circulating air within its membranal structure, perhaps to keep itself inflated, buoyed.

Claude smiled, and he imagined the beauty of this diaphanous sky creature effortlessly jetting through the atmosphere, like a squid through the sea.

Up there so high, is the wind your constant companion? Do you embrace its caress? Do the raindrops feel soft and welcome? Do you flee from our noisy jets?

As he imaginatively, poetically entered its world in his mind, he suddenly felt himself an intruder from the realm outside of where this creature called home.

But why are you down here? On Nobo Savu? So far from the upper atmosphere.

To spawn? Claude guessed. Was this thing like the island's crabs? Hearing the alluring siren call of the sea. Distancing themselves from their natural habitat. Did the rhythm of nature beat so strongly that it could even move such an immense creature as this such a fantastic distance?

No... It was something different. Something quite the opposite. Claude sensed—somehow he knew—that the great sky creature was dying. He guessed that this life-form must have responded to the pleasantly alluring sight of Nobo Savu as an old and sick seagull or albatross would respond to an inviting landfall, and the safety that it offered.

From this, Claude concluded that this sky creature was native to Earth. Whatever birthed it may have come from elsewhere, but it was born here. For no life would die so far from its home by choice. This creature lived in the atmosphere, but it must have instinctively sought the safety of the ground when its time came.

Claude wondered if he should run off, to find Sinclair. *No*—he reasoned that reporting the presence of this beautiful, fragile thing would be like tearing apart a flower.

Instead, he rose and moved closer to it. He walked right up to the thing from the sky, without fear, with only the deepest empathy he had ever felt. *So beautiful, she is indeed like a flower...*

Standing there, Claude felt that her end was near. That her world was dimming. He sensed that her entire universe of perception had shrunken down to just herself and him. The open vastness she had once roamed at will was now irretrievably lost to her senses.

Claude felt safe enough to touch her, and he did. She was soft, like a cloud made tangible. The contact imbued Claude with a palpable sense of her inner beauty: *I am the sky and the sky is me.*

Claude stood there, his hands gently on what would have been her face if she were something other, a form more familiar. She settled more firmly upon the forest floor, losing her magical weightlessness.

As she breathed, Claude breathed. A breath… a breath… a breath…

Each breath of hers seemed less forced, gentler, as if worn softer and softer by the purity and intimacy of their connectedness.

Her age was too far forward in time. Her spirit for life too fatigued to continue.

One last breath and her head dropped gently forward into Claude's arms, her weight coming to rest fully upon the forest floor. Her time was over.

And Claude stood there, just holding her. And he began to cry. For her and for himself. If these great glowing beings died, surely one day he would as well. Suddenly he was less than nothing, his ego squashed down beneath the heal of reality. His true self was revealed to him and fully realized; his eyes opened to a reality that had previously evaded him. And he grew inside, to become more and less than he had ever been before.

"Thank you…" he said to the sky giant. "Oh… thank you…"

Holding her in his hands, Claude watched as her tenuous essence began to glow softly and evaporate, floating off and winking out of existence like dissolving bubbles of soap.

Claude glanced about, feeling the utter loneliness of the moment. It was only he and the night shapes, the crabs, the mute million eyes of Nobo Savu, who bore witness to this ephemeral leaving.

And Claude thought of how the universe far transcended what man could sense, what man could organize into thought, what man could assign a purpose to. In reality, man received into his brain but only a few narrow bands of the gigantic spectrum of messages dispensed by the cosmos. And outside of those narrow bands, only slightly widened by technology, man sensed nothing and understood very little.

Claude would tell only his wife about what he had discovered, and swear her to secrecy. He wanted no recognition, no fame, no part of alerting mankind to the existence of these wondrous sky creatures, so that man could chase them for documentary or sport. No, he would never reveal the secret of UFOs.

Acknowledgements and Identifying Notations

• Nobo Savu is a fictional island. Nobo Savu's crab migration is based on the crab migration that occurs annually on Christmas Island of the Indian Ocean, where over 40 million land crabs make their way to the sea.

• The hypothesis of an atmospheric unknown life-form being the possible explanation behind UFOs was presented as one of four possible explanations by Ivan T. Sanderson in his article titled "UFO—Friend or Foe," published on pages 4–12 of the August 1957, vol. 8, no. 2 issue of the magazine *Fantastic Universe.*

• The dream sequences and the information and speculations on UFOs in "The Million Eyes of Nobo Savu" were drawn primarily from the collected nonfiction writings on the subject by Swiss psychiatrist and psychoanalyst C. G. Jung, collected in the book titled *Flying Saucers: A Modern Myth of Things Seen in the Skies.*

• When the protagonist of this story critiques radar, his criticism is based on that of American science-fiction author and editor Lester del Rey, as expressed in his article titled "The Saucer Myth," published on pages 21–29 of the August 1957, vol. 8, no. 2 issue of the magazine *Fantastic Universe.* (Author Niko Zinovii envisioned the protagonist's research into UFOs as having covered a broad spectrum of expressed opinions, including Lester del Rey's.)

• Civilian Saucer Intelligence was an actual short-lived research group founded in New York in 1954, in operation until 1959.

• The optical illusion of sea gulls being mistaken as flying saucers is based on the description given by science and science-fiction writer Arthur C. Clarke when he recounted such an experience on Long John Nebel's radio show. The relevant episode aired on February 1, 1958.

• The protagonist's idea of the brain sending messages to the eye, making the eye not a camera but something akin to a television screen, was first expressed by science and science-fiction writer Arthur C. Clarke.

• When the protagonist early on defends his belief that UFOs are not extraterrestrial, part of his defense is based on a response given by astronomer Carl Sagan during a March 18, 1974, *People* magazine interview titled "Carl Sagan Searches for Neighbors Out There in Space." (Author Niko Zinovii envisioned the protagonist's research into UFOs as having covered a broad spectrum of expressed opinions, including the thoughts of astronomer Carl Sagan.)

• The protagonist's wife expressing her belief that UFOs are an unknown phenomenon is based partly on musician Frank Zappa's thoughts on the subject of UFOs, as expressed in a 1991 interview.

• The protagonist's philosophical musing near the very end of the story is based on the thoughts of the renowned French undersea explorer and scientist Jacques-Yves Cousteau as expressed in his book *Lessons of Light,* one book of the twenty books composing the set *The Ocean World of Jacques Cousteau,* published in 1975 by the Danbury Press. (Author Niko Zinovii envisioned the protagonist, being French, as having read Cousteau's works and incorporated Cousteau's philosophical thoughts on life into his worldview.)

Cousteau: "The universe far transcends what man can sense, what he can organize into thought, what he can assign a purpose to. Man receives into his brain only a few narrow bands of the gigantic spectrum of messages dispensed by the cosmos. Outside these narrow bands, only slightly widened by technology, man senses nothing and understands very little."

• "The essence of the independent mind lies not in what it thinks, but in how it thinks." —Christopher Hitchens

• The UFO radar contact in "The Million Eyes of Nobo Savu" was based on two UFO/radar incidents:

1. The December 26, 1980, UFO incident at RAF Bentwaters, in Suffolk, England

2. A radar incident at RAF Lyneham in Wiltshire, England, just before Christmas in either 1994 or 1995

A Note from the Author

This author hopes the reader enjoyed this highly speculative tale on the subject of UFOs, painted against the lightly detailed backdrop of a practopian settlement of little people pursuing the colonization of the sea. (Laron syndrome dwarfs do exist.)

The story was inspired by:

1. The title "The Million Eyes of Nobo Savu," which was imagined before a story existed.
2. The nonfiction writings of Swiss psychiatrist and psychoanalyst C. G. Jung on the subject of UFOs.
3. Jacques-Yves Cousteau's attempt at colonizing the sea.

A note of interest:

In the 1960s, undersea explorer Jacques-Yves Cousteau undertook an ambitious attempt to establish manned undersea research stations as stepping stones to the exploitation and colonization of the sea:

Conshelf I: 1962, the world's first manned undersea habitat, submerged thirty-three feet beneath the Mediterranean, off the coast of Marseilles. Two oceanauts spent seven days in Conshelf I, under the sea.

Conshelf II: 1963, a half-dozen oceanauts lived for thirty days, thirty-three feet beneath the Red Sea. In addition, there was a smaller "deep cabin" located at a depth of one hundred feet, where two oceanauts spent a week.

Conshelf III: 1965, six oceanauts lived in this habitat at a depth of 336 feet beneath the Mediterranean, between Nice and Monaco, for three weeks.

The Conshelf projects were funded in part by the French petrochemical industry. After Conshelf III, Cousteau could secure no further support and investment to colonize the sea.

Since Cousteau's golden age of undersea habitats, more than sixty underwater marine labs have been built and operated around the world, all defunct except for one to three small undersea laboratories that remain in operation today, located in the Florida Keys.

Man has yet to make a serious, sustained effort to colonize the sea.

Niko Zinovii
Santa Monica, California
20 January 2018

Niko Zinovii

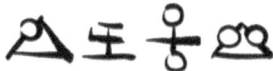

Hollow Boat

Japan, 1803, the Edo Period:

Oda Yoshida crossed the flooded riverbank barefoot, his sandals in hand. The cool water and soft mud felt soothing to his sore and tired feet, and he welcomed this small pleasure. The sun was setting now, and he welcomed this too. For he was a poor, middle-aged bamboo cutter, and he had been chopping young stalks all day in the heat. His arms and back ached.

Only today left of spring, Oda thought. *My walking ended it.* And he felt spring passing in the cry of the birds, in the tears in the eyes of the fish…

Nearby:

In an old pond
a frog plunged into
the sound of water.

Oda turned north and headed toward Harashagahama of the Hitachi Province. As he did so, he thought of his puppets, which awaited him in his rickety shack by the sea. He thought of how he needed to re-dress the puppets, repaint them, to prepare them for the next show. For in his free time, he was a *ningyōtsukai*—a puppeteer—of the Osaka tradition, employing *ningyō*—hand puppets, half life size. Dressed entirely in black, Oda would stand behind the puppets during a performance, politely accepted as invisible by his audience.

It took three puppeteers to move a ningyō. He was the *ashizukai*, the puppeteer limited to operating a doll's legs and feet, working in coordination with two other puppeteers: an *omozukai* operating the puppet's right hand, and a *hidarizukai* controlling the left.

Although he was older and of lower class, it was still Oda's secret ambition to one day rise to become an omozukai. But for now, it was just the legs and feet. And he was charged with maintaining and preparing the dolls. It was hard work, but he took great pride in doing his very best.

~

At sunset, Oda finally reached his lonely shack on the beach of Haratono-hama, where the air was filled with the scent of the sea and of drying nets and fish.

Oda lit one candle with another candle. Next he lit his old lantern, and he watched the nearby yellow chrysanthemums lose their color.

While a shot of sake passed his throat, the moon appeared. He thought of how, even though he was treated as an outcast by the rich and educated, at least he shared the same moon. And he smiled at this thought, for it uplifted his soul.

Eating dry rice cakes, Oda began the *koshirae* process of re-dressing his puppets, altering their colors, changing collars, sashes, robes, and inner kimonos. He then focused intensely on each *kashira*—head. For preparing the hair, made of yak tail, was an art unto itself. He used water mixed with bee's wax to alter and style the hair, in order to distinguish the dolls from one another, reflecting differences in gender, age, and social class.

As he repainted the faces, giving the dolls new personalities, he marveled at their mechanical eyes—vital for the *sanbāso* performances.

While working, Oda noticed that the garment of one of the puppets was torn, and that underneath the cloth, it had a damaged leg. This would be difficult to repair, for he would need to replace the small bamboo rods within the leg's casing.

And so Oda worked diligently into the night, sipping on sake, nibbling on rice cakes, glancing from time to time at the fishing boats and at the sea:

> Escaped the nets,
> escaped the ropes,
> moon on the water.

Later, in the darkness, as the sea swelled and fell and swelled, Oda dreamed of the unknown world lying outside Japan, beyond China. For since 1603, under the shogunate, Japan was *sakoku*—a closed country—having purposely isolated itself, trading only with China and the Netherlands, avoiding all other foreign interactions and influences.

To Oda, in this third year of *Kyōwa*, in this Year of the Ox, the world beyond the sea was a complete mystery.

~

Oda awoke and heated tea. He felt like a monk, sipping morning tea in the early silence, amongst the chrysanthemum flowers. It made him think of his favorite poet, Issa, and how the man's name meant "a single bubble in a steeping tea."

Oda noticed the morning wind, which sent water lapping against a heron's legs. There would be no cutting bamboo today. Instead, his gorgeous kite would rise from his beggar's shack.

Oda smiled and walked stiffly toward the water's edge.

> Along the shore,
> mixed with small shells,
> petals of bush clover.

It was then that Oda noticed the strange object that had washed ashore down the beach. It looked like a small boat, but it was unlike any boat he had ever seen. He joined the half-dozen fishermen who were already cautiously approaching the oddity.

Round like a ball and disc-shaped, it looked rather like a rice-cooking pot. Or a large, covered incense burner—a *kōbako*. It appeared large enough to fit within it two or three men...

"*Utsuro-bune*," Oda heard one of the older fishermen say—hollow boat.

Together the men crept up close to the strange hollow boat. Its top was made of glittering glass or crystal, patterned like folding screens. Its sides were of what looked like red-lacquered rosewood, or sandalwood, only it wasn't wood at all but something else entirely.

There was a thick rim encircling the craft. This seemed to be coated with black paint, only it was not paint... The bottom of the strange boat was ribbed by sturdy metal bands and wide plates, perhaps made of bronze or iron. It must have been made of metal of the highest Western quality, remarked several of the fishermen, for the boat to have survived crashing against the rocks that lined the shore. Yet there was not a scratch on the metal.

A hatch swung open on the top of the boat. *It must be hinged with a hidden latch*, Oda thought. Out of the craft emerged a woman. She was not Japanese, but the strangest and most beautiful woman Oda had ever seen. Even in the most unfavorable light she would have looked beautiful.

Yet there was an odd blankness, a lack of expression on the countenance of this strange vision of morning glory.

"You are the butterfly,
and I the dreaming heart
of Sōshi?"
Oda heard himself remark aloud.

And the woman responded, speaking in an unfamiliar language, one unlike anything they had ever heard before. The fishermen speculated on where this foreigner might have come from. "A princess from a far distant land," one guessed. "A Russian spy," guessed another, "coming to persuade us to trade with them."

Oda observed her closely as the men argued. He noted the details of her beauty. She was young, perhaps no older than twenty, and elegantly dressed in a fine kimono of a strange fabric never before seen in Hitachi.

Most startling was her face, which was a very pale pink, as if she had never seen the sun. Her conspicuous face was accented quite dramatically by her hair and eyebrows, which were fiery red in color, as were her lips.

Oda felt his eyes drawn more closely to her hair, which was extraordinarily long and hung straight down her back. It seemed lengthened by animal fur or some kind of fabric—these extensions covered by a fine powder, white like flour.

Her hands appeared unusually slender, attractively delicate, and within them she held a small rectangular box unlike anything found in Japan. Was it a gift? One of the fishermen tried to accept it from her, but she held on to it tightly and resisted, maintaining possession of it, oddly continuing thereafter to hold it there in front of herself, waist high.

Well mannered, this mysterious woman seemed content to simply stand before the men as they tried again and again to communicate with her, unsuccessfully. In response to their many questions, she merely smiled enigmatically and looked back at them calmly, with her blank face.

~

The fishermen decided to take the secretive foreigner to their village, and Oda accompanied them. He would not be flying his kite today, not with such a remarkable stranger in their midst.

Oda found himself nodding in approval at how their visitor walked: with the daintiest, most careful steps. It was almost as if she were not used to walking. He wondered how long she had been at sea.

On the way to their village, Oda noticed a fallen blossom returning to the bough, he thought—but no, a butterfly. He smiled at nature's trickery. And he saw their visitor smile too, expressing similar appreciation.

Singing, flying, singing, a nearby cuckoo was keeping quite busy. The foreigner smiled again, as did Oda.

Next they passed flowers offered to Buddha, floating down the river. To each beauty offered by Japan, their visitor smiled, observing and appreciating the sights like a newborn, always turning her mysterious box toward what she was observing.

As they entered the village, a plum-scented breeze, in the land of haiku, gently blew over them.

> Green willows,
> painted eyebrows on the face
> of the cliff.

In the village, Oda noticed their visitor attentively noting everything about their settlement, as if carrying out a careful inspection. The village elders observed her with equal curiosity and scrutiny.

She was offered food and drink, but she abstained. Oda wondered how she could make such a long voyage and not thirst or hunger. She was so very puzzling to him. Unknowable.

"Perhaps she is from China," one of the elders proposed, only to be met with the most incredulous expressions from his peers.

"Does not China lie beneath the selfsame sky bound in misery?" the elder defended himself.

Oda looked over their visitor again, her pink skin, her fiery red hair and eyebrows. *She is certainly not Chinese.* He felt convinced of this. Oda wondered if she might be Russian, as one of the fishermen had earlier suggested. Could her clothing and hairstyle be of Russian origin?

Finally, the oldest and wisest of the elders offered an explanation that seemed to fit the circumstances. The elder proposed that their visitor was indeed a princess from an unknown foreign land. That she had betrayed her powerful husband by having a torrid affair with a local peasant. Her husband had wanted her put to death for her unfaithfulness. But due to her beauty, she was loved by her people, and this stayed her husband's hand. Instead of execution, she was mercifully exiled, banished forever from her land, set adrift, left to the fate of the sea.

"What about the box?" someone asked.

The wise elder's face grew most serious. "It contains the head of her executed peasant lover."

Oda felt himself take a nervous, hushed step back, as did nearly everyone else.

The elder's explanation, the strangeness of the situation, and their inability to communicate with their visitor suddenly made them all quite afraid, for they knew full well the rule of the Tokugawa shogunate prohibiting any contact with foreigners.

The elders began to whisper to each other their concerns about properly dealing with this situation themselves, before the *bakufu*—the local government—found out about their visitor and they risked punishment.

The elders decided that the fishermen were to bring this unwelcome foreigner back to her hollow boat, tow her out to sea, and set her adrift. She would be left to the sea, as was her originally intended fate.

This seemed so terribly cruel to Oda. But he understood the law, and so he could not find his voice to protest. Instead, he somberly joined the fishermen in silently escorting the foreign princess back to the sea.

~

Oda sailed with the princess and the fishermen as they used one of their boats to tow her strange craft far out to sea.

When land was almost lost from sight, the fishermen ordered the princess to return to her hollow boat. But she did not understand, so Oda decided to help her. He was surprised at how slender and light her arm felt as he gently took hold of her and stepped down with her upon the crystal top of her bobbing utsuro-bune.

As the foreign princess was about to enter her odd boat, the sea pitched and she misstepped, falling into the interior. Concerned, Oda followed her down into the craft.

Inside, Oda was surprised to see strange, unfamiliar symbols, writing encircling the craft's inner wall. The script was exquisitely beautiful and totally mystifying. Something he had no hope of deciphering, for he was not a *bonkajin*—an intellectual.

Oda felt a strange sponginess beneath his feet, and he saw that he was standing upon a carpet-like thing that was very soft and of an unknown material.

He then noticed the princess standing before him, staring at him, her pale face painted with its usual blank expression. She was holding her box facing him. Pointed at him.

"Please," he asked, motioning to the mystifying box.

She understood his curiosity and held the box out to him to open it. Oda felt himself cringe. Was he about to see the gruesome, decapitated head of a slain lover?

Smiling, the princess gently opened the lid, and Oda's mind flooded with all the images of the fishermen, the beach, the walk to the village, and the village itself. The box had somehow magically recorded her visit, collecting, capturing all the sights and sounds.

She is a spy!

It was then that Oda noticed the tear in the garment of one of her sleeves, the result of her fall. The tear revealed her pale white arm, which had a similar injury to it, a deep gash. But her arm… it was hollow like bamboo, with shiny metal rods within.

"Not utsuro-bune," Oda exclaimed. "*Utsuro ningyō!*"— Hollow puppet!

Oda looked at her pale pink, expressionless face, and he suddenly felt very afraid. *She is not alive!* He then glanced about wildly.

But who was the ningyōtsukai—the puppeteer? *Where is the puppeteer? How is he invisible?*

Oda yelled out in panic and frantically climbed up out of the craft, leaping back aboard the fishing boat. From there, he saw the hatch on the hollow boat silently close. A moment later the craft began to glow like a *kongming*—a Chinese fire balloon. All the fishermen began to murmur in confusion.

Oda's imagination raced. He expected to see the hollow boat lift out of the sea and float up into the sky. To take its place amongst the clouds? The stars?

But instead the hollow boat submerged—it did not sink like a damaged boat might—rather it slowly submerged in a controlled and purposeful manner.

Glowing majestically beneath the waves, the craft then wobbled and swam away like a great round fish. Deeper and deeper it swam, until its glow disappeared and it vanished from sight, as if it had never been.

Where is it going? Oda wondered. *To the bottom of the sea?*

Oda then asked a more profound question. *What… are the puppeteers?*

Who lives under the sea besides fish? Fish-people?

The world outside of isolated Japan was suddenly far more perplexing and unknown to Oda than he had ever previously imagined. And frightening. For the first time, he felt himself thankful that Japan was closed. It offered him a sense of security. He found the incident so unexpected, worrisome, and confounding that he retreated from it—turning his back on it, he gave it up:

> "It doesn't matter
> what I understand,
> oh universe…"

Acknowledgements and Identifying Notations

• The Japanese folklore tale "Utsuro-bune" has been told in three texts: *Toen shōsetsu* (1825), *Hyōryū kishū* (1835), and *Ume-no-chiri* (1844).

• Japanese haiku poetry was presented in "Hollow Boat" both as full poems and as words and sentences taken from haiku poetry. Authors of these poems: Matsuo Bashō (1644–1694), Yosa Buson (1716–1783), Kobayashi Issa (1763–1827), Iio Sōgi (1421–1502), Arakida Moritake (1472–1549), Nishiyama Sōin (1605–1682), Ihara Saikaku (1642–1693), Yamaguchi Sodō (1642–1716).

• The ending haiku poem in the story was generated by this author paying homage to a similar poem by American haiku poet Mike Dillon.

A Note from the Author

This was an exceptionally enjoyable story to write. This author hopes the reader likewise enjoyed reading this simple, haiku-style sci-fi tale. It was based on early 19th-century Japanese folklore, specifically the legend known as "Utsuro-bune." The Japanese word *utsuro* translates to "empty" or "hollow," and *bune* to "boat."

In writing this tale, this author aimed to stay true to many of the descriptive details of the folklore, while taking artistic license to craft a new and entertaining tale.

Regarding the red hair color of the visitor in this story: Interestingly, of the colors of the visible spectrum, red light has the longest wavelength and thus the least amount of energy. Water absorbs different wavelengths of light to different degrees. The longest wavelengths, with the lowest energy, are absorbed first. Red light is the first to be absorbed, to disappear underwater as depth increases. Deep-sea animals that are red actually appear black and thus are less visible to predators and prey.

Some ufologists have proposed that the story of Utsuro-bune depicts an actual extraterrestrial encounter that took place in Japan in the year 1803. This author is not under that impression.

Niko Zinovii
Honolulu, Hawaii
9 June 2018

Hollow Boat

The Psychonauts

~1~

What they were going to do to him was appalling, diabolical.

This, he announced to himself with a mental shiver, *is going to be hell...*

~2~

One thousand years and four months later... he found himself struggling through the surf as he made his way ashore, a sea-battered wanderer.

The sand was scorching hot beneath his bare feet, but he cared not about the pain, so disassociated was his mind from his body. His awareness of the outer world existed distinctly apart from his awareness of himself as a psychic being. He was not the same as the legs that carried him. His legs were somewhere else, out there, as was the rest of his physical body.

Who cares about the body?

And he stood there motionless in the bright sunlight, dripping seawater, basking in the glory, in the wonder, in the unfathomable mystery of pure being. Embracing the infinite value of unadulterated existence.

How long have I stood here like this? Had minutes passed? Or was it centuries? Suddenly he felt himself under the terrible, crushing weight of infinite time, only to in the next moment be swept away by an inner tide of indifference. He half glanced at the watch on his wrist. *Who cares?* his thoughts rumbled. His watch was in another universe.

Without care for or interest in time, existing in the perpetual present, he strode off, carried forth by an insatiable force that he had no control over and that he understood not at all. In him there was an intense feeling of far-wandering homelessness, of a half-remembered unfinished journey. And of a desperate, weary determination to complete it.

He watched on without drawing a breath, thunderstruck, as his inky-black shadow crept across a lone sunbather. He found himself staring passionately at the fabric of her bikini, marveling at the innumerable fine shades of color, at the manifold complexity of the creases in the soft material. The texture of the cloth, how deeply and mysteriously sumptuous it was. Deep, dark, glowing dots of blackness fixed within the yellow brightness of the sun itself. *This leopard pattern.... will I ever forget it?*

The immensely long and slender shadow of a migratory albatross drifted over them in utter silence. He found the moment absolutely enchanting. The bird's darkened shape seemed to possess a burning intensity of significance. Beauty flowing into ever-heightening beauty, meaning deepening into ever-deepening meaning, and all in such sharp, exquisite clarity, more natural than natural.

"... This is how one ought to see," he whispered, interrupting his own gazing moment of timeless, limitless bliss. "How things really are."

"Who are you?" the young, dark-browed blonde snapped as she sat up, surprised, her privacy intruded upon by this trespassing stranger who outrageously stood there towering over her, with one wet, sandy foot sinking into her blanket.

Yet, barefooted, barelegged, bare-chested, there was a whiff of eroticism to this intruder, and it caught her. He was a fit man, without being muscular. Pleasingly broad shouldered, with a slightly sculpted chest, his shorts tightly girdling his narrow hips. She sensed—more than she saw—a strength in his arms. A strength born from will rather than brawn. Tall, aristocratic, he had the strangest faraway look in his eyes, that of an inconsolable hero-wanderer.

"I asked... who are you?" Her words came out more civilized this time, as she found herself restrained by his piercing look, his attractive, smooth, moderate jawline.

"How can you waste time on questions," he responded evenly, unhurried, "when there is unspeakable beauty in the pattern of your garment? How the pattern changes... every time you move your legs, your arm..."

His odd words and his mildly accented voice drew her in further.

"You do have a name, don't you?" she insisted amiably, casting out her own smoldering beauty to net him. "What's your name?"

"Nobody," he answered.

She rose, and in a flash he grabbed her tightly about the wrist, his grip like steel.

"You're hurting me," she cried out in surprise.

"Yell, then," he prompted, glaring at her coldly. "Scream to the world that *Nobody* is hurting you. And they'll think you to be alone and insane."

He felt no pain as she bit down hard into his wrist. He simply held on to her, unflinching, until she released her bite.

"... What's wrong with you?" she demanded, angry, confused, afraid.

"You're the nymph Calypso," he half growled. "I knew it.

But how are you here? So soon? This isn't Ogygia. Not yet! I expected Circe or Polyphemus!"

He yanked her close to himself, and his countenance flooded with arrogance, his voice emanating unbridled hubris. "So you want to know my name? You know my name! The great Odysseus!"

"Paul," interrupted a voice.

The great Odysseus, Paul, turned to face a man—fully clothed, complete with shoes—who was walking up to them, dripping wet, also having come from out of the sea.

"Your voice…" Paul whispered. And Paul closed his eyes tightly, struggling to recognize the man. With his eyes closed, his inward field of vision filled with brightly colored, constantly changing geometric shapes.

He opened his eyes wide, rejecting the inferiority of such a closed, dull universe.

"Paul, let go of her."

To Paul, the man's rich, calm voice seemed to open a door that led back to the limited world of man, a place that he did not wish to return to.

"Autolycus?" Paul guessed at the man's name, unsure, grasping at remaining where he was, adopting a bold stance, steeling himself, preparing himself to stand his ground.

"No," the man said kindly as he stepped up to them, his enunciation elegant, precise. "It's Emil. Emil Lom, your friend. Your doctor. Your name is Paul. Paul Kassa."

Paul noticed recognition of his name flash across the girl's face.

"Paul Kassa…" Paul mumbled, numbly repeating the name. And doing so jarred part of his mind back to three months ago, to cold and distant Tibet, where he had first met Emil, in Lhasa.

"You do trust me, don't you?" Emil asked Paul.

Paul found himself nodding.

"Turn off your mind," Emil instructed Paul. "Relax, float downstream. Drop back."

Paul felt himself relinquishing his will. His face went blank, emotionless, lifeless, as he stared at Emil, transfixed.

"Relax, float downstream," Emil repeated, placing a reassuring hand upon his friend's arm. "Drop back."

Slowly, the life came back into Paul's eyes, which now shone with a far gentler disposition. His grip became like a child's and he released his captured Calypso. As he did so he went slope-shouldered, looking rather feeble, ill, the living embodiment of a million battered egos. Stooped forward, he weakly clasped his hands together in front of himself, utterly helpless. The transformation was startling.

"… I was off on my journey again?" Paul more stated than asked, feebly.

Emil nodded, his naturally saturnine look and penetrating gaze settling upon Paul in a most concerned manner.

"My name is Jean Stewart," the girl introduced herself to Emil, her eyes sympathetically on Paul all the while. "I'm a nurse, on holiday. Can I help?"

"Please," Paul mumbled to Emil, "just… take me back to the boat…"

~3~

The boat was a restored classic motor yacht, circa 1920, named the *Menekülni*, anchored off the sun-drenched Liguria coast of Italy, where it floated lazily, sleepily. Emil and Jean had taken Paul out to the craft in a small motorboat they had procured.

"This way, please," Emil instructed Jean, and together they helped Paul below deck and over to a nearby sofa, where he stretched out, exhausted, sinking into its cushions, closing his eyes.

Emil went for something and Jean stood there, looking at Paul inquisitively. *Such a gentle-looking… handsome man,* she thought. *Noble.*

"He's really Dr. Paul Kassa?" she asked Emil as the doctor returned with a syringe.

Emil nodded and injected Paul with something.

"He'll sleep now," Emil stated, somewhat relieved, feeling Paul's pulse. It was steady.

Jean noticed a glass medicine cabinet, filled with drugs. *Mescaline?* And across the room there stood what looked like an upright, broad iron coffin, with a windowed faceplate. Hoses were connected to its sides, apparently to fill it with water.

"A sensory deprivation tank," Emil explained, wearily.

"What are you doing here?" Jean asked, walking up to the odd tank. "What are you doing to him?"

"It's complicated," Emil answered, rolling his shoulders, shaking his head.

She sat down across from Emil. "I'd like to know."

"Exploration of the psyche," Emil answered hesitantly. "Using lucid dreaming, hypnosis, meditation, sensory deprivation, hallucinogens…"

"Why?"

"You remember what they did to him." Emil shuddered. "Excuse me. I have to go change into something dry. When he suddenly dove overboard, I jumped in after him. Nearly drowned myself. He's a far stronger swimmer than I."

Emil left and she sat there staring at the infamous Dr. Paul Kassa. At the first and last man ever sentenced to serve a thousand-year prison term. At the time, it had been viewed as a fitting punishment for his unprecedented crime against humanity. But afterward… it had forced society to rethink its attitude on punishment. On what was just. And on what was horrifically inhumane.

"How did they do it?" Jean asked Emil as he re-entered the room wrapped in a robe, his feet slippered. "Have him serve the thousand years in a single day?"

"A cocktail of psychoactive drugs"—Emil cringed—"combined with a network of nanobots injected directly into his brain. The combination increased the speed at which his mind functioned, distorting his perception, his sense of time, forcing a dilation of time, tricking him into experiencing a far greater passage of time than is normal.

"In essence, they created a prison cell out of his own skull. An artificial hell. Forcing him to endure a millennium of thinking alone, utterly alone. The most horrific solitary confinement ever devised. Christ, it must have seemed an eternity."

"What did he mean about being off on his journey again?" Jean asked.

"It's complicated."

"You've said that already," she stated, intent on learning more about this Paul Kassa. For she felt herself incredibly drawn to him, more so than she had ever felt toward any other man. She found this surprising, and deeply troubling, knowing full well what this man had done to the world. "I noticed the mescaline in the cabinet. You're using it on him? A psychedelic alkaloid? Its effects are comparable to LSD."

Emil nodded, raised a finger, and slowly sat down, explaining: "Science has known for some time that in each of us, our bodies can naturally produce minute doses of a psychoactive, mind-altering drug: adrenochrome, a byproduct of the decomposition of adrenalin. Adrenochrome is capable of acting as an intense hallucinogen, mimicking mescaline intoxication. Actually, this isn't surprising, as adrenalin itself bears a close chemical similarity to mescaline."

"So?" Jean insisted.

"Well," Emil continued, "after they finished tinkering with Paul's mind, they removed the nanobots, flushed his system of the drugs they had pumped into him, and set him free… Free to suffer from how his body had uniquely altered itself, chemically, in response to the catastrophic trauma of experiencing a millennium of psychological distress in a single day.

"Somehow, Paul's body now irregularly produces copious amounts of a substance biochemically similar to lysergic acid, a profoundly potent hallucinogen, causing him to continuously slip into intermittent holotropic states. He's on a bad trip, with no end in sight. I'm helping him find his way out of it. To heal him, psychologically. To rebalance his chemical composition—"

A groan interrupted Emil. It came from Paul. Jean found herself moving to him.

"No," Emil called to her sternly yet calmly, "leave him be."

"Where is he now?" she asked. "In his mind. Somewhere on his journey?"

"Yes." Emil nodded. "I suspect he's about to encounter Polyphemus…"

~4~

To be strong is to be alive! To be weak is to be dead!

Paul felt good holding his head up high, proud. Strong. Not beaten down by a million, million blows—to be alone but to not feel alone. For all that had ever happened to him, all that was happening everywhere in the entire universe, was now flooding into his brain, into his mind at large. Such heightened sensory perception. How could he hope to contain it all?

He cried out for reduced awareness. And it came to him, his brain, as a matter of survival, filtering, reducing the deluge down to a narrow, almost pointless trickle. It returned him to this world alone. Allowing him to think.

I'm back on the beach? It was the same beach from earlier that day. Only the girl was now gone. The beach, however, like before, was a world of intense beauty: colors radiant, shadows profoundly lovely, profoundly important.

Paul smiled. Even with his awareness dimmed, he felt himself perceiving all the secrets that lurked behind what was normally visible of reality and nature. The incomprehensible mysteries of existence were no longer imponderable to him, but lay open to his examination.

A passing shower dotted the sand with the most delicate imprints of raindrops, which Paul studied in his long light of time without limit. And his inflated ego and overconfident bullishness dropped away as he felt an ever-deepening, uncanny insight into the nature of all things.

But then, as the raindrops vanished into the sand, leaving behind fossil-like imprints, he sensed disturbing portents in their tiny craters. And as before, he suddenly felt himself under the horrible, crushing weight of infinite time. It forced him to remember who he was, Odysseus, son of Laertes of Ithaca. Slowly, his gentle disposition faded away and his chest swelled with pride and arrogance as he recalled his victory at Troy. Yes, *his* victory—for it had been his brilliant scheme, his Trojan horse, that had won the war.

And after Troy: *The raid on Ismaros... The storm... The island of the lotus flower... And now here... But why am I alone?*

"Perimedes? Elpenor? Eurylochus?" Paul called up and down the beach, looking for his crew. "... Polites?"

But only the cry of distant gulls gave answer.

Paul's timeless dimension abruptly lost all its enchantment. He looked heavenward and cried out to his protectress, "Athena, I'm alone... Alone..." And he felt himself the frailest of all mortals, a captive plaything in the hands of the gods—a helpless thing to be tinkered with and tortured to no end.

Goats?

The bleating sound was coming from a small, verdant isle that lay just offshore.

Paul found the disassociation between his mind and body melting away as he vigorously splashed into the waves. He was a physical being once again. It felt good. He sensed an intoxicating power in his arms as he swam out to the strange island. It reminded him of how he had felt when gifting his great wooden horse, and what lay so cleverly concealed within it.

The rugged, wooded isle was blanketed by tall, soft grass. The trickling of water from unseen springs filled the air, as did the bleating of goats.

A flock of sheep.

Paul felt his stomach growl, ravenously. He caught the scent of roasting meat in the air. And the sight of smoke, coming from somewhere down the shoreline, drifting softly up into the sky, wavering there like some paranormal living thing. Instinctively, he headed toward the smoke.

The sand soon grew rough and stony beneath his bare feet, and the shore steeper and dotted with the debris of life. *So many shells…*

Something in his mind told him to look back, and he did, to find that the waves had completely effaced his footprints, washing away all sign of the way he had come. He trembled, feeling himself now absolutely incapable of going back. He could only go forward. Yet before him stretched a nightmarish coast that seemed to invite only storms and shipwrecks.

He felt so utterly alone, lost, an orphan, as if he had somehow set foot upon the moon, distancing and separating himself from all of humanity, forever.

A terrible tension crept over him, and he felt himself cower.

But with a surge of determination, he set one deliberate step in front of another.

The smoke...

It was coming from inside a vast, desolate cave, its mouth yawning open to the sea.

"*Polyphemus...*" Paul whispered to himself, suddenly realizing that he was on the island of the lawless race of giant blacksmiths who had built Olympus for the gods. The cave before him belonged to Polyphemus, the cyclops... son of Poseidon.

Paul felt himself physically stiffen, his soul harden, and his mind flush with vengeful rage as he imagined the man-eating creature, its vulgar single eye glaring outward from the middle of its monstrous forehead.

Eating my men! Paul growled viscerally as he stamped toward the cave, absolutely fearless, on the way tearing a branch from an olive tree, as long and thick as a club, envisioning ramming it into the cyclops's lurid eye. He only wanted to hear Polyphemus's cry of horror echo over the whole of the island.

"Polyphemus! It is I, Odysseus, raider of cities! Laertes's son! He who makes his home in Ithaca!"

But within the cave, there was no cyclopean son of a sea god. Instead, Paul found himself facing a colossal one-eyed idol carved from speckled, coarse-grained igneous rock. A false god of centuries lost, with the posture and frown of a baleful, maleficent judge, its dark visage whispering the absence of a primordial entity yet to manifest itself.

Paul walked up to the idol slowly, cautiously, ignoring the flickering firelight and the cave's mocking shadows, which seemed to cling to him, web-like.

Slowly, the idol's ancient diorite eye opened and shone with the light of Pharos. Paul found it difficult to face the brightness, behind which there seemed to be power undreamed of. Yet he forced himself to look into the light, into the eye, and he beheld the universe…

"What manner of being are you?" Paul stammered under its gaze.

It was the ensuing silence that gave answer, announcing simply that this was a god never to be understood.

Paul shivered as he felt the eye forcibly peer into his soul. The idol then asked a terrible question:

"Was it you who fathered the rain?"

The invisible puffs of sound, the petty little words, caused a transfiguration to sweep across Paul's countenance, one that felled him to his knees in abject submission.

"… Guilty…" Paul babbled the word like a child. "Guilty…"

And Paul looked up to see that there were now billions of eyes covering the idol, all glaring down at him judgmentally.

In his mind he heard the words of the blinded Polyphemus of myth: *"Father Poseidon, look upon Odysseus, the son of Laertes of Ithaca, and grant me this revenge: let him never see Ithaca again! Yet, if he must, may he come late, without a friend, after long wandering, to find evil abiding by his hearth!"*

The idol released an invisible vaporous spell, and Paul felt himself stiffening. He struggled against the penetrating magic, but to no avail, for he was sentenced to fall into a petrified state, his body frozen, but his mind remaining active—to endure a *long wandering*.

"Zeus, give me the strength!"

~5~

Paul awakened with a desperate jolt, falling off the sofa and to the floor.

"Are you all right?" he heard Jean ask, her voice controlled as she cautiously moved to him, helping him up.

"… Thank you," he responded weakly, bewildered, feeling spiritually brutalized and physically fatigued. As he sat up, he struggled to steady himself, to catch his breath, to stop his heart from racing. *I'm back on the boat?*

Jean left and quickly returned with a glass of water for him. As he drank it he slowly calmed, and he carefully looked her over, appreciating the glossy, bright shine of her hair, the extraordinary lightness of her blue eyes.

"You're from the beach?" he asked, unsure.

"You're not going to grab me again, are you?"

"You're real… I remember now."

She nodded and made purposeful eye contact. "I suppose I'd better introduce myself."

"You don't need a name," he offered, his gentle, poetic soul radiating. "I've always known beauty."

She hesitated before responding, doing so somewhat softly, yet assertively. "Then why did you grab me like that? Why not go after things in a nice way?"

He looked deeper into her eyes, to find her. She resisted for a moment, but then allowed him to gain a glimpse of her inner being.

"You're not afraid of me?" he asked her. "The 'abominable Dr. Kassa.' Convicted by the International Criminal Court of widespread and systematic atrocities, crimes against humanity…"

She shook her head "no," as she stared at him, silent, studying him.

"I thank you for that," he whispered, distracted, appreciating the temporary uncompromised clarity of his perception. But then he trembled slightly, as lurking just beneath the surface he could also sense Odysseus, still there, an integral part of him, on a hair trigger, waiting to emerge, to take control. *Oh, how I hate him! Oh, how I couldn't have survived without him… How I can't find my way back without him…*

"Why not tell me why you did it?" Jean asked evenly, peering deeply into his eyes, wanting to understand him, to know him.

Once again, he swiftly caught her by the wrist, only this time he did not squeeze, he simply held her, firmly.

"Please, don't look for me," he answered. "You'll never find me."

"Why?"

Slowly, his gentler, true character resurfaced, and he released her. "Because… I'm lost. Utterly lost."

And Paul suddenly felt the world wobble dizzyingly. He reached out to Jean like a child to a mother, feeling helplessly confused, his mind seemingly floating off through space to somewhere else. *To where this time?*

He tried to hold himself there, aboard the *Menekülni*, but the barriers between the real world, hallucination, and memory fell away and he found himself once again entering Lhasa, Tibet for the first time, several months ago, in the dead of winter:

~6~

It was night and terribly cold. So cold Paul found himself desperately clutching and reclutching himself as he walked, while taking in the shortest breaths possible, his instinct for survival cautioning him against freely inhaling the frigid mountain air of this high Tibetan altitude.

The winding backstreet alley before him was blanketed with fresh snowfall. Climbing over a drift, he slipped and tumbled forward, sliding down to rest prostrate upon a temple-lined street, exhausted, fighting off hallucinations. *Stay focused! You have to find him…*

Slowly, Paul lifted his face to a spotted visage of a confusion of falling white flakes, spiraling, twirling, down, down, down to strike him wetly, softly, upon his blinking eyes. *What's that?*

The air in the old town was imbued with the wafting scent of warm incense, exotic and ancient, seemingly from a millennium ago. *Time has stood still here?*

And Paul rose, weakly, trembling, the flickering light from nearby butter lamps subtly warming him, their radiance dancing across his countenance. It was at that moment that he caught his first sight of the Holy City's gleaming white Potala Palace, etched so very dramatically into the steep mountainside that soared so high above him. Its red rooftops seemed to touch the eternalness of another world. Lhasa was truly the place of the gods.

And also of monks and pilgrims. And of men. And Paul was searching this night for one man in particular. *I have to find him…*

With ungloved, trembling hands, Paul pulled out a small directional device, allowing it to guide him through the whitewashed old town. He went from door to door to door. *No… No… No…*

His vision blurred, making it difficult to read his little mechanism. *This door?*

It was a large, ornate wooden door, massively solid. He banged upon it desperately. The wind howled and sank its teeth into his bones. Paul shivered uncontrollably and banged again and again, louder and louder. But there was no answer.

Maybe it's best to simply lie down… and die here and now… in the snow… end it… finally…

But the door suddenly opened, and Paul found himself collapsing into the outstretched arms of Dr. Emil Lom.

"Please," Paul pleaded weakly, at the point of losing all hope. "Help me…"

~7~

Jean watched on, still holding Paul's hands, as Emil examined him.

"Dilated pupils," Emil noted. "Increased heart rate. Trembling in the hands. Sweating. You're a nurse, you didn't notice these withdrawal symptoms?"

"No…" Jean answered, embarrassed at how distracted she had become in Paul's presence, as a woman, how she had forgotten her training as a nurse.

Paul's eyes fixed on Jean and he whispered to her softly, his sense of reality clearly distorted: "A seagull told me about you. No, it was an albatross. You steal men's hearts. I see a drop of moonlight, a mermaid's tear, a pearl in you. How does it feel to be the only true woman in all the world?"

"The flashbacks," Emil explained to Jean, "are due to his prolonged exposure to the endogenous hallucinogen his body now produces. They often occur after the level of the substance drops off, after its effect wears off."

Emil proceeded to fill a syringe with half a gram of pure mescaline. "His body has run low on its natural psychedelic. I need to relieve his craving with this. To try to control the intermittent holotropic states that he's subject to slipping in and out of. So that he can continue to explore his altered state of consciousness. To reach the end of his journey—it's his only way out."

"His only path to recovery is you keeping him in a hallucinatory state?" Jean asked incredulously.

"It was Polyphemus!" Paul growled out.

"Steady him," Emil instructed Jean.

"Curse you, Poseidon!" Paul yelled out to the sea, banging angry fists against the bulkhead behind him. "Who do you think you are? To do this to me!"

Emil quickly administered the mescaline, followed by a sedative. He then filled the syringe again, drawing from a yellow-tinged 50 ml bottle labeled "Boldenone Undecylenate."

On the bottle was the silhouetted image of a stallion and wording in Italian.

"A veterinarian steroid?" Jean asked disbelievingly.

"It was all I could get my hands on," Emil responded. "It's a structurally altered form of testosterone. It's perfectly safe. I need to keep his strength up. His endurance. If he's to survive this."

"Why did Paul come to you?" Jean asked, suddenly viewing the doctor in a very different light—questioning the man's appropriateness for Paul's care.

"Because I'm a psychonaut," Emil answered directly, as he prepared an IV to hydrate Paul intravenously.

"I don't know what you mean."

"A mind sailor," Emil explained. "I routinely subject myself to a variety of mind-altering substances. I've done so for decades."

"Why?"

"To induce and explore altered states of the mind, by transforming consciousness. To journey out beyond our little-understood frontier of perception. In order to gain deeper insight into the nature of consciousness. To earn a deeper scientific understanding of perception and reality. One who engages in such exploration is known as a psychonaut."

"A psychonaut," Jean repeated the term aloud, scrutinizing it in her mind, struggling to remain objective. "As a doctor, as a scientist, you trip out?"

Emil sighed defensively. "I subject myself to drug-induced temporary psychedelic experiences in the name of science."

"… Is Paul one also?" she asked. "A psychonaut?"

Emil paused to consider it. "Yes. Yes, I imagine one can consider him to be a psychonaut now. The same as one might imagine a Tibetan Buddhist master a psychonaut, when such a master purposefully journeys across the boundary that separates life and death to spiritually experience the in-between realm."

Some moments passed before Jean realized that Emil was simply standing there, waiting silently, patiently, his eyes on her.

"I'm sorry," she apologized for her momentary absence.

"Believe me, Jean," Emil stated reassuringly, honestly, compassionately, "I'm the only one in all the world who has the knowledge and expertise required to help Paul. To bring him back fully intact, permanently. You need to trust me."

"I wish I could," she heard herself reply, her voice low, concerned, a multitude of thoughts racing through her mind.

"Come," Emil instructed her, "help me prepare the isolation tank."

~ 8~

"Thank you," Paul stated softly, with aristocratic refinement, as Emil and Jean walked him to the sensory deprivation tank.

Emil nodded, smiling slightly. "In you go."

"Yes," Paul sighed, "in I go."

Paul then turned to Jean, looking longingly into her eyes. "Stay close, don't leave me."

"I won't," she assured him.

Paul stepped inside and donned a full-face mask with a built-in respirator. He would breathe naturally, using both nose and mouth.

Emil sealed the tank and turned a heavy valve.

Jean could hear the seawater being pumped into the tank. She watched on in silence until the level rose up to cover Paul's face, submerging him completely.

"You're certain he'll be all right?" she asked.

Emil nodded, walked backward, and took a seat, not taking his eyes off Paul.

"What are you doing?" Jean asked as she saw Emil take a flat, dried cactus head, approximately an inch in diameter, and begin to grind it, using a mortar and pestle, into a fine powder.

"Peyote," Emile stated matter-of-factly. "Natural mescaline."

She glanced to the cabin's large portholes, looking anew at the many pots of short, round cacti decorating the inside of the yacht. Nearby, on a table, were cut-up cacti drying into peyote buttons like the one the doctor was grinding.

"They can be chewed"—Emil nodded to the buttons—"but they're quite bitter."

She watched on curiously as the doctor carefully poured the powder into a capsule.

"It's for me," he announced, holding up the capsule. "I'm going on a spirit walk. Would you like to join me?"

"What?"

"Would you like to have a psychedelic experience? Become a psychonaut?"

She thought about it.

"It's perfectly safe," he reassured her. "Peyote—mescaline—lacks the chemical properties to make it a physically addictive drug. There's no chance of brain damage, even after prolonged use. The toxicity is very low. No withdrawal symptoms even with abuse."

"How long will it last?"

"Six to twelve hours. The plasma half-life is six hours."

She turned to Paul, who was floating before them in the tank in silence, his eyes closed. "Is he…"

"Off on his journey again? Yes," Emil answered.

"Yes. I'd like to try it. To understand all this."

Emil nodded and retrieved a syringe. "I'll inject you with mescaline intravenously, to precisely control the dose. Just a quarter of a gram."

Jean felt her heart race as she extended her arm to the doctor. She saw that Emil sensed her unease.

"Think of it as a chemical key," he said to her solemnly, in a calm, fatherly voice. "A key that can open the mind to the realities of expanded consciousness."

"For scientific, research purposes..." she said, steadying herself.

"... And spiritual," Emil added.

~9~

Half an hour later, Jean felt an indifference to space and time infuse her perception and awareness, locking her into an everlasting present moment. Simultaneously, the world became... different.

The walls, ceiling, and floor seemed no longer to join together properly, but her eye no longer had any concern for spatial relationships. Distances, context, and positioning were all of so little interest.

It was the growing intricacy of the world that mattered.

The rays of sunlight entering the cabin took on a lively, sumptuous, golden glory. The stacks of nearby books glowed with the intensity of gem stones heavenly lit. The glow, the colors, were alive, breathing, as if produced by the cry of music. The world was fabulously lovely, profoundly meaningful, vibrating with energy. It was beyond what any artist could ever hope to express. Jean could almost hear the colors and see the singing of the universe.

Reality broadened still further. In every cell of her body, Jean felt a great change in her place in existence. She sensed herself apart from everything, yet when she looked at the books, she also felt herself being the books. *All is in all...*

And she shed a single tear, the seemingly extrasensory perception granted to her by this chemical key making her feel as if... the innocence of an adult childhood had fallen away.

"It's not pleasing?' Emil asked, his watchful eye on her.

126

"Too pleasing," she whispered, surprised to find that she could actually think straight, her intellect seemingly unimpaired. She was experiencing a stream of multitudinous thoughts, but she found that she could quite easily focus on but one while watching the others simply flow past her.

Emil began to talk. Jean, suddenly feeling no desire to do anything in particular, sat back, listening in timeless bliss as the doctor described the ritual of the Tibetan clear light phases that Paul was working his way through.

Chikhai Bardo: The first phase of transcendental awareness, free of roles and objectives.

Chonyid Bardo: The second, hallucinatory phase of a deliberately induced psychosis.

"It's the Chonyid phase," Emil explained, "that Paul has transitioned into. It's where one surrenders to extreme uncertainty and fantasy takes on real form. It's where Paul's journey is being played out by his unconscious dominants. Despite my guidance, he's fallen into an ego-dominated game pattern. He's Odysseus off on his mythical journey. Paul's subconscious mind is using Homer's *Odyssey* to direct and control his hallucinatory journey."

"Why?" Jean heard herself ask.

Emil shrugged. "It's impossible to guess at this point. Hopefully it will lead to attaining a level of understanding, an enlightenment that will guide him to his liberation. And normalization. This re-entry, this return to the self, takes place in the third and final phase: *Sidpa Bardo*.

"This third Bardo is the stage of rebirth. Paul will remain in Chonyid Bardo, struggling to regain reality, until his mind permits the transition from transcendent reality to the reality of ordinary life.

"Paul trusts me. This allows me to serve as his guide and protector, to prevent entrapment. But I can only do so much.

As the voyager, it is Paul who must follow his visions, until he genuinely pronounces judgment upon himself in his unconscious, innermost thoughts, in his heart and soul. And he must gain enlightenment on that judgment to attain peace. Only when his mind reaches this point will he enter the third Bardo to be reborn. It is in Sidpa Bardo that his body chemistry can normalize."

Jean turned her attention to Paul, who was still floating there before them, his inner Odysseus off somewhere on his Chonyid Bardo hallucinatory journey.

"What's next for Paul?" she asked. "In *The Odyssey*."

Emil recalled the literature and ran down the list: "The hospitality of Aeolus. An encounter with the cannibalistic Laestrygonians. Circe and a visit to the underworld. The Sirens. The straits of Scylla and Charybdis. Then Calypso… Phaeacia. And finally home, to Ithaca."

Within the silence of the sensory deprivation tank, deep within Paul's mind, Odysseus smiled as he was gifted an ox-hide bag by the demigod Aeolus, the Keeper of the Winds, king of the floating isle Aeolia, which lay upon the waves of the Tyrrhenian Sea off the coast of Sicily. For within the bag stirred the harsh winds that could prevent Odysseus's homeward journey. Odysseus knew not that this welcomed boon would soon be torn open by his curious men, allowing the winds within to escape and storm… and that his long wandering would only continue.

~10~

Later that night, as Paul slept in his cabin, strapped to his bed for his own protection, Jean took a peek in at him. Still under the influence of the mescaline, she perceived glowing waves of light rising and falling gracefully along the contours of Paul's handsome and noble face.

"Find your way to Sidpa Bardo, Paul," she whispered. "Please find your way back…"

She then heard Paul growl in his sleep, and she witnessed his chest and arms strain against the straps that held him secure. He was off on his journey again, although she knew not where. If she could somehow have viewed the visions in his mind, she would have seen that Paul's inner Odysseus was fleeing from a race of powerful giants, the Laestrygonians, who had speared and eaten most of his men and sunk eleven of his twelve ships. Only Odysseus and those on his personal ship would be fated to escape. This surviving Homeric vessel would continue onward with but three: Odysseus, Emil, and Jean.

~ 11 ~

The *Menekülni* had dropped anchor in the sheltered cove of an old fishing village. There was a small gathering of Italians on the shore, men, women, and children, standing here and there, dotted about under the midday sun. They were all looking out to sea and skyward, their focus on something in particular. They paid little attention to the *Menekülni*'s small utility boat as it made its way toward them, Paul rowing, Emil and Jean seated aft.

Jean found her eyes falling upon Paul's bare chest and arms, so handsomely natural and aesthetic was his build. The contour of his legs, the flow of the lines was so pleasing, so attractive. His bare feet so tan and strong, like his hands. It was as she looked up from his hands that she noticed the expression on his face, one of utter weariness and sorrow.

"Paul?" she asked.

"Speared like fish," he moaned.

She did not understand.

"My men," he explained. "Dreadful deaths…"

"At the hands of the Laestrygonians?" Emil asked to clarify.

Paul nodded, and he wept a single great tear.

Jean felt her heart breaking. She thought of the emotional strain Paul was being subjected to in his altered states of consciousness. She wanted to somehow rescue him, comfort him.

The boat beached itself upon the sand and Paul leapt out. Splashing through the shallow waves, he strode ashore purposefully, a sad and solitary figure yet a man who was in his mind already leaving behind the tragedy that had befallen his fellow Ithacans, his chest swelling with the bold and reckless confidence of Odysseus, his soul rising in readiness to meet his next challenge.

"Aeaea…" Emil said to Jean. "He must believe this to be the land of Aeaea. Circe's isle."

Paul soon stopped and stood motionless, his feet slowly sinking into the wet sand of the strange sea beach upon which he stood. Before him lay a huge pale blue boulder, which rose to the height of a man. At the sight of it, Paul beamed, feeling that its presence somehow allowed him to wrest a measure of control over the universe, for he suddenly embraced a penetrating insight into enigmatic reality. This rock, although it trembled on the brink of being supernatural, was there to distract him. And so he turned from it and headed down the beach, toward the Italians, some of whom stood alone, others clumped together in small groups.

Dogs—two, four, five, six of them—bounded toward Paul. They were quite large, and in Paul's mind he saw them as wolves, mountain lions, a cheetah, and a panther. He was about to step back, but the animals wagged their tails and nuzzled him tamely, like pets.

"Grrr!" Paul's inner Odysseus growled at the beasts, and they scampered off, whimpering. *Another distraction*, Paul thought. And he walked on.

Paul noticed flowers growing wild. As he knelt to pick one, Jean stepped up to his side. "For me?" she asked.

"No," he answered, and he yanked a flower from the earth. "The gods call this moly." And he showed the flower to her. It petals were as white as milk, its roots as black as coal. "Most mortals can't uproot it. I need it. Its magic will make me immune to Circe's charms."

And Paul tucked the flower into the top rim of his shorts. He then turned to the sweet, lyrical sound of a woman singing in a beguiling, silvery voice. To Paul's ear the song was eerie, inhuman. Something about the melody made him momentarily lose all desire to return home to his Ithaca. Instead he felt overwhelming curiosity and an urge to pursue glory. Unafraid of women, he sought out the source of the music.

It came from a lone golden-haired artist. She was attractive, perhaps thirty years of age. The sand castle that she was painting on her canvas seemed to Paul an otherworldly palace of polished stone.

Paul stepped up to the woman, his eyes full of lust, suspicion, and recognition. Surely behind this false face was the divine daughter of the sun god Helios and Perse, daughter of the Titan Oceanus.

"Your beauty is famous all over the world," Paul said to her, quietly.

The woman turned to Paul, looking him over approvingly. She then reached out and touched him with a single fingertip, pressing lightly upon his shoulder.

"You're burning," she said, her accent thick, her voice sultry.

In a flash Paul swiped at her painting, knocking it to the ground, his hand like the paw of a lion. "Your magic won't work on me, witch-goddess! Nymph! Pigifier of men!"

Jean rushed forward and grabbed hold of one of Paul's arms, struggling to restrain him.

"And now you'll want to have intercourse?" Paul demanded an answer from the artist. "And I'm to make you swear that you won't harm me?"

"Dog!" the woman cursed him. *"Pazzo figlio di puttana!"*

And the sky suddenly darkened, forebodingly, eerily.

Jean spun about, taking hold of Emil, who had approached her from behind. Together they witnessed the Italians raising their eclipse glasses to their eyes to view the moon's passage before the sun.

"The power of the sun…" Paul mumbled aloud as he staggered on his feet, tumbling deeper into his hallucinatory state, his psychedelic experience about to give way to pure imagination.

The Mediterranean sun dimmed still further, and darkness fell across the land. A rooster crowed from somewhere off in the distance. It became night, but the beach seemed lighted by bright moonlight, the light of the sun's corona was so intense. It grew cold, and Paul felt a wind blow over him.

"Sea witch…" Paul shivered and growled at Circe. "You're sending me to hell! Again!"

In the otherworldly moonlit darkness, the sea of Paul's world transformed into the river Styx and glowed a dim red as the portal to the House of Hades opened, revealing the mythical land of the dead. The dogs on the beach merged and transformed into the monstrous Cerberus, the lion-clawed, three-headed guardian hound of the underworld.

What now? Mighty Hades and Persephone? … The dead?

Cerberus scampered off. And Paul stood there alone to face not the dead but the shades of the unborn, the powerless ghosts of those who would never be. Billions of eyes glared at him hauntingly.

In secrecy the shades whispered to Paul's heart: *Why? ... Why?*

Echoing through his reeling mind, Paul then once again heard the question asked by the colossal, baleful idol of Polyphemus's cave:

"Was it you who fathered the rain?"

Paul stiffened and collapsed into the sand in wretched submission.

"Yes, yes, it was I... Odysseus, king of Ithaca! It was my Trojan horse that won the battle..."

It began to rain. And as the rain pounded down upon Paul, it cast its spell over him. Odysseus fled. Paul, utterly alone, became petrified, absent any strength, his mind active but without the will to endure his long wandering.

Somewhere in the blackness, he heard Emil's familiar voice:

"Turn off your mind. Relax, float downstream. Drop back."

~12~

Paul awoke to find himself back aboard the *Menekülni*, once again securely strapped down upon his bed. As his eyes adjusted to the evening twilight, he recognized Emil and Jean, both standing over him, concerned.

"... Let me regale you," Paul whispered to Jean weakly, making dreamy eye contact with her, "with a tale of the Trojan War."

"Is this Odysseus speaking," she responded, sitting down beside him, "or Paul Kassa?"

Paul thought for a moment. "Both... Neither. Mostly Paul."

"A lost Paul..." she added sympathetically.

Paul nodded, painfully aware of this fact.

"Paul," Emil stated, "you should rest now, sleep."

"To continue my mad journey?" Paul grumbled.

Emil nodded, soberly reassuring Paul: "Patience, my friend. Hold tight. I believe your difficult and unpleasant situation may soon be approaching an important moment, nearing its end. It may be difficult to see the light at the end of the tunnel, but it is there. I assure you."

As Paul struggled to believe the doctor's words, he felt Jean take hold of his hand.

"I'll be right here," she assured him. "Through the night."

"Thank you."

"Do you want me to give you something?" Emil asked Paul. "To sleep?"

"… No," Paul heard his own fading voice answer. "Tired… So tired…"

He blinked once, twice, and then his eyelids closed on him, sending him back into darkness.

"He'll sleep now," he heard Emil's voice say, so distant, so faint.

But he did not sleep. He was somehow fully alert and on his ship's deck, sailing west-southwest in the Tyrrhenian Sea, feeling a soft wind caressing his face as it gently blew over the summertime waters. But it was not the waters of modern-day Italy. No, it was the waters of a sea most ancient. Paul was once again in the world of Odysseus, in the age of gods and heroes and monsters and epic wars.

But why am I bound? Tied to the mast?

He looked for his crew. Emil and Jean were right there, staring at him.

Paul ordered them to free him, but they appeared not to hear. *Their ears,* Paul noticed, *plugged up with beeswax…*

He then heard a distant, magical song, at first so faint it was like a whisper, an echo of an echo. And Paul saw that a mere stone's throw away, off his vessel's starboard side, loomed the sharp rocks of the isles of Sirenum scopuli—where lived the dangerous and beautiful Sirens.

It was their singing voices, their seductive song that bewitched passing sailors, luring them to their deaths by shipwrecking on this rocky coast. Paul shivered at the sight of the lurid white bones of the countless dead men littering the shoreline.

But as the alluring song grew louder and louder, Paul felt its sweetness enchanting his heart. He suddenly longed to plunge into the sea and swim mightily to the Sirens, to hold them in his strong arms, to embrace their beauty.

Odysseus welled up within Paul and Paul strained against his bonds, but he was tied so tightly to the mast. He could not break free. He cursed Emil and Jean and ordered them again and again to set him free. But they ignored his demands.

The Sirens—Paul could see them now. *They're as beautiful as Helen of Troy!* He strained with all his strength, growling against the pain of his bindings cutting deeply into the flesh of his chest, shoulders, and arms.

The pain unexpectedly granted Paul a moment of clarity. Suddenly he was just Paul again, and he saw the Sirens as they truly were, vile creatures with crooked claws and horrid female faces, figures with feathery legs of birds and scaly feet.

Paul calmed. Quite sanely, he told himself to *hold tight,* that this moment would pass, that he would survive their song. That this was part of the process of his unconscious mind, of his soul unburdening itself. He was a voyager, his journey one of these visions. He was still in Chonyid Bardo, but he was apparently gaining some measure of control over his hallucinatory journey.

The Sirens had tempted him in their song with the gift of love. They had promised to soothe away his anguish and bring him peace, to recognize him as the wisest and bravest of all heroes. And yet he had gained clarity and found that he could ignore their calling.

Am I now closer to enlightenment? he wondered. *Will I soon enter the third Bardo and be reborn?*

Over the waning song of the Sirens, Paul heard Jean and Emil talking, but the voices came not from his two-member crew standing loyally before him but from elsewhere, from the world beyond his dream journey. The voices were faint but clear, first Jean and then Emil:

"Punishment without forgiveness—and after what he had also gifted humanity."

"Don't forget what he took away from it."

"Why did he do what he did?"

"You need to know?"

"Yes."

"Why?"

Paul strained to hear through the ensuing long moment of silence, which was finally broken by Emil's voice again:

"You've fallen in love with him?"

"… Yes."

The voices faded, disappeared, and the sounds of his dream journey returned. And Paul steadied himself, mentally, spiritually, as his Homeric vessel sailed past Sirenum scopuli. Up ahead, he could already see the straits of Scylla and Charybdis, where awaited Odysseus's choice between a six-headed sea monster and a whirlpool. Calmly, Paul instructed Emil and Jean to avoid the whirlpool and hold their course tight against the cliffs of Scylla. They would face the monster. It was time for him to face his monster…

~13~

Paul awoke in comfort, free from his bindings, with Jean sitting beside him, still holding his hand.

"You stayed through the night?" he asked.

She nodded, fatigued but alert and focused on him. "Where are you now?"

"Here," he answered. "With you."

It was then that Paul realized his unusual state of mental clarity. "I feel as if something has changed. I faced something during the night... and somehow... I'm changed."

But was it only another temporary state of lucid perception? Or had he during the night entered the final stage of Sidpa Bardo? Had he gained his liberation, his normalization? He swung his legs out of bed and sat there beside Jean, fearful that his clarity would soon slip away, struggling to maintain it.

"I'm Paul Kassa... Dr. Paul Kassa... What I did, I had to do..."

And Paul found himself rising, only it was not him alone, it was also the enraged Odysseus that dwelt within him. "And for it they labeled me abominable! Sentenced me to one thousand years! Inside my own head! Damn that court!" he growled.

"Paul!" Jean pleaded.

Paul psychically held back, struggling against his desire to fully release Odysseus in order to enjoy the feeling of indomitable will and strength that accompanied the mental metamorphosis.

"I'm... I'm all right..." he stated, embracing the relief that he was able to subdue his inner Odysseus and maintain his mental clarity.

But it was then that he felt his heart rate increase. His hands began to tremble. *Oh no... Not again...*

Like before, he held on to Jean. His perception wobbled and his mind lifted upward, soaring through space and time, leaving the real world far behind. His endogenous hallucinogen, having lost its potent effect, sent him tumbling into a withdrawal-induced flashback. Once again, he was in his laboratory, in Budapest, Hungary, the day they came for him.

~14~

Paul calmly turned to the sound of the footsteps racing in through the door that he had purposely left unlocked, invitingly wide open. For he had been patiently waiting through the night for TEK's arrival. He was surprised that it had taken the *Terrorelhárítási Központ* as long as it had to send in their paramilitary police.

The TEK point man yelled loudly as he tossed the flash-bang grenade toward Paul. Paul had not expected this, and the explosion of light and noise and the concussive force knocked him to the floor, disorientating him.

He only half noticed the other team members rushing in, dropping into their various positions, pointing their weapons at all parts of the laboratory.

"I'm alone," Paul tried to tell them. But his words came out muffled as he was forcibly turned face down onto the floor, pinned and cuffed, captured, neutralized.

Paul felt hands roughly searching all over his body.

"No weapons!" one of the officers yelled.

The abominable Dr. Paul Kassa was apprehended without casualties, without a single shot being fired.

At last, Paul thought, relieved, *it's over...*

But it was far from over. Paul felt himself flipped onto his back. Lying there supine, helpless, he said not a word as the officers dragged him to the center of the room, where one by one they switched off their body cameras.

The long, terrible assault that followed was unspeakably vicious and brutal. It was if the entire population of the world were taking its revenge upon him. *Can a man survive this?*

~15~

Paul felt his legs trembling as Jean helped him ascend the cabin stairs, up to the boat's outer deck. It was midday, and the sun was warm and bright. Paul saw that the *Menekülni* was anchored off a small and apparently uninhabited isle.

"Consider it Ogygia," Emil stated as he unwrapped a peyote button, his natural mescaline. "The mythical isle of Calypso."

"And I, still the fabled Greek hero Odysseus?" Paul responded, weary.

"Paul says he feels different," Jean informed Emil. "Since last night's journey."

"A sense of clarity?" Emil asked Paul. "An unusual calm?"

"Clarity yes," Paul answered. "Calm, no."

"There was another flashback," Jean added.

The doctor carefully examined Paul's pupils, took his pulse. "I'm going to hold off on administering any mescaline. At this point, your clarity could signal re-entry. Rebirth unfolds as an unconscious process. First there will be an unusual sense of clarity, sometime later an unusual calm."

"And then?" Paul asked.

"If you are in re-entry, if you have entered the third and final Bardo, your unconscious enlightenment should soon surface. When it does, you'll suddenly instinctively know that your journey has indeed ended. And you'll become aware of what you need to do to be able to move on."

Paul nodded slowly, hoping rather desperately that he had entered Sidpa Bardo, that his journey was nearing its end. Feeling a need for calm, he found his eye drawn to the peace of the lagoon. Odysseus stirred, and Paul found himself walking to the bow, where he silently disrobed and dove naked into the sea.

Emil broke his peyote button in two and offered half to Jean. "It's bitter, but it can be chewed quite easily."

"Mind sailing?" Jean asked the doctor.

"A short spirit walk."

Jean accepted the peyote. Placing it into her mouth, she walked to the bow, stepped out of her clothing, and followed Paul into the sea.

Paul waited for her and then together, side by side, as if engaging in a ritual of love, they swam toward the island's alluring golden beach, the water beneath them all the while glistening resplendently, magically in the sunlight.

As they left Poseidon's sea, they took each other's hands and slowly walked ashore, their bare feet sinking softly, deeply into the fascinating sand. And they turned to face one another, to see the longing in each other's eyes.

There was a slight rumble, and the beach shook. The small earthquake sent them falling into each other's arms, their naked bodies pressing against one another. The earth settled and quieted as their passions rose to heights undreamed of.

"Perhaps that quake will set the world right," Paul murmured, locked in their trance of love. "Why have you opened your heart to me? How can you forgive Paul Kassa?"

"I owe my life to you," she whispered, lost in the feeling of their shared warm and wet embrace, the feeling of his chest, of his body against her own. "Part of what you did saved my life."

"You…"

She nodded. "I was dying. Doctors had given me less than six months to live."

Paul felt himself about to surrender to the moment—the pleasure of her naked body against his own was so intense. "Odysseus remained on Ogygia for seven years. He made love to Calypso for seven years… Can we love for seven years in a single afternoon?"

She nodded, and Odysseus and Calypso kissed. Entwined in overwhelming passion, they slowly, gently collapsed upon the sand, where they made timeless love.

~16~

That night, a large motor yacht anchored in the lagoon beside the *Menekülni*. The captain of the craft took the initiative to learn the owner of the *Menekülni*, and when he found that it was Dr. Paul Kassa, he cordially invited Paul, Emil, and Jean aboard for dinner.

Paul felt himself smile slightly as he piloted their small utility boat toward the nearby motor yacht. It felt so pleasant to continue to experience such mental clarity. He looked at Emil and Jean, both dressed somewhat more formally for dinner, as he himself was, and he felt as if for the first time a great smothering pressure had been removed from his life, and that he could breathe freely, normally again.

He then thought about his journey, and what would come next, if anything. Sequentially, Odysseus was due to find himself washed ashore on the isle of the seafaring Phaeacians, where he would recount his travels to their king and queen.

Aboard the opulent visiting yacht, after introductions and innocuous pleasantries, as everyone began dining, the captain slowly sat back and studied Paul.

"Forgive me, Dr. Kassa," the captain said with courtly politeness and restrained curiosity. "But I can't help asking. Why did you do it?"

Paul gripped the table as all eyes turned to him, especially Jean's. He suddenly felt as if he were once again under the judgmental scrutiny of the billion eyes covering the ancient diorite idol of Polyphemus's cave.

"You can speak freely," the captain added in a mitigating manner. "My wife and I, our families, we were all home on Santorini when it happened. Due to drought, the water there now comes wholly from desalination and purification plants. We were unaffected."

"Do you feel guilty?" the captain's wife asked Paul bluntly.

It was the tone and directness of her question that sent Paul's mind reeling back in remembrance of the day when the court's sentence had been carried out on him. For a terrifying moment, Paul relived it all once again:

He wanted to scream out as he helplessly watched them inject the numerous psychoactive drugs into his strapped-down arms. But the sheer horror of what the drugs would soon do to him kept him voiceless. The nanobots were next injected through small holes earlier bored through his skull to allow delivery of the microscopic machines directly into his brain. He could not actually feel the nanobots, as the human brain has no pain receptors, but his imagination felt them crawling uglily through his mind. This did make him scream, again and again.

The drugs and the nanobots would together speed up the rate at which his mind worked, causing him to experience a millennium of thinking in a single day. He would face a thousand years alone, within the solitude and confinement of his own skull.

It was appalling, diabolical. It was going to be hell. And there was absolutely nothing he could do about it.

Paul suddenly found himself back at the dinner table, shivering. "Guilty?" Paul answered the woman, his voice trembling, cracking, his throat so dry. "Guilty of what? Saving the world from itself?"

Odysseus, on a hair trigger, erupted within Paul in all his vainglory, and hands and arms empowered by the might of the son of Laertes, the king of Ithaca, sent the dining table flying up into the air, flipping it over completely. As it came crashing down upon the floor, Paul's inner Odysseus growled, and together Paul and Odysseus strode out of the room.

As Paul left, he felt himself experience a sudden unusual calm, and he fully re-entered the world. His psychedelic journey had ended. He had pronounced judgment upon himself in his heart and soul. His unconscious enlightenment had surfaced, and he had found peace. And more, he now knew what he needed to do next to move forward.

~17~

At his summer home on the Greek isle of Ithaca in the Ionian Sea, birthplace of Homer's Odysseus, Paul stood silently before the hologram projector that Emil had focused on him. Dressed in a light cotton shirt, matching shorts, and brown leather sandals, Paul appeared more the image of a humble, sun-bronzed fisherman than the physician, medical researcher, Nobel laureate—and international criminal—he was.

Paul glanced once at Jean, who was standing beside Emil, and he then looked directly into the camera and lucidly addressed the whole of mankind:

"This is Paul Kassa... broadcasting to the world. To the world that pronounced judgment on me... and punished me so terribly.

"To the very same world that I bestowed my welcomed discovery upon. Yes, do not ever forget that it was I who discovered the cure for cancer, and gifted it freely to the world, as freely as the sun gifts us with light and heat, with life."

And Paul paused, remembering in his thoughts how he had novelly delivered his cure by developing an aerosol carrying mechanism capable of suspending his cure in liquid droplets within the atmosphere. The planes of the many countries of the world, under the direction of the United

Nations, had seeded Earth's clouds with this unique aerosol. Later, when it rained, his cure had been delivered equally to the wealthy of the world and to the poor of the world, held within those tiny precious droplets. The rainwater only needed to be ingested.

Yes, it was he who had fathered the rain. It had been his gift to humankind.

"As a doctor," Paul continued, "I am a healer. I treat the unwell. I heal the sick. The possibility of healing humanity of cancer on such a scale made me realize that my duty as a healer extended beyond diseases of the body.

"It extended to man's *disease* of maximum self-expression without self-restraint. Before my rain, human beings were on a pathological path of self-destruction, practicing harmful and lethal excesses: overpopulating the planet, causing mass species extinction, environmental degradation, excessively preparing for war. Man was walking the knife's edge, threatening to vanish altogether from this world, to slip off in an apocalyptic fashion.

"Humankind needed to be healed. And so, within my cure-carrying aerosol, I also concealed the cure for man's lack of restraint. The aerosol became my Trojan horse. And when it rained around the world, not only was cancer eradicated… ninety percent of humanity was also sterilized."

Paul thought back to how utterly alone he had been in doing what he had done. How frightening the decision had been. How making it had distanced and separated him from humanity, for the rest of his life. How the path that he had chosen had offered no way to go back. And yet he had felt compelled to take it.

"We were ten billion people, on our small Earth… There was starvation, limited fresh water, unending territorial disputes, conflicts over resources, constant war. The threat of nuclear annihilation. Global fisheries were on the verge of collapse. Man was destroying the coral reefs, the rain forests... causing the extinction of species at one thousand times Earth's natural background rate."

Paul's voice trembled with emotion as he then rattled off fact after fact after fact, shooting the data forth like arrows from Odysseus's bow, intellectually slaying any who would stand in opposition to certain truths.

"There could be no illusion as to where this all would eventually end. In our lack of self-restraint, we had condemned ourselves to utter catastrophe, extinction by our own hand.

"I could not blind myself to the truth. Was I to simply sit by and watch in helpless horror? No. I am a healer. So, I fathered the rain.

"In doing so, I've provided humankind with additional time, with the chance to learn if we can master aspects of our own nature, develop ways to regulate our behavior, sublimate our runaway desires, curtail our limitless, destructive lack of self-control.

"Our population is now rapidly decreasing. It will continue to do so for a long time. Eventually it will drop to a sane level, compatible with our environment and resources. What we do then is in the hands of a future generation. It is my belief that future man will look back at this event and recognize it as a precious gift, one that bestowed upon them the opportunity and the responsibility to extend man's presence on Earth by practicing self-expression with self-restraint.

"Only the future can and will truly judge me properly."

Emil switched off the camera, and Paul silently walked out onto a whitewashed balcony overlooking the timeless wine-dark sea of the ancients. He heard Jean walk up to him and felt her lovingly take his hand. His inner Odysseus stirred and rose within him, present but under control. For although his body chemistry had normalized and his mind was clear, Odysseus, his millennia-old alter-self, generated by his mind as a survival mechanism, would forever remain a part of him.

"Let us love," he whispered softly, romantically, to Jean, "a thousand years, in the short day that is our lives."

Acknowledgements and Identifying Notations

• The term *psychonaut* is derived from the ancient Greek words *psychē* (soul, spirit, or mind) and *naútēs* (sailor or navigator); thus, a psychonaut is a "mind sailor."

• The story was partly inspired by philosopher Rebecca Roache proposing to *Aeon* magazine in 2018 that future technologies might transform criminal punishment by utilizing psychoactive drugs to distort a person's sense of time in order to make that individual feel as if he were serving a thousand-year sentence in less than a day.

• The psychedelic experiences of the characters in "The Psychonauts" was based on writer, novelist, and philosopher Aldous Huxley's nonfiction philosophical essay detailing his experience of taking mescaline that was released in his book *The Doors of Perception*.

• In crafting "The Psychonauts," this author exercised significant artistic license when drawing from the manual titled *The Psychedelic Experience*, by Timothy Leary, PhD, Ralph Metzner, PhD, and Richard Alpert, PhD.

• Some of the descriptiveness in the protagonist's dialogue at this story's end was loosely based on remarks and writings of physician, medical researcher, and virologist Dr. Jonas Salk.

• This author drew upon science and science-fiction author Isaac Asimov's strong views on the problem of overpopulation, as expressed in his writings.

• *The Odyssey*, by Homer.

A Note from the Author

This author hopes that the reader appreciated aspects of Paul's unusual Odyssean, psychedelic journey.

Regarding the fact that adrenochrome, a byproduct of the decomposition of adrenalin in the human body, is capable of acting as an intense hallucinogen, mimicking mescaline intoxication, this author cannot help but suspect that this might explain certain incidents of people claiming to have had supernatural sightings of ghosts, angels, the Blessed Virgin Mary, etc. This author is not aware of anyone else ever having suggested this possible explanation.

For the record: This author is not advocating the use of psychedelic or psychoactive drugs. He himself has never taken such drugs as of the publication date of this work, with the sole exception of alcohol in moderation.

Niko Zinovii
Santa Monica, California
27 June 2018

Niko Zinovii

To Rise Again

David Alt, silent and aloof, walked away from the hospital, away from the commotion of its doctors and nurses who were busily moving to and fro, and strolled into the institute's garden, where he sat himself upon a soft pine bench, alone. He welcomed the coolness offered by the large shade tree overhead, despite his impression that its dense, dark green foliage gave the plant a rather sad look.

Glancing back at the hospital, David thought of his shyness, of how he often felt awkward when interacting with others. And of the relief that he had felt when he had been instructed to wait in the garden. In the hospital he had felt quite out of place—his manner of dress, his blond hair, blue eyes. He must have cast quite a European presence. Little did he realize that in actuality it was the sensitivity and inquisitiveness in his eyes, his intelligent mien, and his quietly solemn features that had drawn the stares of the doctors, and the nurses—who found him to be intriguingly handsome.

And now I'm in Mumbai, India… David thought. *Surrounded by lots and lots of people…*

Leaning back, David disappeared into himself as he questioned his restlessness, his uncertainty as to what he was actually pursuing. He had studied, traveled, read so many books, and yet when faced with a foretaste of death, something in him had changed.

Two years ago, during his formal study of geology and paleontology, he had had a bad fall when hiking in the mountains of Sweden, in the province of Västergötland, where he had been surveying for outcrops of conglomeratic limestone in which fossil trilobites of the lower and middle Cambrian might be collected. Severely injured, unable to move, he had believed he would die in that harsh, remote area where he had fallen. Fortunately, he was found and rescued, but the experience had left him traumatized. It forced upon him a rejection of pursuing a conventional life in favor of a search for experience and meaning. He wanted, needed... something more. And so, he had taken this job, so that he could continue to travel, experience, to learn still more, to search for whatever it was he was looking for. *The meaning of life?*

And David recited to himself, in his mind, a poem that he had read during his recovery:

> *Before fate strikes you down by surprise,*
> *Order them to bring you rose-colored wine.*
> *Oh silly fool, you are not gold*
> *That they bury and dig up afterward.*

An odd noise, a sort of squawk, pulled David out of his contemplation. The sound seemed to have come from a crown of shining green leaves capping a nearby tree, one that was decorated by white, very fragrant drooping flowers.

David heard the squawk again, only this time it changed into a sort of whistling sound, like something that might be made by a tropical bird.

The foliage shook, and David's eye caught an Indian giant squirrel coming down the tree. It was a true giant. David estimated it to be nearly three feet in length. So large was it, in fact, that it cast the impression of a squirrel version of an orangutan. Lending to this illusion was how beautifully colored it was, the fur of its body and extremely long tail dappled in dark browns, oranges, rich rusts, creams, blacks, and hues of maroon and purple.

This improbable squirrel was so utterly different from the gray squirrel that David routinely saw in Europe. *What a weirdly wonderfully beautiful rodent.*

The squirrel jumped from the trunk of the tree and into the grass. Its round rusty ears were panda-like; its cute, cream-colored paws disproportionately large, with powerful claws for climbing.

"And what are you up to," David whispered, his empathy for the natural world rising, "my magic purple squirrel?"

And David wondered if India's giant squirrels gathered and stored nuts to last them through the winter. India did have a winter. The country had no fall, but instead, summer, winter, and then monsoon.

No, the squirrel was moving cautiously toward the garden's bird feeder, which sat quite high atop a tall pole. Beneath it was something that resembled a downward-turned tin umbrella—a device obviously installed to prevent unwelcome animals from gaining access to the seeds from below. *Now this should be interesting.*

The squirrel reached the bottom of the pole and paused to look up.

David felt a shiver tingle over him. *He's thinking… He actually stopped to think.*

The squirrel then ascended, and with body and soul it met every struggle, first clinging with its huge paws to the smooth, slippery, swaying pole, then grasping the tilting umbrella bottom to next flip itself up over the barrier and onto the bird feeder—where it quietly and delicately feasted.

David made a low whistling sound, trying to imitate the call of the Indian giant. The squirrel turned to him. And for a fleeting, dreamlike moment, he and the squirrel gazed into each other's eyes. In that heartbeat of time, David felt a reflection of distant humanity, a connection from whence man had come all those vast eons ago. He thought of man's distant warm-blooded ancestors, the little mousy mammals of the underbrush that had been left after the eclipse of the dinosaurs. And David wondered about the shining little brain of India's giant squirrel, while appreciating its dexterous, skillful, hand-like paws. He then marveled at the uniqueness of what had become the human mind. Man was truly the genie that had come out of the bottle.

The sound of talking, behind David, ended his moment of intimacy and appreciation. Two men were wheeling out the casket of the woman whom David had arrived to collect. One of the men was a Hindu attendant from the hospital, the other a technician of World Corp, the company that also employed David. David walked over to them.

"She was placed within the Cocoon immediately after the pronunciation of death," the young technician stated matter-of-factly.

"Good." David nodded soberly, checking the electronic paperwork that he was handed for the transfer.

It was as David prepared to provide his digital signature that he glanced down into the transparent casket and saw her for the first time. She was Indian, early 30s, dark-skinned, breathtakingly attractive. So much so that David felt her beauty move him, even in death. In fact, he found himself momentarily frozen in place, just staring at her as if time and the movement of the world had somehow stopped.

There was something about her still, poised countenance that exuded a captivating air of dignity, grace, and calm. It made her appear mysteriously discreet and reserved, yet her gently closed eyes and relaxed lips echoed the deepest warmth of love. This charm that was hers alone seemed to reach out to him like a soft kiss from beyond the veil of death.

Such a gentle soul, he thought.

"It's an E-model," the World Corp technician stated, referring to the odd Cocoon, which was composed of a hard, translucent, synthetic material. "So you'll need to confirm the seal before you sign."

"Yes, of course." David redirected his focus and typed a code into the small console atop the casket.

SEAL CONFIRMED

The technician nodded. David nodded in return and took possession of the Cocoon, wheeling it toward the transportation that he had arranged to drive him and his unusual cargo to the airport.

~

Rising, rising, rising, the fifty-foot-long, twin-engined, extended-range World Corp jet lifted off from Chhatrapati Shivaji Maharaj International Airport.

A high-speed aircraft, it was soon far away from Mumbai and its grand architecture, chaotic streets, outdoor bazaars; its multitudes of people, stray dogs, and exotic birds.

David, singly piloting the jet, soon leveled off its ascent and smiled slightly, feeling the freeing exhilaration of flight and the opening up of the horizon, for before him stretched an endless panorama of puffy white clouds and blue sky. Despite the sky being so very beautiful, he found himself glancing at his console's cabin video monitor. The jet's short, seatless cabin contained no living passengers, only four

Cocoons, three empty. The Cocoon from the hospital was on board, properly secured beside the others.

David thought of how the majority of Hindus must have believed that preserving the body in hopes of rising from the dead one future day was utterly wrong, sacrilegious, for Hinduism preached that the body was made up of the five elements of nature and that these elements must be returned to nature after death, to release the body and allow for spiritual reincarnation.

"She must have been very unique," David heard himself conclude aloud. *To have had such a sensitivity to newly born ideas.*

David then forcefully refocused his thoughts, examining his flight plan. From Mumbai, he was to cross over the Himalayas into Russia, landing in the Siberian city of Krasnoyarsk, located on the Yenisei River. There he would wait to pick up his second passenger, a terminally ill elderly Belarusian man who had made his fortune in the production of aluminum. Then it was onward to China, Japan, and finally across the Pacific to San Francisco and the headquarters of World Corp, where the company stored the preserved bodies of its clients.

~

As David flew on, monitoring his instruments, his thoughts began to wander. The clouds seemed so distant, his destination still so far away. He noticed his eyes continuously drifting over to the cabin video monitor, to glance at his cargo. He soon found himself envisioning in his mind's eye the overwhelming loveliness of the deceased woman whom he was transporting. The charm and beauty of her remembered countenance stirred something within him. His heart tugged at his mind and he switched on the autopilot.

The cabin lights flicked on automatically as David entered and approached her Cocoon. He stood there, over her, his hands behind his back, staring down at her through the casket's transparency. And once again he felt her remarkable silent and still presence reach out to him with the gentle touch of timeless, ethereal love.

He truly felt as if she had somehow come to him from another world, from beyond the stars, transcendent, pure, of unimaginable beauty. Magically bringing with her the essence of love.

A true sleeping beauty, yet he could not hope to awaken her with a kiss, even if he had been a prince from some impossible fairy tale, which he was not.

He felt like saying aloud, romantically, poetically: "Please look at me, and hear me, I'm here just for that. To be your moon, your moonlight too. Your flower garden, and your water too."

But instead he stood there in silence. And he soon found himself thinking about flowers. How he would have liked to have gifted this Indian woman flowers. The way evolution had gifted Earth flowers. Once upon a time, long ago, there had been no flowers on Earth: only a monotonous stretch of green across the land, all plants and trees possessing no other color. But then, late in the dinosaur age, flowers had appeared and forever changed the world.

David felt that his life, in terms of women, had been similarly monotonous, until the unexpected presence of this woman, who figuratively ushered forth the appearance of flowers into his life. Her presence was that singular to him.

"It's so odd. I sense your presence in my heart," David whispered to her. "Although I realize you no longer belong to the world…"

Suddenly an elegant white swan with an eight-foot wingspan flashed past the starboard portholes, one after the other, like something out of a dream.

A surprised half smile lifted upon David's face. "A swan?"
Then another swan flashed by. And another.

David felt the sheer panic of the realization of the moment surge through him. The terror sent him racing back to the cockpit in a mad dash. As he clumsily dropped into the pilot's seat, a thirty-pound swan crashed into and rolled up and over the jet's polycarbonate windshield, sending hairline cracks spiderwebbing across its transparency.

"Oh no…"

Directly before the jet, heading toward it in a dispersing V formation, was a high-flying flock of several hundred giant whooper swans. David glanced at his altimeter.

"At twenty-seven thousand feet?" he mumbled in disbelief. David knew that pilots had reported flocks of high-flying migratory birds, but he had never expected to encounter such birds, not at nearly 30,000 feet. And such large birds: swans—and so many of them. It seemed impossible. But it was happening.

There was the terribly unpleasant sound of a swan colliding with and being sucked into the jet's port engine. Followed by another. And then one went into the starboard engine.

The World Corp jet coughed, jerked forward, and decelerated in a shocking and distressing manner.

David struggled with the control wheel as it suddenly became so dreadfully heavy in his hands, so unruly.

"Oh damn…" he muttered, his voice submissive, powerless, as the plane suddenly plummeted downward.

David noticed a flash in the distance, far below, a change in brightness—sunlight reflecting off a glacier. The Himalayan region of India possessed a number of the world's most notable glaciers, tremendously high, stretching for miles in length. Flat topped. Snow covered. *Yes.* David realized it was his only chance. He needed to somehow land upon one of the glaciers below.

Straining with all his might, he slowly turned the jet while gaining some control over its rapid descent, his eyes all the while focused on one particular long and invitingly straight river of ice and snow. The glacier, flowing north to south, lay within a chasm, bordered east and west by incredibly lofty mountains.

David glanced at the altimeter as he struggled to level the plane: 20,302 feet and descending rapidly.

He kept the landing gear up as he came in, nose slightly elevated, following the glacier up into the mountains. Slower and slower, lower and lower, until he heard the initial rush of snow making contact with the belly of the fuselage—and he, as gently as possible, put the jet down upon the mass of glacial ice.

The roar of the jet's failing engines died completely and the craft thumped hard once, twice, thrice. The sound of its rush over the glacier's surface became deafening.

A deep groove in the ice caught the jet and spun it violently. David found himself thrown against the pilot's port hinged window and its framing. He blinked once, twice, and lost consciousness.

~

Hours later, David regained consciousness; after his disorientation and confusion subsided, he found that he remembered nothing about how he had successfully landed the jet. From this loss of memory, from the ringing in his ears, his dizziness and headache, he reasoned that he had likely suffered a concussion.

Yet he found that he had the presence of mind to check the transponder, the craft's robotic radio that would automatically transmit a response if it received an inquiry signal. It was on. It had power, for now.

David next read the altimeter: 17,035 feet above sea level. He was beneath the death zone for mountain climbers, which was approximately 26,000 feet, the altitude at which the amount of oxygen available in the air was insufficient for humans to breathe.

I'll be able to breathe…

But at 17,000 feet, although he would be able to breathe, the amount of oxygen in the air was less than half that at sea level. He would be subject to altitude sickness, something that was potentially lethal. For some, the sickness was fatal within hours due to fluid collecting in the lungs, in the brain, while others suffered nothing more than something akin to an awful hangover.

I'll need to limit my physical activity…

Nevertheless, David fought to rise, struggling against a lack of coordination and poor balance—additional signs that his self-diagnosis of a concussion was correct?

He put on a warm jacket, opened the jet's starboard door, and stumbled down onto the snow-covered glacier, collapsing to his knees. Rising unsteadily, he fell back to his knees as he saw how severely damaged the jet was, its fuselage intact but perforated, its wings shredded. He then noticed the ugly splattering of blood over the engine nacelles. And he felt bad for the swans that had lost their lives…

It began to snow lightly, the soft flakes encouraging David to look up at the towering, sprawling mountains to his left and right.

He was not far off course. He could be found. Rescued. But these high mountains flanking him… Any searching plane would have to fly directly over him, directly between these mountains, to sight him, to trigger a response from his transponder. His face grimaced and a deep concern gripped his psyche.

He turned north and looked up the glacier. Its accumulation zone lay somewhere unseen beyond the mountains. He looked south. The ice flow continued for as far as the eye could see, the glacier's terminus lost somewhere many miles in the distance. The harshness and silence of the land was numbing.

Standing there utterly isolated from civilization, David found himself recalling the words of impressionist artist Paul Gauguin, who had once written: "I shall take my paints and brushes and reinvigorate myself far from the company of men." David had memorized these words because they were how he had felt after his accident in Sweden, only in his case he wished to take his "books and mind" to reinvigorate himself far from the company of men. But now, he found himself suddenly longing for the company of someone, anyone...

And if I'm not found? David's spirit collapsed as he thought of all the things he would never come to know and understand, of all the life experiences he would never have. And an unpleasant wistful sadness, a helpless sorrow, crept over him, stilling his soul.

"But who am I... against the backdrop of eternity?" he humbly asked himself aloud, feeling a wound open within his psyche as deep as a well. And he looked down at his shadow, feeling that his existence was as ephemeral.

Suddenly it was Sweden all over again. He had attempted to continually flee from that traumatizing experience, but now, here near the top of the world, it had caught him, forcing him to face it again, perhaps once and for all.

Feeling the cold, and a coming shortness of breath, David climbed back into World Corp's downed jet, wanting only to close its hatch to the world and seal himself inside.

~

Fatigued, David sat himself clumsily in the cockpit, stumbling as he did so. He consciously assessed his mental state. *Am I confused? No… No, I don't think so… Am I?* He gently felt the injured side of his head, concerned, wondering if his lack of coordination, his weakness, the dizziness he felt were all symptoms of a concussion or… the early signs of serious altitude sickness, specifically fluid on the brain. Such altitude sickness could be fatal within a very short time. If he began to feel drowsy, experience excessive emotions… it would indicate severe altitude sickness. The drowsiness would occur shortly before the loss of consciousness and death… The only treatment was specialized medicines, which he did not have on board, and an immediate descent—an impossibility.

David rose and procured an oxygen cylinder, holding its connected mask over his nose and mouth. *Oxygen could buy time…*

As he breathed from the mask, he stared blankly out the porthole before him, at the whiteness of the mountain glacier. He could not help but think of Ötzi, the famous 5,000-year-old prehistoric man of the Copper Age, who had been found frozen in the ice of the Alps near the Italian–Austrian border, naturally mummified, remarkably well preserved. Ötzi the Iceman could never have guessed that millennia after his death he would lie on display, naked, without dignity, in the South Tyrol Museum in Italy.

David shuddered. His past trauma, his present situation, the possibility of impending severe altitude sickness, and his disbelief in a timely rescue all coalesced in his mind. And he sensed that this was to be his end.

He thought of the dignity, grace, and calm that he had perceived on the face of the Indian woman whom he had taken on board as his cargo. Longing to see her again, he awkwardly made his way to her Cocoon, where like before he silently stared down at her, at the woman who had so touched his heart and soul. He felt as if flowers were blooming. He removed his oxygen mask.

"Tell me what to do?" he asked her, half realizing the madness of his question, half wondering if it was proof of his suffering from a high-altitude cerebral edema.

And he waited with a silent passion for one impossible gesture, one impossible glance from her.

"I long for your love," he then went on with a shortness of breath, saying aloud what he truly wanted to say, romantically, poetically, a growing lassitude in his mind dismissing all his concerns. "I long to kiss your lips. I desire you more than life."

Love is what matters most...?

Strangely, an unexpected calmness descended upon him. And he understood what he needed to do, reciting aloud:

"Before fate strikes you down by surprise,
Order them to bring you rose-colored wine.
Oh silly fool, you are not gold
That they bury and dig up afterwards..."

Focusing his mind, David typed instructions into the small console atop the empty Cocoon resting beside his sleeping beauty. The empty casket's transparent lid opened. Struggling against increasing dizziness and oncoming drowsiness, David crawled into and lay down within the Cocoon.

"I'm no longer separate from you," he whispered. "Together we'll sleep away the winter..."

The Cocoon's lid closed over David and he heard it self-seal, the synthetic material of which it was constructed bonding to itself, merging inseparably, creating an airtight, impenetrable time capsule.

David then heard the hiss of the release of World Corp's patented Richards Gas, which would soon invisibly fill the casket, replacing and altering the air within, to perfectly preserve his body.

David reminded himself not to panic, that before he would suffocate, the Richards Gas would euthanize him without pain or suffering. He would simply experience a loss of consciousness.

And so he waited, calmly. He closed his eyes and wondered if he would be revived in the future, and if so, how far into the future. World Corp's Cocoon was constructed entirely of a nondegradable synthetic. Theoretically it could travel any distance into the future intact, transporting its occupant forward through the ages perfectly preserved, a time machine for the dead.

As David felt his thoughts slowing and his body becoming hopelessly immobilized, he imagined pages falling off a calendar, and himself traveling into the future. He wondered: if he was fortunate to awaken in the far future, would there be flowers?

And David surrendered himself to the loss of consciousness, and death.

~

The far future:

David sensed something in the awakening darkness of his mind. It was an odd psychic sensation, but also one of the body. It felt as if he were a raindrop, being forcefully pulled from the heavens, falling and falling, to finally reunite with the sea, to be replenished by the sea, where he floated weightlessly, coming back to life. Slowly, he came to feel fully revitalized, his mind clear. And he found himself struggling to open his eyes, blinking, his vision straining to focus.

He remembered losing consciousness, dying. But it seemed to have happened only moments ago. And yet he understood that time must have passed. As his vision cleared, this understanding was confirmed, and David gasped at his first glimpse into the world of tomorrow.

Standing before David was a gigantic, golden mechanical being, its highly polished aluminum skin glistening with dreamlike, manufactured perfection. The being was startlingly massive, towering over seven feet in height. David guessed that it must have weighed nearly 500 pounds—its tremendous bulk supported upon two seamless, tubular legs, unreal in their straightness. Humanoid in appearance, it had a strikingly large rectangular torso topped by a wide, elongated head, with an unmoving face. Two smooth, glistening arms hung straight at its sides. So surreal was its appearance that it looked more like something brought to life by magic than science, like the golem of Jewish legend.

David felt the golden golem regard him with its benign photoelectric eyes, and he relaxed. This automaton meant him no harm.

There was a loud electrical whine and one of the golem's arms moved. With a wave, the golden giant motioned for David to rise.

David noticed for the first time that he had been seated upon a furnishing that appeared to have somehow grown up out of the floor of the small room that he was within. Oddly, there were no other furnishings or objects of any kind within the room. *They undoubtedly resurrected me using some future technology, but it wasn't done here. Is this some sort of recovery area?*

David's eyes moved over the curved walls of the room. They appeared to be composed of stone, yet there was an organic style to the construction that gave David the impression that he was within the hollow trunk of a huge tree. The room appeared so oddly primitive and natural in comparison to the glistening, futuristic, mechanical automaton standing before him.

The golem motioned again for David to rise.

David rose and found that he was barefoot and cloaked in some type of furry animal hide, naked underneath.

The golem motioned once more, this time for David to follow it, and it began to turn, to leave.

"Wait," David heard himself call to golem, suddenly realizing something most important. "There was a woman with me. She was preserved also. What became of her?"

David waited for an answer, but the golden giant only stood there in silence. David looked over its unmoving metal mask of a face, wondering why it had a wide nose molded upon it if it did not breathe, why it had a slotted opening for a mouth if it did not speak.

The golem motioned once again for David to follow it, and it exited the small chamber.

David felt his heart drop as he followed after the mechanical thing, stepping outdoors, where he immediately welcomed the luxurious warmth of his shawl as he encountered the cold, dry air of the future.

The light of the rising sun momentarily blinded David, then he saw that they had stepped out onto a kind of pedestrian walkway, one that was elevated several stories above ground level, a sort of bridge that connected the many clusters of dwellings that sprawled out around them.

David was deep within some type of a city, built upon a mountainside. But the architecture was unlike anything from the past. The structures were organic in style, without uniform shape, surreal in appearance. So much so that as David followed the golem, he felt as if he were not on Earth but on some dreamlike parallel world.

But then David realized how the architecture must have been paying homage to man's arboreal past, to man's distant ape ancestors who had once, millions of years ago, lived in the trees. Most of the dwellings sat upon thick columns that were reminiscent of trunks of giant oaks. This imbued in David a comfortable, nostalgic reaction, arising from the preferences passed on to him evolutionarily by his most distant ancestors. He found himself emotionally embracing this futuristic city of tree houses, open spaces, and cliff dwellings.

Yet David found himself puzzled. The innate primitiveness of the city, born from its stone and wood construction, its use of natural forms, was in such stark contrast to its futuristic place in time as symbolized by the golden giant that he found himself following.

The golem led David past a tall dwelling, and a magnificent view of the surrounding landscape opened up to their left. Ancient and immense trees like giant sequoias rose up into a startling blue sky that was filled with beautiful wispy clouds. Groves of other conifers that looked like pines and cypress dotted the landscape, as did innumerable clumps of broadleaf oaks. Close to the city, steam was venting up out of small domed structures that must have capped underground geothermal power stations. Beyond this stretched farmland and then prairie grasses, which extended to the horizon, speckled by tiny daisies and meadows of flowers of every color. And finally, off against the distant skyline, towered mile-high gleaming white glaciers of ice and snow, their melt waters streaming liberally across the land.

A new ice age, David realized.

And David then noticed the megafauna populating the distant prairies, large mammals that resembled llamas and camels, elk and bison, wooly rhinoceroses and fur-covered elephants—evolved once again.

How far into the future am I? David wondered. *How much time has passed? Ten thousand years? A hundred thousand years? A million years? Ten million years? Will the clever men who survived the ice look different? Has man physically evolved further?*

But then a troubling thought struck David. What if the men who had created this robot were no more? What if he was alone in the future? With this silent automaton…

A second huge golden golem suddenly appeared to their right, coming from an adjoining walkway. And following behind this golem—the woman whom David had picked up in Mumbai.

The sight of her took David's breath away. He found himself instantly running to her and they embraced one another as if they were the last two humans on Earth who had suddenly, unexpectedly found one another. *There are flowers in the future.*

David looked down at his awakened sleeping beauty, and once again he felt her beauty move him. Feeling the potential promise of her love, he stood there entranced, looking into her gentle eyes, completely captivated, feeling as if time had frozen, as if the movement of the world had stopped. He could not help but think of Rumi: *Lovers don't finally meet somewhere. They're in each other all along.*

"You're alive," he finally said to her.

"Yes," she said, her soft voice delicate, lovely, frightened. "Where are we? Are there any others like us?"

David shrugged, and they heard the loud electrical whine of the arms of the golems motioning for them to follow.

David put an arm around his dream woman and together, barefoot, clad in fur shawls, they followed the giant golden automatons.

"My name is David," David whispered to her.

"Talia," she whispered her name to him.

The golems opened an enormous, decoratively carved wooden double door and proceeded into the largest of the city's structures. David and Talia followed, welcoming the warmth that was within, their curiosity growing.

To their left and right were dimly lit chambers of vast libraries, stacked with books. *Do these automatons read?* David wondered. No, he did not think so. These hulking mechanical giants seemed to only possess narrow artificial intelligence. They did not appear sentient. *They must be robotic servants…*

David surmised that he and Talia must be nearing the men who had gathered these libraries, who had built these robots, who inhabited this unique city. And he was correct. A great hall opened up before them, like a fantastic cathedral within an impossibly enormous hollow tree, beams of sunlight radiating down from above.

The huge golden golems stopped and motioned to David and Talia, instructing them to continue alone.

David felt Talia take his hand, and together they proceeded into the cathedral, fearful but with dignity and grace. There were figures up ahead of them, in the shadows. Not seven-foot-tall mechanical giants, but human-sized figures. *Thank God.* David heard the relief of his inner thoughts echo forth in his mind.

David and Talia stopped, and the new men of tomorrow stepped out into the sunlight.

Improbable man-sized squirrels they were. Big and gray, furry, fluffy, and handsome, their craniums human-sized, their eyes so alive, shining with intelligence, their hand-like paws marvelously dexterous.

The leader of the squirrel-men focused on David benevolently. And for a long, dreamlike moment, David and the squirrel gazed into each other's eyes. In those heartbeats of time, David thought of all the life that in the past did fall, and gleaned the meaning of it all. The meaning of life was to go on. Evolution was Nature's way of finding a means for extending the persistence of life on Earth, and apparently for allowing sentience to rise again.

The squirrels of the trees had arisen after the eclipse of man. David found himself smiling with admiration for Nature's continued ingenuity. Nature had let the genie out of the bottle yet again. When man could not endure the ice, these winter-preparing mammals survived and then evolved to the greatest heights of sentience in the noncompetitive absence of man.

Here in the distant future, with Talia, David would be able to reinvigorate himself far from the company of men.

A Note from the Author

This author hopes that the reader appreciated this story of science and love and time travel via death into the distant future. The story was partly inspired by and pays homage to anthropologist Loren Eiseley's essay "The Fire Apes."

Talia is the name of Sleeping Beauty in Giambattista Basile's version of the fairy tale "Sleeping Beauty."

Whooper swans are among the highest-flying birds in the world, recorded on radar flying at 27,000 feet above sea level. During migration, the swans form flocks that can contain thousands of birds.

The poem cited in this story was written by the twelfth-century Persian mathematician, astronomer, and poet Omar Khayyam:

> Before fate strikes you down by surprise,
> Order them to bring you rose-colored wine.
> Oh silly fool, you are not gold
> That they bury and dig up afterwards.

This author also drew upon the writings of the thirteenth-century Persian poet Rumi.

The philosophical scientific statement:

"As a process, evolution seems to be Nature's way of finding means for extending the persistence of life on Earth."

was presented by Jonas Salk in his book *The Survival of the Wisest*.

This author would like to leave the reader with this parting question: is it man's dominance of the planet that has prevented sentient intelligence from evolving in other animal species?

Niko Zinovii
Santa Monica, California
18 October 2018

Niko Zinovii

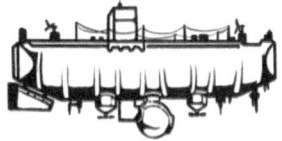

Down, Down, Down

~1~

The deep-sea diving submersible the *Dīpukujira Maru* broke the surface, rising quite high in the water, amply buoyed by its large gasoline tanks. As the bathyscaphe was lifted still higher in a swell, the hatch of its conning tower swung open and Alec Urashima emerged from within, smiling.

Climbing down to the vessel's fairwater deck, Alec vigorously took hold of the life rail's safety lines, steadying himself against the rocking of the craft. He then allowed a soft spring breeze to turn him about to witness parting clouds revealing Mount Fuji, which suddenly loomed godlike over Suruga Bay, its majestic white crown of snow towering so unbelievably high, up, up into the heavenly blue sky. The dreamy, perfectly shaped volcano seemed so much larger than the entire bay, otherworldly.

"Fuji-san..." Alec uttered, his breath taken away, his velvety, resonant Anglic voice filled with awe and reverence. And Alec felt himself bow his head as he sensed the familiar connection to Fuji flood his soul, so special a place did this near mythical, sacred mountain occupy in his heart. There was no wonder in Alec's mind as to why Mount Fuji had been immortalized in countless works of art, for he simply could not imagine Japan without *Fuji-no-Yama.*

Too many men talk too much, Alec heard his innermost thoughts whisper as he appreciated the moment, *hearing only the sound of their own voices, never the pregnant silence of the living world.*

Alec nodded as he further appreciated the grand generosity of Nature's beauty: Japan's highest mountain poised over Japan's deepest bay—and what a bay, its seabed a labyrinth of submarine canyons inhabited by a fabulous diversity of exotic deep-sea marine life.

And Alec looked up into the sky, thinking that at sea level he was living at the bottom of an ocean of air. He then looked down, gazing into the deep blue water of Suruga Bay. He thought about the unseen drama of life unfolding in its depths, wondering about the mysteries that lay hidden in the darkness. Was the most fantastic of all sea creatures yet to be caught? He had just observed giant Japanese spider crabs twelve feet across, and a phantom-like abyssal cusk eel, which seemed like a graceful ghost from another world.

Alec waved to the crew of his approaching support vessel, barking out orders to them in fluent Japanese, directing the men as to how to best secure the *Dīspukujira Maru* for towing back to port. It was quite startling how Alec's commanding personality was at such odds with his rather plain, ordinary look: that of a common middle-aged Englishman—with a hint of Japanese ancestry in the shape of his eyes.

"No," Alec corrected a young Japanese sailor who had jumped aboard the submersible with a towrope. "Connect it to the tow pad, beneath the bow thruster."

Alec took the rope from the sailor, dragged it forward, and attached it himself. The sailor watched on silently, his attention fixed on the purposeful Wagnerian grandeur that projected from Alec. There was something palpably imperious about Alec—about who he truly was at his core. His passions, when released, were eye catching, thrilling, even thunderous, very much the opposite of the contained Japanese character, although that Japanese character was also there in Alec.

~2~

Aboard the support vessel, Alec spread open a chart and showed the boat's captain the diversion he wanted to take on their route back across the bay to Shimizu Port.

~3~

The diversion was a stop at a small and rocky land-tied island, connected to Honshu by a long, narrow sandbar.

The support boat, towing the *Dīpukujira Maru*, anchored in deep water, and Alec and two Japanese archeologists were transported over to the island by skiff.

Ashore, Alec pointed out to the archeologists what appeared to be ancient ruins of prehistoric construction: sloping stones that had been long ago polished, likely to enable small boats to be pulled up onto the rocks.

Alec directed the scientists to search for artifacts, and the men walked off, doing so.

Alec started to follow but found himself distracted as he noticed very simple little flowers growing nearby. He knelt and touched the flowers. He picked a few, smelling them, appreciating their mild fragrance. As he moved amongst the flowers, associating with them, slowly he became aware of a hidden entrance to a small cave—a cave that the two archaeologists had passed without noticing.

Alec shook his head. Just by looking at flowers, he had made the discovery. It reaffirmed to him his belief that specialists so narrowly focused saw little. That to really see things one needed to be deeply attached to the Earth.

The cave contained a primitive temple within. But the site was Neolithic, from Japan's Jōmon period, circa 10,000–300 BC. Alec shook off the disappointment. This site was too old, for he was searching for clues to Yamatai-koku, Japan's Atlantis… of the late Yayoi period, circa 300 BC–300 AD.

Another false lead.

~4~

While docking, Alec found himself unusually relaxed, aimlessly gazing about, visually taking in the beauty of the scenic port of Shimizu, a town known for its tea leaves and spectacular views of Mount Fuji. He looked for Fuji—for it changed every time he set his eyes upon it. In the winter it was brilliant white with snow, in the summer almost blue. Its shimmering snowcap often glowed red, reflecting the light of the sun. Fuji also changed daily, even over a single day.

He saw that Fuji-san was shrouded by clouds, as it often was. *It's hiding.*

Nearby, upside down in the sun, a cat stretched out, far from bashful.

Farther down the dock, a group of young Japanese boys were playing with a very large red and brown and pale-yellow loggerhead sea turtle they had caught. The turtle was a beautiful specimen, three feet in length, likely weighing over 300 pounds.

"You need to return her to the sea," Alec instructed the boys sternly, in Japanese. But then he grinned. He understood what it was like to be a boy here in Shimizu and to catch something so dinosaurian from the bay. He had spent his own boyhood here, fishing, boating, swimming. He walked over and knelt beside the boys, turning over in his mind the best way to deal with them.

"You see how her tail is short and slender, and how her lower shell is long?" he asked the boys. "A male would have a longer, thicker tail and shorter plastrons. She's mature, you can tell by her size. She'll lay over a hundred eggs every several years. And she can live to the ripe old age of sixty-five."

Alec paused, suddenly at a loss of understanding, realizing that he was now sixty-five years old. Yet he did not consider himself to be at a ripe old age. He was healthy, trim, full of vitality. He did not see any difference between the capabilities he enjoyed now and the capabilities he had enjoyed twenty years go. But time was moving on him. He wished he could stop time, at least for a little while, until he could catch up with all his ambitions.

"She's also the progeny of a long line of honorable ancestors," Alec went on, his richly textured voice sounding like trickling tears, "that traces its way in time back to over a hundred million years ago. And sea turtles, they passed Nature's difficult test of the Cretaceous extinction, which ended the lives of all the dinosaurs. The sea turtle offers much to respect.

"Now, I'm sure you're all good boys, respectful of nature. This turtle, she has no name, and her life is a mystery to you, but I'm sure you must feel for her. Let me help you return her to the sea." And Alec waited for an answer, feeling that he had won the boys over with his thoughtful appeal, delivered with such a kind smile.

The oldest of the boys answered. "Give us some money for the turtle."

Alec stood, affronted, ready to take matters into his own hands by force. But then he dismissed his reaction, shrugging it off entirely, as if he had merely been play-acting. And he laughed, genuinely, openly, congenially.

He reached for his wallet and winked at the boys. "Buy anything you like with the money. You can do more with this money than you could ever do with this poor turtle."

~5~

Alec bicycled from the dock to his traditional although elaborate Japanese home, which was perched on a cliff, overlooking a small and tranquil private beach. As he approached his sizeable residence, he dismounted his bike and walked it in leisurely, for a moment feeling himself a child again. For this had been his paternal grandfather's home. It had been handed down to Alec's father, and recently to Alec. It was what had prompted Alec's return to Japan.

Alec nodded in approval at the towering and picturesque line of *kuromatsu*—black pine trees—that ran along the southeastern boundary of the walled property. In Japan these pines were a symbol of longevity and abundance. But more importantly, aligned as they were, they provided a formidable windbreak. He had barely heard the wind of last night's storm.

Between these beautiful, mature pines and his new home stood thickets of bamboo and plum trees. *Suihan Sanyou*: pine, bamboo, and plum blossom, the Three Friends of Winter. Grouped together, they stood as a symbol of the traditional values of steadfastness, perseverance, and resilience—the ideal characteristics of a scholar-gentleman, which Alec's grandfather had aimed to be.

"Oh…" Alec heard himself utter as he noticed the half-dozen reporters, all men, all Japanese, waiting before the gated entry of his estate, intruding upon his private world.

"Urashima-sama," one of the reporters addressed Alec, "why do you believe you can find Yamatai-koku?"

"I never said that I would find Yamatai-koku," Alec corrected the man. "I said that my research would reveal the truth about it."

"Urashima-sensei," a second reporter asked, respectfully, "are you stating that the lost kingdom of Yamatai did not actually exist?"

Alec nodded to the reporter, flattered by the man's use of the honorific title *sensei,* a title reserved for addressing a figure of authority. Usually Alec heard Urashima-san—Mr. Urashima—or the more formal Urashima-sama.

"There certainly was something to the origin of the legend," Alec's velvety voice trickled out, "and that's what I'm investigating. The Chinese records of Wei are all we presently have to go on, but I find it… curious that nothing is mentioned in Japanese records, scanty as they may be. It almost seems that Japan went out of its way to leave Yamatai-koku and its ruler out of the historical record. I believe this is a subject that people would like to know the truth about."

"Is it true that Yamatai-koku was ruled by the shaman-priestess Queen Himiko?" asked another reporter.

"Imagine that." Alec smiled mischievously, appreciating the irony. "A female ruler in Japan."

It began to rain, and the reporters sent up their umbrellas. It was the typical light, drizzly rain of spring. Alec felt soothed by how softly it fell. Rain was such an integral part of Japan, indispensible to life. Of course it also brought disaster. Summer, approaching, was the typhoon season.

"Excuse me, gentlemen." Alec bowed politely and stepped past the men, disappearing through a roofed cherry-wood gate—the entrance to his home.

~6~

Alec stepped into the *genkan* of his home—its entryway—exchanging his shoes for slippers, turning his shoes about to leave them pointing toward the door through which he had come.

After walking the length of a long, timber-floored hall, he slid open a wooden-framed panel of opaque paper painted with decorative calligraphy. Stepping out of his slippers, he entered the spacious living room of his family home, where he stood

179

motionless for several moments, just soaking in its traditional Japanese ambiance: the reverence of beautifully grained wood, in the framing, the ceiling, the intricately carved transoms; the stylized walls and sliding doors covered by white paper—*fusuma*—some sections painted with flowers and landscapes; the other walls and doors of translucent paper framed within decorative wooden lattices—*shoji*—through which came the diffused natural light of the day, all the main rooms of the house facing south; the *tatami* flooring that he now stood upon, respectfully in his stocking feet, the thick, woven grass of the matting feeling so welcoming.

Alec especially appreciated the home's intimate contact with the outdoors, the aesthetic provided by way of the views offered of the bay and Mount Fuji. And the home's broad wooden *engawa*—veranda—that opened to the garden.

Alec held out his hands to better sense the air in the room. And he smiled at his grandfather's foresight of having laid nearly twelve thousand pounds of charcoal beneath the floorboards to regulate the moisture in the home, maintaining a pleasant humidity level throughout the year.

Walking over to the open window that viewed the bay, Alec picked up a pair of binoculars and focused them down upon the stretch of beach beneath his house, looking for something or someone.

"She there again?" asked a gray-haired, elderly Japanese man as he entered the room.

"What? Who?" Alec fumbled a bit, taken by surprise.

"Oh, nothing." The old man smiled, displaying kindness and a happy energy toward life.

"*Ojisan,* I was only looking out at the bay." Alec winked. "Can you please help me into my kimono?"

"The senators?" Alec's ojisan—uncle—asked.

Alec nodded. "For tea."

"Later, help me mash the rice?"

"To make *kiritanpo*?" Alec asked.

His uncle nodded.

Alec smiled. "Of course."

~7~

Alec felt rather dignified in his kimono, reflective of Japan's sense of beauty—even though the kimono was a plain, uniform smoky gray in color. For up close, the rich pine-needle pattern of the fabric was quite eye catching. It was remarkably impressive in its subtlety.

To reach the tea room, Alec had to pass through the garden. Having to take this walk was intentional in the design of the estate, to allow one to leave behind the noise and distractions of everyday life in order to properly compose oneself for the tea to come.

The artfully positioned stepping-stones of the garden path, still glistening wet from the earlier rain, led Alec past ferns and blanketing mossy greenery. Above, the sunlight fought to flicker down through the overhanging tree branches, so profusely were they interwoven, like a fairy-tale forest.

A single butterfly, fanned along by the softest of zephyrs, fluttered and drifted across Alec's path. And Alec paused to allow the butterfly safe passage and to appreciate the beauty alongside him: a small pond containing *nishikigoi* (koi), the fish decorated with the most attractive splashes of white, orange, and black, as if painted by the hand of God. To Alec these moving works of art, these swimming jewels, were the living embodiment of Japanese aesthetics.

Around the pond, here and there, were potted bonsai trees, miniature yet picturesque living works of art crafted by the human imagination. One of the bonsai was a fine-needled pine five hundred years in age, truly a symbol of the ceaseless march of time.

The stone path curved in front of him, imbuing in Alec a sense of anticipation for what lay ahead: a gate of bamboo. Alec had to stoop as he passed beneath and through the gate, which was purposely made low, to force one to adopt a posture of humility.

Beside the entrance to the tea room, beneath a giant camphor tree, rested an old stone basin filled with rainwater. Alec ceremonially washed his hands and mouth, to purify his spirit before entering.

But before doing so, he paused to listen to the *shishi-odoshi* as it rhythmically interrupted the silence of the garden, its bamboo rocker arm hitting upon a stone each time the device was filled by the water trickling into it. *Knock... Knock... Knock...* The sound was most pleasing, especially when accompanied by the scent of chrysanthemums, as it was.

Bowing his head to the garden in a gesture of appreciation, Alec entered the tea room, in the right frame of mind: clear, humble, relaxed yet focused.

~8~

An hour into the tea-drinking ceremony, the bond between its participants developed and conversation grew more open.

"How is it," Alec asked the eldest of the three senators present, "that so much money is presently scheduled to be spent to explore distant things that have so very little to do with our lives while so much remains unknown about our oceans, which need so much funding but receive so little?"

"I'm convinced that our duty is to explore outer space," answered the senator, in a relaxed yet stately manner. "Other nations will soon have communities in outer space."

"Forgive me," Alec responded respectfully, thoughtfully, "but I don't think that is a desirable way of life, to live off planet. I feel very attached to my planet, and I think others do as well, and that this will be true for generations to come.

"Man is still a backboned animal, whatever else he thinks he may be. And the origin of all backboned life traces its path back to the sea, to our fish ancestors. Yes, evolution has changed us in significant ways, but we're still essentially fish out of water.

"The old sea salts are still bottled up inside us, flowing within our tissues, our veins, our cells. The sea is still in us, and we belong in the sea. Not in outer space. It would be much more desirable to live in underwater cities. And a submarine town would be far more feasible than a similar outpost on the moon."

As Alec waited for the senator to respond, he glanced behind the man at the decorative focal point of the room: the elevated alcove known as the *tokonoma*. On its wall, Alec had hung a *kakejiku*—a hanging scroll.

Alec had taken great thought in making his selection of which scroll to hang, for the scroll would convey a message to the room's guests, providing them something to ponder while drinking tea. Usually selections were pictorial, invoking a seasonal theme. Instead, Alec had hung a *hanshi* scroll decorated with Zen calligraphy, the kanji symbols stating: *The past is prologue*

The simplicity was quite deceptive, as the words held a much deeper meaning for Alec.

"I am trying to see you," the old senator stated, staring at Alec inquisitively. "A former lieutenant of our Maritime Self-Defense Force; an archaeologist, treasure hunter, marine biologist; an author of so many books on science; a poet and painter... You are so many that I don't know who you really are. Who are you?"

"I don't know," Alec answered sincerely. "I only know who I would like to be."

"And who would you like to be?"

"Ideally? A manfish. A future human *Homo aquaticus*. A sea king with gills, adapted to life in the sea, able to live in fantastic domed cities at the bottom of the ocean."

"Even today," one of the other senators stated with a critical shake of his head, "that sounds like fantasy, like science fiction."

"And what's wrong with science fiction as a presentiment of reality?" Alec calmly defended his position. "Ever since Jules Verne, and lots of people before him, the informed human imagination has projected what is to come."

"Milking whales?" the third senator chimed in. "Underwater cities? Aqua-farmers?"

Alec nodded. "Yes. And kelp farming. Oceanic dairies—"

"You are a utopian?" the eldest senator interrupted, still attempting to properly appraise Alec.

"Let's instead say a realist with a vision. The past is prologue, gentlemen. I believe it indicates our most appropriate path into tomorrow. Given our biology, our evolution. I see the destiny of humanity, the most natural option for humanity, being a return to the sea, living in the sea, not up in outer space."

Alec rose and stepped over to the room's tokonoma. Beneath the scroll that hung there was Alec's chosen ornament of beauty, also on display. Tea ceremonies usually were decorated with a flower arrangement, or a decorative rock, or a bonsai, or even a single burning stick of incense. But Alec had chosen something quite different for the decorative ornament of this tea gathering. Something extraordinary in its uniqueness: a thirty-million-year-old praying mantis, perfectly preserved, locked within a splendidly clear, pristine block of amber.

Alec took the amber and handed it the eldest senator to hold up to the light and examine, and then pass along to the others.

"Imagine"—Alec's rich, velvety voice filled the silence of the tea room—"to meet every struggle with heart and soul, only to be smothered alive in an ooze of amber, just when you must have felt your moment of life was at its height... To be encased and frozen in time for all eternity without thought or movement... with only the silent echo of the cruel beauty of Nature calling out that you had ever existed...

"Nature has a power that cannot be ignored, gentlemen. Our ancestry, our evolution, should also not be ignored."

~9~

Later, when Alec's guests left, they did so exhibiting genuine, respectful appreciation and contained anticipation for their next tea gathering, which Alec had already invited them to. Alec's aim was to slowly convert them to his vision of the sea as man's next logical frontier, and through them turn Japan in that direction.

As Alec meditated, alone, the last of the pine and sandalwood incense burned out, and in the absence of these exotic wooded fragrances, he suddenly felt himself drawn to the sea. Smiling, he set out toward the steep stone steps in the back of his property that led down to his private beach.

Plum blossoms, still in bloom, so late in spring?

~10~

Slender and elegant stalks of green bamboo lined the steps descending to the shore, their rustling leaves softly, ever so softly, whispering to Alec's heart a presence that seemed to convey the very essence of Japan.

Alec glanced northward. Fuji-san was still concealed by clouds.

The beach was awash with shells, sun-dried seaweed, and driftwood, all deposited by last night's storm. Alec knelt and picked up a rather attractive shell, turning it about in his hand, appreciating its simple beauty, its strong ocean fragrance. He thought of how the shell was empty, of how the life that had once inhabited it had either abandoned it or made its exit from this world... And he felt a deep connection to Earth and its life flood his soul. It reminded him of why he liked to walk the shoreline after a storm.

The sun broke the clouds and Alec suddenly saw her, on the beach up ahead, her presence like a single flawless gem against the backdrop of the world. He stood there motionless for several long moments, just quivering like a drop of mercury. This was the first time he had actually seen her in person, and not through his binoculars. Her beauty literally took his breath away.

Focused as she was on the easeled canvas she was painting upon, she had not yet noticed Alec, and this gave him the opportunity to absorb her presence unabashed.

To Alec, her beauty was startling. The contrast between her pitch-black hair, which fell in soft waves, and her porcelain-white skin was haunting. And more, there was the most exotic European glamor to her presence. She seemed a highborn queen, a seductive princess, and a femme fatale, somehow all combined in one woman.

For moments, when concentrating on her painting, her countenance became so still and unemotive, like a blank slate of pure beauty frozen in time...

Finally, she turned to Alec. And Alec saw the ocean in her light gray-green, pooling eyes. Her eyelashes went on forever. Her lips were so full, her mouth like a poppy in heavy bloom.

"Hello," she said in English, in a lilting Viennese accent, her voice feminine, delicate yet seductive, suggesting a titillating past, despite her young age. She was magnetism with warmth. Her very presence seemed to display most eye-catchingly the European art of being womanly.

"Hello," Alec responded, and he walked up to her and placed his seashell in her hand. "A present. I found it."

She ran a finger over the shell, her bejeweled wrists contrasting sharply with her rather plain and worn painting clothes. "Soft." And she looked up at Alec, into his eyes. "Thank you," she said. "Who are you?"

"Oh, someone, no one. I live right up there." He pointed up to his home. "Call me Alec."

"Irene," she reciprocated. "Irene Kiesler."

Alec turned his eyes to her painting, curious.

"The rose is opening," she explained her work, "because it has felt something."

Alec turned back to her, his creative intellect aroused.

"The painting," Irene went on, "it doesn't answer what the rose felt."

As she spoke, Alec could hear nothing in his mind but the sound of her inimitably accented soft voice.

"It only asks the question: can the most beautiful things in the world be seen or touched, or must they be felt by the heart?"

Alec just stared at her for a moment. The enchanting beauty of this raven-haired goddess suddenly seemed more a mysterious mask that concealed a complex and creative mind than simply Vienna's gift to men.

Alec looked back at her painting, feeling it, and he gave his own interpretation, poetically. "Let me leave aside my worries, the flowers are blooming."

"Interpretation is a connection with the spirit," she responded thoughtfully.

"As is love," Alec added. But then he turned away from her, wondering what he was doing, reminding himself of his age and of the fact that she was likely no older than twenty-two or twenty-three. She could be his granddaughter.

Yet he heard himself then ask: "Are you married? I don't see a wedding ring."

"I was married. He was an absolute monarch. I was like a doll. I was like a thing, some object of art, which had to be guarded, imprisoned, having no mind, no life of my own. I couldn't go on living like that. And you?"

"A widower."

"Oh."

Alec turned to face Suruga Bay.

"You're staring out to sea like a seagull," Irene said gently as she stepped over to him. "Are you in love with the sea?"

"Very much so. Earlier I was thinking about last night's storm. I was wondering if it was the sea asking for respect."

This time it was Irene who was drawn in further, her artistic intellect aroused by his words. "Your eyes…" she said. "You see things differently. What do you do?"

"Oh, I travel the seas, to touch hands with the universe."

"Does a man so wide awake do much dreaming?" she asked.

"I have my dreams. Things can haunt the mind."

"These dreams are important to you?"

Alec felt himself pull back, uncomfortable with his intentions, due to their significant difference in age.

"They give one something to hang on to in life," he began, but her smile stopped him. "Yes, they're important. To me."

And for a long moment they fell silent, saying nothing, just listening to the sound of the waves together.

"I have to go now," Alec finally said. "I promised my uncle I'd help him mash rice. It was very nice meeting you, Irene."

And Alec walked off with his shadow leaning away from him, his heart feeling the siren call of love and yearning to remain behind.

~11~

Later that night, after mashing rice and eating the kiritanpo, as dumplings in soup, Alec, alone, watched the moon sink behind Mount Fuji.

~12~

The next afternoon, Alec returned to the beach. Irene was there, painting again.

"This is private property, you know." Alec winked.

She laughed gently, melodiously.

In response to her silvery laughter, Alec handed her daisies he had picked.

"Thank you. How are you?"

"Oh, the usual. Lack of sleep."

They both reacted to a distant flash of lighting, out over the sea.

"Those who see lighting," Alec commented, his velvety voice filled with resonance, "without thinking of transience... How admirable."

"But we need to be happy for this moment," Irene turned his thought. "This moment is our life."

Alec noticed that she had laid open near her a book on fish and a book on birds, both turned to pages displaying the fins and wings of each. On her canvas she was painting something new, startling, unique. An imagined flying fish soaring over the sea, its membranous pectoral fins enlarged yet shaped like those of the fastest fish, but the fins were flapping like the wings of a bird.

Alec had once wondered if flying fish could have ever evolved sustained flight, to become true wing-flapping aerialists, if they had not been so restrained by their water-breathing requirements. And here on this canvas, his wondering had been brought to life by Irene's imagination.

Alec turned his eyes upon the porcelain-skinned beauty before him. He thought about her mind. And how she looked so glamorous, even when just painting.

"Would you like to see something?" Alec asked her.

"See what?" She smiled.

"My boat. I think you'd find it interesting."

~13~

Walking to the port, Alec took a short cut, leading Irene through a small area of wilderness, where wild sunflowers were reaching for the sky. Within the greenery, they passed a boulder surrounded by roping, which created a sacred space for the rock.

"In old Japan," Alec explained to Irene, "it was believed that all rocks had deities dwelling within them. It's believed that some still do…"

Alec noticed something beneath a clump of ferns. He stopped and picked it up. It was a teakettle-sized rock. Conical in shape, it was reminiscent of Mount Fuji. It inspired a deep feeling of appreciation in Alec.

"This *suiseki* will be the decorative ornament for my next tea ceremony," Alec stated, his voice trickling with enthusiasm. "Until then, I will put it beside my bed. And dream of cuddling it in my sleep."

Irene laughed delicately.

"Why are you here?" Alec asked her. "In Japan. Why have you come to Japan?"

"Japan is special."

Alec nodded. "Yes. It is."

"Why are you here?"

"For that very reason. And more."

She looked at him, for more.

"I was born in Japan," Alec said a bit wistfully, adding, "later lured back once by beauty, and recently again by death."

Irene was about to ask more, but Alec stopped her with a commanding yet gentle gesture of his hand.

"In time," he offered, respectfully.

~14~

At the port, Alec walked Irene up to his docked bathyscaphe, the *Dīpukujira Maru*.

"My undersea boat," he said with pride.

"You have your own submarine?" she asked in disbelief.

"Bathyscaphe," Alec corrected her gently. "Wouldn't any boy who could afford it acquire his own submersible?"

Irene approached the craft, her eyes filled with wonder. She reached out to touch the bathyscaphe, running a hand over its name. "*Dīpukujira Maru*—what does it mean?"

"Deep Whale," Alec answered, moving to her side.

"You go down inside this thing?"

Alec nodded.

"Is it claustrophobic?"

Alec nodded again. "Yes. One needs to fight the fear. But there are certain things men must do, to remain men. I must be a bit insane. But I'm so amazed at what I see."

"What is it like? When you go down, so deep?"

"Oh, there's a strange silence that you can almost hear. A wonderment that you can feel, but that you can't see or touch."

And they turned to face each other, their souls connecting.

"What do you want out of life?" she asked him.

"Too much. And you?"

"I would like to find a person to come into my life by accident. But remain in my life on purpose."

Alec reached out and took her hand, gently touching and moving his palm against hers. It felt so good to touch her. It was heaven. Yet he felt himself pull his hand away. *What are you doing?* he asked himself in his thoughts. *You're old enough to be her grandfather. Regardless of how vigorous you believe your state of health to be. Remember that!*

~15~

That night, however, as Alec looked at the moon, alone, he thought of how sometimes there is a kiss that one wants with one's whole life.

He found himself opening the window, and in his imagination he asked the moon to come in and press its face against his, so that he could pretend it was Irene.

"I never knew love could make me feel like this," he groaned. "Carrying me so helplessly in its tide, out to sea…"

And in his mind flashed an image of cherry blossoms bursting into bloom, petals gently scattering, falling to the ground.

"Cherry blossoms. I want to sit beneath cherry blossoms with her."

And Alec laughed out loud at himself, in disbelief.

"I'm so small," he moaned out his window to the distant, majestic silhouette of Mount Fuji, "I can barely be seen. How can this great love be inside me?"

The answer seemed to waft in upon a breeze, although in actuality it came from Alec's deeper thoughts: There are things that can take over our minds.

Employing his strength of will, Alec fought against the spell that had caught him. He forced the possibility of being with Irene out of his heart. "No… Not everyone is meant to be in our future. Some people are only passing through… to teach us some lesson in life." *Humility?*

Alec straightened himself, gaining some control over his longings.

"Tomorrow, I go down into the deep."

~16~

Alec could hear the *Dīpukujira Maru*'s ballast tanks flooding with seawater. Soon the craft would begin to submerge, and sink down, down, down into the abyssal depths of Suruga Bay. Before leaving the bright light of the surface world, Alec thought of how each flower that he had bicycled past this morning on his way to Shimizu's port had reminded him of Irene.

Thirty-three feet. Alec read the gauges, forcing himself to focus on his descent. *Two atmospheres, pressure doubled. Sixty-six feet, pressure tripled.*

As the *Dīpukujira Maru* dropped still deeper, Alec found himself entering a world of silence so profound it momentarily stilled his soul. To drop down into the deep so utterly naked of possessions... It was almost like being born again. Alec wondered if this was how the terrestrial ancestors of whales and dolphins had felt when they left the land all those millions of years ago to return to their mother the sea. And Alec believed he could sense the salt from those long-ago seas in his blood, coursing through his veins, celebrating the consanguinity of life.

Jellyfish, tiny and diaphanous, undulated past the large Plexiglas viewing port of Alec's observation cabin. *So small,* Alec's thoughts whispered, *and yet Earth belongs to them as much as it belongs to me.*

Behind the tiny blobs floated a single huge moon jelly, motionless, as if suspended in a spell.

Alec's submersible dropped still deeper.

A churning cloud of sardines—as large as the *Dīpukujira Maru*—rolled past the bathyscaphe, the hundreds of thousands of tiny silvery fish within sparkling with mesmerizing beauty.

Then, suddenly, a school of large-eyed Japanese horse mackerel, gleaming yellow, flashed before Alec's view, heading toward the surface, a loggerhead sea turtle following them up.

Diving deeper and faster than Alec's craft, big eighty-pound Japanese amberjacks torpedoed past the *Dīpukujira Maru,* vanishing into the deepening blue water of Suruga Bay.

All around Alec there was now a treasure trove of fish, and it would be this way until he reached the depth of 660 feet, for ninety percent of the life in the sea lived between the surface and that depth.

At 656 feet, Alec was treated to a scattering of Sakura shrimp, and he felt a painful longing in his heart. For *sakura ebi* translated to "cherry-blossom shrimp," named so because of their translucent pink color. Alec could not help but see cherry blossoms in his mind, and Irene. *No,* he told himself. *That's not meant to be. We missed each other in time... One can let things go in life. People come and go. And you know what, life goes on.* But this was not truly his own voice speaking to him...

Alec increased the rate of his descent; he would drop down deeper today than he had ever gone before.

800 feet. The *Dīpukujira Maru* passed the maximum dive depth of most nuclear submarines.

1,044 feet: the deepest depth recorded by a scuba diver. Alec was now in the kraken's world. Alec thought of how amazing it was that a human skin diver had reached this depth, as the pressure here would crack the hull of all but deep-sea submersibles—and nuclear attack submarines. He found himself deeply appreciating the marvel of living tissue, in that it was mostly water and thus almost incompressible. It was only man's air-filled lungs that prevented him from going still deeper. Fish, without lungs, experienced no difficulty with the tremendous pressure of the deep.

At 1,962 feet Alec slowed his descent, startled, his eyes filling with awe. Circling his bathyscaphe was a magnificent sperm whale, holding its monstrous head pointed down, its body nearly vertical in the water. Closer and closer the great whale maneuvered itself to the *Dīpukujira Maru,* looking in at Alec.

Alec felt a shiver of amazement run through him as he sensed the mind behind that great eye that stared in at him. In that eye Alec saw intellect, and emotion. He saw a soul. And he felt a spiritual connection, he and this whale sharing a glimpse into one another this day, at this great lonely depth.

Alec knew that sperm whales dove this deep, even deeper, down to over 7,000 feet, but he had previously only encountered them near the surface. Here, in this whale's more private, silent world, in the depths of Suruga Bay, the experience was quite different.

Alec sat there awestruck, and he felt a reflective sadness creep over him when the magnificent aquatic lifeform finally swam off, its dusky gray body—spectacularly splotched and streaked by white—disappearing into the dark twilight water of the bay.

Alec increased the rate of his dive, determined to venture still deeper, to see what other wonders he might find.

The *Dīpukujira Maru* passed 2,000 feet in depth, and Alec thought of the giant Japanese spider crabs he had observed at this depth during his previous dive. Along with a Japanese pancake devilfish, and a horrid yellow goosefish. But last time he had descended to a sea bottom lying at this depth. This time he had his submersible positioned in the bay over an area where the bottom lay more than 8,000 feet beneath him.

Alec ran calculations in his head, figuring his rate of descent, taking into account distance and that his craft contained enough air for nine hours.

Jet propelled, a Japanese flying squid soared past Alec's viewing port. *You're a bit deeper than usual... So am I.*

And Alec thought of all the accounts of animals that had been found so far from their natural habitats. He thought of the bleached skeleton of that elephant found 16,000 feet up the slope of Mount Kilimanjaro, shy of the mountain's 19,340-foot summit.

Why did that elephant ascend so far up the Great White Mountain? Alec shrugged imperiously.

And why is this human today going to descend to the very bottom of this great blue bay? Because he is!

~17~

The *Dīpukujira Maru* rocked as it dropped through a strong undersea current.

At 3,280 feet in depth, the last trickle of sunlight winked out, leaving Alec in a midnight world lighted only by the bathyscaphe's huge incandescent and thallium iodide floodlights.

4,100 feet. Suruga Bay, the deepest bay in all Japan (and nearly the world's deepest) was, at its greatest depth, 8,202 feet. The *Dīpukujira Maru* was now halfway to its bottom. Men in bathyscaphes had ventured much deeper. Jacques Piccard and Lt. Don Walsh, in 1960, aboard the *Trieste*, had descended to the bottom of the Mariana Trench, reaching the depth of 35,800 feet. James Cameron in 2012 had descended to 35,756 feet in that same trench. But no manned submersible had yet ventured to the very bottom of Suruga Bay. For Alec, it would be like landing on the moon.

Alec sat up in surprise, treated to an exceptionally rare sight. Swimming before him was a deep-sea-dwelling frilled shark, nearly seven feet in length, its ferocious mouth containing over three hundred teeth, aligned in twenty-five rows. This species of shark had swum the seas of Earth eighty million years ago, and here one swam today, before Alec, virtually unchanged.

Tyrannosaurus rex, brontosaurus, and triceratops had all fallen into the dead cellar of time over sixty-five million years ago, but somehow this dinosaur-era shark had managed to go on, swimming millions and millions of years forward in time, into the age of man. And Alec thought about that immensity of time, finally shrugging in submission, unable to fathom such an expanse.

For a time there was nothing but darkness. Alec began to wonder if it would be like this for the rest of his journey to the bottom.

~18~

7,000 feet and still the view was but a curtain of blackness.

No... What's that? Alec noticed a simple, small glow out there in the dark.

He took the *Dīpukujira Marui* off course from its vertical drop, following the glow horizontally, thankful that his bathyscaphe was self-propelled.

As he neared the glow, he saw that it was not a single light but several small glowing objects.

Jellyfish? At this depth?

The mysterious jellyfish, lit by bioluminescence, were like nothing Alec had ever seen before, so eerie and dreamlike they were. Within the translucent bell of each jelly there were yellow egg-shaped objects, softly aglow. *Gonads?* Stretching down the sides of their bells ran bright red canals, likely part of their digestive system, Alec guessed. But most amazing was how each jelly traveled with its glowing purple-white tentacles hanging down, outstretched like fishing nets cast out to catch unsuspecting prey, deep under the sea. *They're fishing.*

So ethereal and otherworldly were these mute creatures, so alien to his human sensibilities, Alec could only conceive them as part of a dreamscape, not denizens of the real world.

And yet they were. Alec concluded that the jellies must have evolved long ago in the sunlit sea and over time come down here by preference from above.

Alec wished he could touch these dream jellies, pick one up, hold it, as he had the tiny flowers on that land-tied island, where he had accidentally found that cave and its Neolithic temple.

As he followed the jellies, observing them, like that afternoon of looking at flowers, Alec became aware of something: a much larger glow below him. Being so deeply attached to the Earth and to its life had once again led him someplace afield where fate had gifted to him a discovery. This time by just looking at jellies.

A thousand feet beneath him, resting on the sea floor, was what appeared to be a tremendous domed underwater city, aglow with light.

Alec felt his heart pound. *How can this be?*

He checked his sonar. Side-scan sonar would provide details of the ocean floor beneath him. It should confirm his sighting. It did not. The sonar showed only a flat, uniform sea bottom. *Is something wrong with the hydrophones? Unless... somehow, is it disguised from sonar? Purposely hidden? But how?*

No matter. There's nothing wrong with my eyes.

Alec sent the *Dīpukujira Marui* into a vertical descent once again, steering it toward the hidden, glowing city. As he did so, he thought of the mythical sunken Atlantis, and he laughed out loud. He then thought of Yamatai-koku, and he grew most serious.

~19~

8,000 feet: Alec sat astonished within his bathyscaphe, motionless, speechless, thoughtless, as the *Dīpukujira Marui* floated in place several hundred feet distant from the fantastic undersea city that serendipity had delivered him to.

Alec forced himself to think. He looked at the city carefully. Its huge semi-translucent dome—several miles in diameter—was like nothing Alec had ever imagined. He had always visualized submerged habitats as they appeared in the artwork of science fiction: capped by hemispherical geodesic domes composed of a rigid crisscrossing metal framework, filled in by innumerable sections of clear Plexiglas.

But this dome... It looked more like a soap bubble. It even wavered like a soap bubble, from time to time. It looked so beautiful, illusory. *Can it be a visible field of high energy? Somehow holding back the sea... The pressure on it must be... beyond tremendous. How can it last?*

Alec wished he could see through the bubble-dome more clearly. He could see some shapes within, but only as indistinct blurs. It was like gazing through a distant, wavering haze.

As Alec continued to stare, he noticed that the city was not resting flat upon the sea floor but elevated, lying upon a mound of earth that was approximately equal in area to the city above it. The city's protective bubble oddly covered this mound as well, right down to the sea's natural bottom.

The *Dīpukujira Marui* suddenly shook, and its power blinked out, its lights, engine, instruments—everything went dead.

"Oh..." Alec heard himself murmur as he came to realize that the abrupt loss of power must have been the result of an action taken by unknown others against his intrusion into their world. He had been noticed.

As Alec sat there, he began to feel rather odd, and he seemed to sense that he had a visitor, someone who was spying on him... and his thoughts. But he was quite alone in his bathyscaphe. There simply was not room for anyone else. Still, the feeling was quite pronounced and most unsettling. It was if something invisible were trespassing in his mind.

Slowly, Alec felt the imagined or sensed presence disappear, and his submersible jerked forward. Something unseen had grabbed ahold of the craft and was pulling it quite rapidly toward the undersea city, far faster than his vessel was capable of moving under its own power.

There seemed to be a cocoon of some invisible yet tangible force enveloping the entire *Dīpukujira Marui*. Alec surmised this because the water close to his viewing portal, the water in proximity to his craft, seemed completely undisturbed, yet the water fifteen or so feet ahead of the submersible... It seemed as if a space in the sea had somehow opened in front of the bathyscaphe and the craft was continually falling into it, a space that then closed behind the vessel.

Alec smiled in uneasy astonishment. He seemed to be traveling through some type of ever-opening and closing undersea passageway. He wondered if the force that was now pulling him forward was similar to the force that kept the entire bay from collapsing down upon the city he was approaching.

And Alec sat on edge, marveling at the seemingly magical powers on display. Such a command of science and technology seemed so very, very far into man's future, and yet here it was, mysteriously manifest at the bottom of Suruga Bay.

A fabulous blur appeared in front of the *Dīpukujira Marui,* and the craft, still traveling within its ever-changing tunnel, slipped into and through the city's protective bubble, and all became dark.

~20~

The darkness lifted.

From the viewing port of Alec's observation cabin, it appeared that his bathyscaphe was now floating down a sunlit... river?

Alec glanced at his depth gauge. *One and a half atmospheres.* He was barely beneath the surface but sinking fast. Immediately he started the boat's pumps, flushing the seawater out of the ballast tanks, allowing the gasoline in the floats the buoyancy required to lift the *Dīpukujira Maru* to the surface.

Out of the cabin and up the craft's vertical access tube Alec climbed, feverish with curiosity. As he felt the submersible break the surface, he pushed open the overhead hatch and with great vigor pulled himself up and outside, into what appeared to be daylight.

Immediately he leapt from the conning tower down to the vessel's fairwater deck, where he straightened himself to feel a soft spring breeze blow over him, carrying upon it all the floral fragrances of Japan in full bloom.

And Alec found himself smiling broadly as he viewed what lay before him, appreciating in his heart and soul that life was not about how many breaths one took, but about the moments that took one's breath away. He reminded himself to breathe.

For sprawled out for perhaps a dozen square miles was a magical landscape, suggestive of ancient Japan. So remote did it look in time, it appeared like something out of a fairy tale, completely anachronistic with the technology of the bubble that kept it all safe from the sea.

Village settlements dotted the land in the manner of a sedentary society based on the cultivation of rice. Men and women wearing simple pull-over dresses—worn by slipping the head through an opening in the center of a section of cloth— were working the fields and walking to and from primitive buildings composed of wood and stone, raised above the ground on posts, topped by thatched, flared roofs.

Everything in sight suggested a Bronze and Iron Age society, evocative of Japan's late Yayoi period, circa 300 AD, Alec estimated.

The kingdom of Yamatai-koku, Alec reflected, *according to Chinese records, existed in the late Yayoi period… Queen Himiko, if she truly existed, ruled for half a century, until her death in 248 AD… And from shortly afterward, no further mention of Yamatai-koku… As if it had simply vanished from the face of the Earth…*

Alec felt rather like a time traveler. But he was in the present. This was not the past.

He glanced overhead, at the technological marvel of the bubble looming so high above him. It was brightly yet softly aglow, providing this hidden land with artificial sunlight. *Do they have night too?*

Alec noticed that the *Dīpukujira Maru* was still moving, and against the current. Whatever force had brought Alec's bathyscaphe into this land continued to pull the craft along for a while longer and then, amazingly, docked it with precision alongside a long, planked wooden pier.

Also docked at this pier were several odd, small watercraft, constructed of a glittering transparent material and what looked like metal. Round like balls, disc-shaped, and thickly rimmed, the craft looked rather like rice-cooking pots. Alec received the distinct impression that these craft were submersibles, capable of containing two or three passengers. These strange vessels appeared very much the product of a far future technology… like the huge bubble-dome.

Patiently awaiting Alec on the riverbank was a Japanese woman dressed in refined silk clothing. *A woman of status,* Alec deduced. *They raise silkworms here, and weave.*

Alec climbed down his craft's aft ladder and stepped onto the dock. *Cedar*, he noticed.

But then all his focus fell upon the woman, whom he walked up to, somewhat cautiously. She had long, elegant black hair, which she wore in loops, the style of the late Yayoi period.

She smiled gently at Alec and her cheeks dimpled, and her eyes twinkled. Her apparent good nature immediately put Alec at ease.

She said something to Alec, but he could not understand her words. He guessed from the sound and the simple syllable structure that she was speaking to him in Old Japanese.

"I'm sorry," he offered in modern Japanese, "I don't understand."

She gracefully handed him a single long-stem flower she had been holding, and she motioned for him to take it, bring it to his nose, and smell its fragrance. Slightly amused, Alec smiled and did so.

Before he exhaled, he felt rather odd, as if he had been asleep and suddenly awakened. But there he still stood, on the same dock, beneath the same glowing dome. But something was now different. And he realized what it was when the woman spoke to him again.

"Welcome," she said, still in her ancient language, only Alec could now somehow understand her perfectly, "to Yamatai-koku. I am Iyo."

It took a while for Alec to gather his thoughts. When he did, he decided not to question what had just happened. Instead he asked her, in her language: "I am in Yamatai-koku?"

"Yes."

"But how can that be? How can Yamatai-koku still be? How can all of this be?"

Iyo offered a courteous but enigmatic smile. "Please follow me," she instructed him politely, and she walked off.

Alec followed after her. "And where are we going?"

"You will find our land," she responded graciously but without answering his question, "to be a land of beauty and symbols."

203

Now that Alec had had a few moments to recover from his amazement, he wondered if he had inhaled something microscopic that had somehow granted his brain this new linguistic ability. He preferred this explanation to a magic spell. *A drug? Nanobots?*

"You greeted me alone," Alec stated. "You're not frightened of me? A stranger. Coming to your land."

"Men of exalted character rise above the vices of the age in which they exist," she responded.

"You're complimenting me more than I deserve."

She stopped and smiled kindly.

"Thank you." Alec bowed to her, but then he forcefully yet carefully took her by the arm, stopping her from proceeding. "But please understand, Iyo, I have a hundred questions."

Alec noticed that she looked past him, behind him, to the river alongside which they had been walking. Alec turned about and saw young Yayoi men diving from small wooden rafts and surfacing with fish in their hands.

"While the fish sleep at midday," Iyo explained, "when it is the hottest, they are easy to catch."

Alec felt himself smile, appreciating the unexpected and unusual sight. The young Yayoi men eyed Alec curiously, but they kept their distance. It seemed to Alec as if they had been instructed not to interfere.

"Please, come," Iyo coaxed Alec to follow her again. "Enjoy the walk."

Alec considered it. "Yes… I believe I will," he conceded, reminding himself of his recent discoveries when picking flowers and following jellyfish. Reminding himself to always remain open and connected to the Earth, even when at the bottom of the sea.

Iyo led Alec away from the river, along a path that disappeared into thickets of beautiful bamboo, and Alec felt his heart connecting with her land. He thought of how it was impossible to imagine Japan without bamboo. For bamboo, so poetic, so utilitarian, could not even be severed from Japan in thought. And Yamatai-koku was a slice of Japan, from time past—if this really was the mystery-shrouded Yamatai-koku.

"*Take to kurēn,*" Alec said in modern Japanese, by habit, pointing out a white crane amongst the bamboo.

"Here in Yamatai-koku," Iyo said softly, elegantly, "the bamboo and the crane together symbolize long life, rectitude, and constancy."

"*Setsu ri ko seisu o miru,*" Alec added to her thought, in modern Japanese.

Iyo smiled as she waited for the translation.

"It's an old saying, about bamboo," Alec explained. "'When the snow falls, its virtue stands aloft.'"

"I do not remember snow," Iyo whispered as she pointed to several mandarin ducks. The plumage on the birds was striking.

"*Mandarin'ahiru,*" Alec whispered back, identifying the ducks in modern Japanese, continuing with what he had started, feeling how strongly it was connecting him more deeply to her land, to Yamatai-koku. For language was the strongest link to one's culture, and to Alec, Japanese was an imaginative, poetic representation of the thoughts and beliefs peculiar to Japan and the Japanese mind and heart.

"*Yanagi no ki to tsubame.*" Alec pointed to a supple willow tree, gracefully yielding to Nature, obedient to every breath of the wind, and to the docile swallow perched there.

"Consideration and patience," Iyo provided the symbolism of the scene.

They left the bamboo behind and continued deeper into the mysterious and mythical land that was Yamatai-koku, which unfolded before them in a magnificent kaleidoscope of colors and forms of beauty that charmed the mind and soul.

Yayoi boys were flying paper kites shaped like koi fish, colored red, white, and black, the wind above distending the paper, casting the illusion that the fish were unendingly trying to free themselves.

"Our symbol of perseverance," Iyo stated.

"Ours too," Alec replied, his velvety, resonate voice trickling out slowly, carrying upon it notes of suspicion. For the carp had not been bred for color in Japan until recently in history. Alec thought about those small, strange watercraft he had seen back at the dock. And he concluded that this hidden undersea kingdom apparently had contact with the world above—if not formally, then at a minimum it spied on Japan. Perhaps the Yayoi from time to time visited Japan and brought things they appreciated back to Yamatai-koku?

"Only the koi can scale the waterfall," Alec added as he eyed Iyo. "Where they can be caught by white clouds from heaven and transformed into dragons. Living thereafter in the region of happiness above."

He watched Iyo as she glanced upward and silently mouthed the word: *above.*

A breeze blew over the two of them, gently, and Alec found a soft storm of rose-like, fragrant petals snowing down upon them.

Sakura. He silently mouthed the word. Cherry blossoms. And Alec cleared his mind of all distractions and concentrated his whole being on the fragrance, attempting to listen to the scent. And he heard it tell him how, even though he was at the bottom of the sea, so very far away from Shimizu, Irene was still very much in his heart.

Iyo's words brought him back. "There is someone you miss?"

When he opened his eyes, he noticed the purplish clusters of wisteria hanging behind Iyo.

"*Fuji*," he said, the name of the flower in modern Japanese. And he turned about, looking to every horizon beneath the circular bubble-dome. There were no high mountains. There was no Fuji-no-Yama. No stupendous triumph of Nature, towering with a majestic glory over the land. His soul was connecting to Yamatai-koku, but could this small, mysterious land of beauty and symbols ever replace Japan in his heart? Perhaps. *Small is so very beautiful.*

Iyo offered Alec carnations she had just picked, to coax him along. He took them—how could he refuse the "little darling" of Japan's flora.

"*Hasu*," Alec said as he pointed out a lotus flower, rising from a lowly bed of mud yet untainted by the place that gave it birth.

"Yes," Iyo said. "That is you, the lotus. The heart that remains unspotted by the world, rising above the sordidness of life."

Alec felt himself bowing to her again. "You are too kind." And he thought of how the flower bloomed to live but a single day, so sensitive it was to Nature's breath. And again he thought of Irene—such an image of faultless perfection she seemed to him, in her pursuit of beauty through art.

Alec followed Iyo onward, feeling himself slipping into a trance, so connected did he feel himself becoming to the land. *What's next?*

"*Matsunoki to kurēn*," Alec said, indicating to Iyo a pine tree and a crane.

"Stability," Iyo replied, identifying the symbolism. "Faithfulness. And eternity."

Alec nodded. The pine lived for centuries, ever green, ever stable.

"*Ume no ki to naichingēru.*" Alec heard himself identify the plum tree in bloom, where a nightingale perched amongst its lovely, flaky double-white blossoms. The fresh and delicate fragrance gladdened Alec's heart. "The elder brother of the hundred flowers."

Iyo bowed to Alec in appreciation. "The harbinger of anticipated happiness," she said with a calm and gentle smile.

Alec smiled back, feeling that Iyo was as intoxicated by the beauty about them as he was, that they were sharing a special experience in the shortness that was life.

He touched a hand to a maple tree, and then to another, and another.

"The maple tree signifies longevity," Iyo remarked, still smiling.

The maple forest opened up to a hillside of chrysanthemums, yellow, white, purple, red.

"*Kiku*," Alec murmured, enchanted by the colors. "The emperor's flower."

"Happiness," Iyo stated of the flowers, "virtue, repose, longevity."

Alec stepped over to the stream at the foot of the hill. The water was crystal clear, although speckled with fallen chrysanthemum blossoms.

Iyo knelt, cupped water in her hands, and drank. "Those who drink of the stream," she said, "after chrysanthemum petals have fallen into it, receive the boon of long life."

Alec bowed to her, and to the chrysanthemums, and to the stream, and he knelt and drank from it as well.

"Come," Iyo said to him, offering her hand. "We're almost there."

Taking her hand, Alec walked with her along the stream toward a huge, unpainted *torii*—a Shinto gateway—made of beautifully grained wood, standing most stately, so well poised.

"The whispering voices of tradition," Alec observed. "Can you hear them?"

"We treasure them," she answered. "From here the sunshine lights our world."

"Oh?" Alec did not understand.

"Please wait here," Iyo instructed Alec. He remained in place and she stepped up to the gateway, where she proceeded to perform a heavenly, graceful, ritualistic dance.

Alec grew increasingly curious, as he soon had the distinct impression that she was not dancing for him, as he had first assumed, but to capture the attention of someone else…

Her dance went on and on. As it did, the more and more captivating it became. In his mind, Alec imagined hearing soft taiko drumming accompanying her movements, growing in sound and momentum. As she turned and spun, Alec almost felt as if he were becoming drunk on sake.

Then suddenly she stopped, and moving so lightly on her feet, she shuffled off to strike a nearby bell. There was coolness, and the sound of the bell, as it left the bell.

And Iyo knelt to face the torii from a distance, in loving, faithful obedience.

Alec found himself rising, as if on cue. Somehow, intuitively he knew he was now to pass through the gateway, alone. And he did so, his single forward step transitioning him, as if by magic, from the earthly world of Yamatai-koku to the beginning of a long and majestic hall that a mere moment ago had been completely invisible to his senses. *How limited is our perception…*

Alec shivered. Before him stood a pair of immense and imposing statues of Japan's most ancient mythological creatures: Fu dogs, *Kara-shishi*, Chinese lions, the guardians of Japanese temples and shrines, believed to possess the magical power to repel all evil.

"Watchdogs of the emperor..." Alec whispered, respectfully admiring the huge, lion-like heads and claws of the stone figures, appreciating the presence of the guardians. For the shishi dogs imparted to Alec an overwhelming feeling that he had just crossed over a threshold that left behind the mundane and offered him entry into the realm of something fantastic and sacred.

Alec focused ahead, and with trepidation he started down the palatial hall. At its end there were glossy, soft white steps of gypsum. Many, many steps, and Alec ascended them all.

At the top, there was a chamber encircled by a scintillating purple and white crystalline wall, streaked by tremendous translucent beams of selenite. The luster of the walls and floor was exceptionally lovely, instilling a sense of wonder and joy into Alec's heart.

In the center of the room, a mere dozen paces from Alec, was a simple throne of fine-grained alabaster, and seated upon this throne, looking at Alec, was something... ineffable.

At once, Alec knew that this being before him was he who made the sun shine on Yamatai-koku, he who caused the rain to fall on this hidden land, the wind to blow. From this being's still presence radiated power and sovereignty, mystery and omnipotence. It was something ancient and glorious. Alec sensed that it was thousands upon thousands of years old. Why he felt this he could not fathom.

Alec also sensed something utterly astounding, that this being was absolute goodness. It was wisdom, benevolence and mercy, tenderness and caring made manifest in the flesh. It would not tread upon the smallest flower. This was the highest type of… animal creature… imaginable.

To Alec it appeared fabulous, magical, mythical—and amphibious. Alec could picture it swimming with grace and ease amongst the fish of the sea, at any depth, and also walking silently, poetically, across meadows, alongside streams, amongst bamboo, fruit trees, and flowers.

"*Kirin*…" Alec heard himself murmur aloud, in sudden recognition. Could this be the fabled Japanese creature that was the incarnation of the five elements of which all things were once believed composed: earth, air, water, fire, and ether? Only *Tatsu*, the dragon, was more important to the Japanese.

Applying his logical mind, Alec knew that this being could not be an actual living mythological creature. *Is it an alien from a distant star?* he wondered. *Or could it have long ago arisen here, on Earth, in our own seas? Or on land, something that then returned to the sea? Is it just this one being? Or is there an entire race of them living down here, hidden away in the deep?*

"Man from the outside…" the being whispered in modern Japanese, its voice like the soft flapping of feathered wings of beauty. "You are the first from the outside. Come closer."

Alec walked up to the creature, timidly, deferentially, and bowed, feeling himself in the presence of a divine power.

As he rose, he felt his mind and thoughts intruded upon again, as they had been earlier aboard the *Dīpukujira Marui*. This time, however, he did not feel unsettled. Instead he welcomed the contact. It was slightly longer than previously, but without discomfort. When the contact was finally broken, Alec felt himself an open book to this mysterious being. He also oddly sensed that this second probing was necessary for this wondrous creature to confirm what it had gleaned from the first contact.

"Are you Kirin?" Alec asked reverently.

With immutable calm, the magnificent being just stared at Alec, in silence, deeply appreciating Alec, as a naturalist might appreciate encountering a handsome deer in the wild.

"Are you from… elsewhere?" Alec tried again.

"You are to go now," the being whispered, feathery.

"No…" The response was unacceptable to Alec. "Wait… Please, surely the explorer has earned the right to some knowledge about his discovery? How is it that Yamatai-koku is at the bottom of the sea? I must know…"

And Alec waited uneasily for a response to his plea.

After a moment, the being rose and lifted a benevolent and merciful hand, placing it tenderly upon Alec's forehead. Its touch felt warm and good, so very soothing.

Alec felt his eyes close, and in his mind's eye he saw a vision of *Wa*—ancient Japan—of many centuries ago. He saw the ancient island kingdom of Yamatai-koku in all its glory. The kingdom, ruled by the shaman-priestess Queen Himiko, late in the Yayoi period, had experienced contact made by young Kirin beings from the sea.

There was a gifting of advanced technology by these sea beings to the ruler of Yamatai-koku, enabling Queen Himiko to maintain peace in her kingdom by reigning with what presented to the Yayoi as powerful sorcery and magic.

After the passing of Himiko, in the time that came afterward, there was the abuse of the commanding technology gifted to Yamatai-koku, and horrible violence and death and war resulted.

A cataclysmic tsunami born from the sea rushed against ancient Wa, to punish and destroy Yamatai-koku. Kirin elders interceded and managed to save the best of Yamatai-koku and transplant it beneath the sea, where it would be forever hidden, protected, and cared for, a living reminder to the entire Kirin race of the mistake that had been made by their youth.

When the tsunami subsided from Wa, with its receding waters left all the Kirin, young and old, forever.

The vision ended, and Alec felt his eyes open to behold the Kirin elder seating itself, a sadness born from the past creeping across its countenance.

Like Atlantis of myth, Alec heard his own sad thoughts pronounce, *Yamatai-koku fell out of favor with the deities... Most of it washed away into the sea... And what was spared... was brought down to the bottom of Suruga Bay... An underwater terrarium.*

Alec felt his emotions and intellect tug at him.

To live under the sea... Isn't this what I always wanted? No... Not to be exiled to the sea floor, encased and closed off from the sea, but rather to be an aquanaut has been my dream, living amphibiously in the sunlit depths... Freely...

Alec suddenly had a terrible thought. "Can I still go now?" he asked, fearing that the price for knowing the secret of Yamatai-koku might be imprisonment at the bottom of the sea.

"I brought you into Yamatai-koku," whispered the Kirin elder enigmatically, "so that you can truly return."

"Oh?" Alec did not understand. "You trust me to keep your secret—why?"

"Because you will."

"You think that highly of me?"

"You are to go now."

Alec bowed, and when he lifted his eyes, the fabulous Kirin being was gone.

~21~

Alec followed Iyo in silence as she led him back across the beauty that was Yamatai-koku. With each step, despite his love for the surface world of Japan and his aquanaut preference as related to his visionary dreams, Alec felt his heart and mind aching at the thought of leaving such special loveliness and wonder. He began to question if he should have asked the Kirin elder for permission to stay, rather than the opposite.

"Are you happy, Iyo?" Alec asked her. "Here in Yamatai-koku."

"Very happy."

Alec nodded, and his uncertainty and aching increased as the day's end commenced. The tremendous bubble-dome so high above was darkening, simulating a sunset over the land, complete with the rising, growing light of a huge artificial full moon. Yamatai-koku shimmered resplendently in the sunset like a jewel, like a magical fairytale land of beauty and symbols and eternal spring.

It was across the rising moon that Alec saw the cuckoo bird fly. *Fujioki! Fujioki!* the bird cried out.

And Alec knew that he had to go home. He suddenly longed for it so deeply that he momentarily felt like sobbing.

"Even in Kyoto," Alec recited aloud the haiku of Bashō, "when I hear the cuckoo, I long for Kyoto..."

In that moment Alec fully appreciated how true it was, that anyone who hears the cuckoo will instantly think of his home and dear ones, and interpret in his heart the bird's call as "*Return.*"

"*Tsuki to hato,*" Alec stated aloud in modern Japanese—the cuckoo and the moon.

And an image of Mount Fuji flooded Alec's mind, the dreamy mountain looking godlike over Suruga Bay, its majestic, otherworldly white crown of snow towering so unbelievably high, up, up into the heavenly blue sky.

"Fuji-san..." Alec uttered, his velvety, resonate voice filled with reverence and longing.

The image of Fuji-no-Yama was then swept away by one even more breathtaking, a visage of Irene, her porcelain-white skin framed by her soft, pitch-black hair. Her light gray-green, pooling eyes, beneath eyelashes that went on forever, beckoned to him. He ached for the touch of her lips, which were so full, like a poppy in heavenly bloom. He longed for the sound of the lilting Viennese accent of her soft voice, which opened the doorway to her beauteous, artistic mind.

"Irene…" he whispered, wondering how he had ever for a single moment let her out of his thoughts, how he had ever tried to force her out of his heart.

"The cuckoo," Iyo said, her cheeks dimpling and her eyes twinkling, "symbolizes that which has gone before. It reminds us of what is most important."

Alec nodded.

"You will soon be back with the one you miss," she offered Alec.

Alec nodded again, but his smile did not last, not fully.

"Goodbye, Iyo." He bowed to his host.

"Goodbye," she reciprocated, bowing in return.

Alec ascended the aft ladder of the *Dīpukujira Marui*, climbed up to his craft's conning tower, took one last look at the beautiful and mysterious land of Yamatai-koku, winked at Iyo, and descended into his submersible.

~22~

The *Dīpukujira Marui* surfaced in Suruga Bay late at night.

Alec vigorously climbed out of the submersible's top hatch and dropped down onto the vessel's fairwater deck.

An unsettling fog had rolled into the bay. This was quite bad, for Alec's adventure, the prolonged time away, and the ascent had left the *Dīpukujira Marui* completely drained of power. Alec could not reach the shore without assistance, and he would have to be sighted visually to be found.

What to do… Alec considered the fact that even if his support ship had remained vigilant through the night, he had taken the bathyscaphe quite far off course. And the current… He was now drifting out to the open sea. And the great depth beneath him prevented any attempt at anchoring. And the fog could last for days…

"Well," Alec stated rather imperiously, with complete equanimity, "there's only one thing to do. Abandon ship."

After securing the conning tower hatch to keep the *Dīpukujira Marui* watertight, Alec put on a lifejacket, climbed over the safety lines of the vessel's life rail, and jumped into the sea.

The salt water stung his eyes as he surfaced, blinking. "I hope to see you again," he said to his bathyscaphe, which was drifting southeastwardly.

Looking at his compass, Alec turned himself in the direction of Shimizu Port and began to swim.

~23~

After a time, Alec stopped to rest, buoyed by his lifejacket. The fatigue in his arms and legs made him fully realize that he was not the young man he often felt himself to be. *What's a sixty-five-year-old man doing jumping into the sea in the dead of night? Am I that crazy?*

He began to swim again. As he did so, a very large red and brown and pale-yellow loggerhead sea turtle swam past him, heading landward. It was a beautiful specimen, very much like the turtle he had recently paid the boys of Shimizu Port to set free.

Alec reached out and gently but firmly took hold of the supracaudal end of the turtle's shell.

Alec was surprised that the turtle did not dive immediately but instead peacefully pulled him forward. *Is it the fog? The unusually calm flatness of the sea? The moonlight?*

~24~

Alec released his hold on the sea turtle as they entered the surf of the beach together, and they both crawled ashore in their own ways and for their own reasons, the turtle to lay her eggs, Alec to collapse in exhaustion and rest.

Alec could not help but smile broadly at the mysteries and coincidences that life offered. This was his beach, his family's private beach.

Despite his fatigue, he looked for Mount Fuji. Mist and drizzle. Fuji-san would be hidden all the coming day. Still, even the clouded sight was most delightful.

As Alec lay there recovering, he turned to simply watch the beauty of the loggerhead sea turtle digging her nest and laying her eggs. *This beach belongs more to her than it will ever belong to me...*

Alec then found himself reciting in his mind words of T. S. Eliot:

We shall not cease from exploration.
And the end of all our exploring
Will be to arrive where we started
And know the place for the first time.

And Alec fell asleep.

~25~

Alec awoke after dawn to a dream vision of pure loveliness, the porcelain-white face of Irene, staring down at him with such concern and confusion in her eyes.

"Irene," Alec heard himself say, his heart sent afloat by the sight of her.

"Alec?"

With her help, he sat up. "Yes? What is it?"

She reached into her purse, pulled something out, and held it before him.

When Alec looked into the hand mirror, he saw that he was a young man again.

For the longest moment he just sat there, as utterly confused as Irene. Then he remembered it, exactly as it had happened:

~ ~ ~

"The maple tree signifies longevity," Iyo remarked, smiling.

The maple forest opened up to a hillside of chrysanthemums, yellow, white, purple, red.

"*Kiku*," Alec murmured, enchanted by the colors. "The emperor's flower."

"Happiness," Iyo stated of the flowers, "virtue, repose, longevity."

Alec stepped over to the stream at the foot of the hill. The water was crystal clear, although speckled with fallen chrysanthemum blossoms.

Iyo knelt, cupped water in her hands, and drank. "Those who drink of the stream," she said, "after chrysanthemum petals have fallen into it, receive the boon of long life."

Alec bowed to her, and to the chrysanthemums, and to the stream, and he knelt and drank from it as well.

~ ~ ~

"Oh…" Alec heard himself murmur. He then recalled in his mind the whispering, feathery voice of the Kirin elder:

"I brought you into Yamatai-koku so that you can truly return."

And Alec rose, lifting Irene to her feet with him, feeling even more full of vitality than usual.

"Yes, Irene, it's really me," he said. "I've returned from the depths of the sea… so that I can truly be with you." And with heartfelt joy, he bowed toward Suruga Bay, in respectful gratitude for the precious gift that had been bestowed upon him.

Time had been reversed for him, at least for a little while, and this would allow him to truly love once again, as well as time to catch up with all his ambitions.

Alec bowed to the sea once again.

Domo arigatou gozaimasu, Kōtei Kirin.

Acknowledgements and Identifying Notations

• This author drew upon what he has learned about Japan, its history, and culture, partly from the Japanese television program *Begin Japanology*, hosted by Peter Barakan.

• This author drew upon the public-domain work *Mythological Japan or The Symbolisms of Mythology in Relation to Japanese Art*, by Alexander F. Otto and Theodore S. Holbrook, with illustrations drawn in Japan by native artists. Publisher: Philadelphia, Drexel Biddle. Copyright 1902 Alexander F. Otto and Theodore S. Holbrook, and Anthony J. Drexel Biddle.

• Certain poems by the thirteenth-century Persian poet Rumi were drawn upon for this story.

• The sperm whale encounter presented in "Down, Down, Down" was based on a real-life encounter between a sperm whale and the ROV *Hercules* at 1,962 feet below the Gulf of Mexico off the coast of Louisiana in 2015. Encounters between sperm whales and ROVs are incredibly rare.

• It was Jacques Cousteau who discovered an archeological site when once picking flowers on a small island across from the ancient harbor at Knossos, Crete. Cousteau described this experience in a 1976 interview at NASA Headquarters.

• When the protagonist of "Down, Down, Down" advocates the study of the oceans over the study of outer space, some of the protagonist's wording was based on similar yet different comments made by Jacques Cousteau during his 1976 interview at NASA Headquarters.

• It was also Jacques Cousteau who once witnessed divers catching fish by hand at midday, at Cam Ranh Bay in Indochina. (Cousteau described this during his November 1991 interview with the *UNESCO Courier* magazine.)

- Mist and drizzle
  Fuji will be hidden all day—
  How delightful!
  — Bashō
- "The most beautiful things in the world cannot be seen or even touched, but must be felt in the heart."—Helen Keller
- It was assumed by this author that the protagonist of the story was intimately familiar with the writings of marine biologist N. J. Berrill.
- The character Irene in the story states: "I was married. He was an absolute monarch. I was like a doll. I was like a thing, some object of art, which had to be guarded, imprisoned, having no mind, no life of my own. I couldn't go on living like that. And you?"

This was based on a comment once made by screen actress Hedy Lamarr.

- The deep-sea jellyfish the protagonist encounters that lead him to the undersea city were based on the 2016 discovery of jellyfish floating 2.3 miles beneath the surface in the Mariana Trench.
- *Domo arigatou gozaimasu* is a Japanese expression used when one thanks someone for something that has been done to one.
- *Kōtei* is the Japanese title used for non-Japanese foreign emperors.
- The protagonist offering speculations on what if flying fish did not have the respiratory limitations of being water breathers was drawn from the thoughts expressed by ethologist Jonathan Balcombe in his 2016 book titled *What a Fish Knows.*
- Japan's Yamatai-koku remains a mystery to historians and archeologists to this day. As a result, it has been dubbed by some "Japan's Atlantis."

• When the protagonist of "Down, Down, Down" defends science fiction as a presentiment of reality, this was based on Jacques Cousteau who, in 1963, introduced his vision of *Homo aquaticus* to the World Congress on Underwater Activities held in London. His prophecy did not meet unanimous approval. In fact, one official dismissed Cousteau's forecast as "science fiction." Cousteau's response to this was:

"What's wrong with science fiction as a presentiment of reality? Ever since Jules Verne, and lots of people before him, the informed human imagination has projected what is to come."

A Note from the Author

This author hopes the reader appreciated Alec's journey, so filled with perception and appreciation for the natural world and the many traditional things that are Japanese and contribute to defining and understanding Japan.

This author found it a delight to write this tale, which, although an original creative work, was inspired by and pays homage to the eighth-century Japanese folk story "Urashima Taro."

Please consider "Down, Down, Down" an extension of what this author began to imagine and explore in his earlier story, "Hollow Boat."

This author would like to end by thanking Yuri, who introduced to this author certain thoughts and poetry that in some form made it into this story.

Niko Zinovii
Santa Monica, California
19 December 2018

• Addendum: On April 28, 2019, Victor Vescovo, in a submersible named *The Limiting Factor*, set the newest world record for the deepest dive ever completed in the Pacific Ocean's Mariana Trench, diving to 35,853 feet.

Niko Zinovii

Dancing with Sirkka

~1~

John Corey, tall and lean, felt rather lighthearted as he followed the babbling glacial stream down the mountainside. The air about him was full with the scent of pine and beech, oak and fir—the trees composing the surrounding Alpine wilderness. He was so very far from his small hometown of Shenandoah, Pennsylvania, but the verdant forest cast a comforting spell over him, putting his heart and soul at ease. For whenever within the green world of nature, wherever it might be, John always felt that he had found sacred refuge.

A large single raindrop smacked off John's nose and he paused in his hike, touching the wetness that was left on him. He looked at the water sparkling on his fingertips, and he thought about water and how it was truly the magic of life. For the chemistry of life was an aquatic chemistry.

He glanced up at the vaporously thin cloud floating so high above to see it dissolve before his eyes, dissipating into nothingness, leaving behind only unfiltered sunlight. And as he stood there so relaxed, so comfortable, bathed so pleasantly in the gentle warmth of Earth's star, he felt the sunlight without the passage of time. He felt young and eternal, sensing only the present moment, having momentarily forgotten all the troubles of the past, all his concerns for the future.

Then slowly, his quietly intelligent brown eyes stirred and swelled with a sincerity that matched the air of solemn purpose that projected from his dignified and handsome countenance. For in his mind's eye he was recalling his first lecture taken at the University of Vienna a decade ago. His professor of biology had rather audaciously strode into the laboratory, pointed out the window at the rising sun and opened his lecture by proclaiming, "There is my god."

John nodded, slowly, silently, in acquiescence to the truth that he still recognized and appreciated in that statement, and to its further implications. It was that single statement that had so profoundly influenced his formal education. It was the reason he had left his study of evolutionary biology to earn his PhD in astrophysics, becoming a young solar astronomer.

Forever let there be the sun.

The sudden squawking honk of a distant wild goose pulled John's attention back to the mountainside, and he continued his hike with increased enthusiasm, for he suddenly found himself quite eager to reach his frogs.

~2~

John found it challenging to climb down to the small pool, but he managed to do so. There, well off the beaten trail, he found himself entering a hidden world, so much further was he absorbed by nature. The place seemed as alive with secrets as it was with the sounds of trickling water and croaking frogs.

The frogs seemed to be crying out in a celebratory chorus, shouting to the sky: *We're alive! We're alive! We're alive!* And yet, paradoxically, there was simultaneously a palpable, forlorn sadness in their voices, as if their song were nearing its end, forever.

John thought about that sadness. For it was the reason he was there, at that mountain pool, away from the observatory.

Frog species around the world were disappearing at an increasingly alarming rate. Amphibians had flourished for hundreds of millions of years. They had managed to survive the Cretaceous dinosaur extinction. Yet for some reason they were now in peril. Was it due to increased UV-B radiation from the sun? Pollution? *Can the world's frogs be saved?* John was studying this question, in his spare time. It seemed important to him.

John moved to a large, familiar flat stone, sat, removed his boots and socks, and eased his bare feet into the cool, refreshing pool, looking down through its translucent surface at the emerald submarining frogs within. He then took out his notepad and began counting frogs, diligently noting their sizes and number. Next he took the temperature of the water and a reading of UV-B radiation. But then a sad thought gave him pause.

Or… Have frogs simply had their day in the sun… And now suddenly it's all over for them…

And John struggled to make sense of it, of life. He looked to the beauty of the nearby wild edelweiss, Alpine roses, and heather and up at the greenery of Austria's Nockberge mountains that majestically surrounded him, amphitheater-like, seemingly placing him somewhere between heaven and Earth.

He then thought of the impermanence of all things within the immensity of time. Not time as is held in the minds of men but the time of glaciers, canyons, and drifting continents. The vast eons of time that thrust Mesozoic sea floors up into high mountain peaks to unveil fossilized shells for later mountaineers to contemplate.

"Why am I here?" John asked aloud to the cosmos as his mind went still deeper. "What is my place in the universe? What gives transient life meaning?"

Two trillion galaxies out there, he pondered. Two trillion. Two hundred billion stars in our galaxy alone… And probably over twenty billion Earth-like planets just here in our Milky Way. And everything a temporary phenomenon…

What framework of knowledge am I missing? To make sense of it all…

Think, John prompted himself. Consider what we know. John realized he could not turn to philosophy, for the humanities were still being taught almost as if Darwin had never existed. So instead he turned to nature, to science.

He gazed down into his pool. Water. *The magic of life…*

And he thought about the vast age of the planet Earth, 4.5 billion years, and how life had arisen on Earth so quickly once suitable conditions had appeared. *It must not be difficult for life to get started, from chemical reactions…*

John imagined Earth of 3.8 billion years ago, its vast early seas blanketed by floating single-celled aquatic life. *Simplicity…* Just single cells everywhere, floating and floating seemingly forever. So ineffable was that vastness of passing time, it must have so slowly and monotonously crept by hour after hour, day after day, year after year, eon after eon.

Until about 600 million years ago, during the late Proterozoic, when animals—multicellular life—finally arose, likely by blind chance. *Complexity…* It had taken over 3 billion years for multicellular life to come into being. *It must be so very difficult for life to evolve beyond the single cell…*

John considered how early single-celled life had produced and detected chemicals, bringing about coordination between individual cells; of how chemicals were later created to be perceived and responded to by other organisms—this sensing and signaling also occurring between cells within an organism, becoming the basis for the development of the nervous system and the evolution of the brain.

John thought of how this evolving life had somehow survived through the chilling of the planet, algal blooms that had sucked nearly all the oxygen from the early seas, and recurrent incidents of natural catastrophes—volcanic eruptions, surging global temperatures, oceans acidifying, and even a cataclysmic asteroid impact.

"And yet," John reasoned it out aloud, "despite suffering five mass extinction events, Earth has been a relatively stable world for nearly three point eight billion years… allowing life the time required to evolve greater complexity… thinking man being the rare end result of that rise of complexity. But if it is indeed so very difficult for multicellular life to arise… and if most planets do not experience the relative stability Earth has enjoyed… the probability is that we may very well be the only truly thinking life in the entire Milky Way. If so, meaning exists here on Earth only because it means something to us?"

So, infinitesimal man is at the heart of things after all? John laughed softly at the irony that he, a fellow astronomer over four hundred years after Galileo, would speculate such a reversal of man's place in the universe.

But such meaning doesn't imply purpose or provide a point to existence—especially one so ephemeral…

John then looked down at one of his frogs. Intellectually, he understood that 360 million years of evolutionary time separated him and that frog. That was how long ago they had shared a common ancestor. So incredibly distant was he from that frog, and yet so incalculably close was the commonality that they shared.

John glanced up at the sun and once again heard in his mind the words of his old professor, although dimly this time: "There is my god."

Sunlight... And I and this frog, both of us alive today... but both of us soon to be reduced to specks of dust under that sunlight? What is the point to existence?

John had come to this hidden mountain pool to study his frogs, but also for the solitude, to commune with nature pleasantly. He had not expected his thoughts to venture so deeply into the realm of true philosophy. Feeling intellectually overwhelmed, and suddenly quite alone, he decided to head back to the observatory early.

~3~

The Kanzelhöhe Observatory sat at an altitude of 5,000 feet, on the slope of the Gerlitzen mountainscape, on the southern border of Austria. The facility consisted of a main building and three observation towers, with an additional two towers at the summit of Gerlitzen. Affiliated with the Institute of Physics at the University of Graz, the station existed for solar and environmental research.

As John approached the observatory's main building, he thought about all the wondering eyes that had over time peered through the magic looking glasses within, gazing up through protective filters at the marvels of the sun. Eyes of men whose ancestors had, since the depths of prehistory, gazed up at the nighttime stars in awe, imagining, speculating, visualizing how those tiny points of light fit into their reality.

The stars must have felt like friends to those distant men, John thought reasoning that the stars' nightly, eternal presence must have offered a sense of security and reassuring comfort to early man, even though he could not comprehend the true nature of the lights.

And John smiled as he recalled a poem by the eleventh- and twelfth-century Persian astronomer and poet Omar Khayyam:

Dancing with Sirkka

"In secrecy, the Stars whispered to my heart:
'Why ascribe to us the decrees of Destiny?
If we were the masters of our movements,
We would free ourselves from our wanderings.'"

Never in their wildest imaginings could the forebearers of modern man have guessed the thermonuclear-fusion inner workings of the sun—to those ancestors the sun was simply another object in the sky, like a cloud. And stars predetermined events, and controlled men's destinies.

How man's increasing knowledge continually transforms his understanding and perception over time…

~4~

Nearing the observatory's main building, John paused by the grounds' old stone well to look down it. He wondered if there was water in the darkness below. If anything might be living down there, hidden away, existing in such silent, limited perception, beneath such a small circle of sky.

Entering Kanzelhöhe, John heard his footsteps echoing disturbingly loudly due to the emptiness of the facility. He walked past vacant rooms that had once housed mechanical, electrical, and electronic workshops; an optical laboratory, a precision mechanics studio, a lens-grinding shop; the facility's once extensive library and archive.

John felt how it was such a haunting and lonely thing to look upon abandoned works of men, and he shuddered. The observatory had not long ago possessed all the necessary well-equipped workshops to make it completely self-sufficient in terms of infrastructure. All maintenance, repairs, modifications, improvements, and developments of instruments had once been performed on site.

But the recent budgetary cuts by the government to science and research had been severe. It seemed that politicians believed

231

there was nothing new to learn about the sun, and so the Kanzelhöhe Observatory had been scheduled for closure—until the novel idea was put forth to rent out the space of its workshops and library and archives in order to cover the expenses of the facility's continued systematical observation of the sun, though at a greatly reduced capacity. And so Kanzelhöhe was stripped down and reduced to a skeleton station, a skeleton crew, but kept in operation.

That had been nine months ago. Only a handful of the empty rooms had since been rented, and only at reduced rates, and unexpectedly only by artists, musicians, and the like. Apparently the seclusion and acoustics offered by the scientific facility were attractive to those in the arts.

As John thought about the surprise of who had ended up leasing the space, he slowly nodded his head in respectful acceptance of the unexpectedness that was continually offered by life.

He then focused on retrieving his notes, for with such favorable weather he would be driving up to the summit today, to carry out solar corona observations from the second observation tower atop Gerlitzen, which was equipped with the necessary instruments for such chromospheric study.

~5~

John gathered together the many pages of neatly handwritten equations lying atop his desk and placed them into a folder. Certain that he had all he would need, he left his claustrophobic, windowless office and descended back to the station's ground floor.

He nodded hello to a bespectacled middle-aged man who passed him at the foot of the stairs. *The sculptor?* John wondered, curiously eying the man's self-satisfied smile and rather bohemian choice of clothing. *No, I think one of the painters…*

John glanced left to right as he passed door after door, most of the rooms still empty, only a few having been transformed into art and music studios—most of them dark inside, their doors closed, but not all.

The double doors to what had once been the library were open. Standing there in the dim light of the entrance was a woman John had not seen before. She was facing away from him. John noticed this at once as the cream-colored leotard that she wore nicely displayed the perfect posture of her naked back. Over the tight-fitting garment, tied about her slender waist, was a floaty wrap skirt, which covered her hips and derrière while accentuating her shapely legs, which were adorned with thigh-high leg warmers. Completing her outfit were the quietly elegant slippers of an accomplished ballerina. Even though she stood motionless, John perceived a captivating inert grace and liquid sensuality to her lithe figure.

Overcome by curiosity, John walked up to the woman and stood beside her to join her in looking into the room. He was quite taken by surprise as she turned to him, into the light, revealing herself to be much older than he had initially thought. Her hair was silvery grey, her sculpted features tender and elegant, echoing a past beauty that had somehow transformed over time into a magical, casually battered, untended attractiveness, her face and eyes still exuding traces of a glamorous, erotic past sensuality, but now dominated by a dignified loveliness and a mesmerizing, alluring mystique. She had grown gracefully into her later years without worrying about aging, moving through life with grit and acceptance, the embodiment of an exotic, sophisticated woman of the world— her countenance loudly projecting that her life had been a journey of one resilient woman through time, that she had been through it all and was still here.

"I'm sixty-two," she responded to John's inquisitive stare, in a sultry Swedish accent.

"No, um," John stumbled, taken off guard by her directness, still under the spell of her unexpected mature, mysterious, and attractively charming air. "I was, um, wondering what you were looking at."

She smiled and the world lit up. "The canvases."

John looked into the room for the first time. It was full of paintings, having been transformed into an artist's studio. There was an elderly man, an artist, in the far corner of the room, painting.

The woman pointed to the older paintings directly before her and John. "I was thinking about how the playwright Lillian Hellman once described pentimento."

"Pentimento?"

"Old paint on a canvas," she explained, smiling easily, gracefully. "As it ages, it sometimes becomes transparent. When this happens it's possible, in some paintings, to see the original lines: a tree will show through a woman's dress, a child makes way for a dog, a large boat is no longer on an open sea. It's called pentimento because the painter 'repented,' he changed his mind."

John studied her in silent appreciation as he perceived her mind going deeper.

"The old conception being replaced by a later choice, it's a way of seeing and then seeing again, don't you think? The paint has *aged*… it's interesting to see what was there once… what is there now. Like in life. What was there for me once? What's there for me now?"

And she turned back to John, focusing fully on him. "My father was a publisher of books on art, my mother a painter. I'm irresistibly drawn to paintings, to art. You're the other astronomer?"

John nodded, quite taken by the unexpected quality of his interaction with her so far.

"So what does an astronomer think of when he looks at a painting?" she asked him maturely, with genuine interest.

John considered the question. "I think of the Pleistocene, of Ice Age art, of how prehistoric man became an artist, painting on cave walls while glaciers advanced and retreated. Of how the ancestors of those Paleolithic artists would later use their minds and talents to rediscover, measure, and study those forgotten ice ages, and even examine the distant stars sprinkled out there across the mindless, dark glitter of our galaxy, and beyond.

"I think of the illusion of permanence, cast by the art on those walls of Lascaux, the painted reindeer, the bison, calling out to us from such a depth of human time. And I can't help but think of infant, transient man, and how he has changed as Earth has aged. How it's interesting to see what was once there, what is here now. How it's interesting to wonder what was there for us once, compared to what's here for us now."

The silence between them, after John thoughtfully returned her words to her, was so very magical it became deafening.

"And I'll stop there." John forced a smile, suddenly feeling somewhat uncomfortable under the silent, inquisitive stare of this mature woman, of having intimately opened his mind, intellectually, to this stranger so nakedly.

"My name is Sirkka," she introduced herself, eyeing him with unusual appreciation. "Sirkka Torsten."

"John Corey," he reciprocated, shaking her offered hand, which felt so very soft and warm and pleasing. Surprised by the pleasantness of her touch, and by the fact that she continued to hold his hand, he gently, politely pulled away.

"You're a ballerina?" he asked, finding his eyes drawn down to her slippered feet, which were attractively slender, tapered, and with beautiful naturally high arches.

"My feet were once legendary," she confessed in a halcyon tone. "But at the Paris Opera Ballet, retirement is mandatory for women at the age of forty-two. Skimming jetés, high leaps, balancing on pointe, pirouetting—a dancer needs a certain muscular power, a certain flexibility in the hips and ankles.

"We're all conditioned to accept that when we reach a certain point in life, we're entering old age. And it's frightening for a woman, because you get put aside, even sexually, so you feel weaker.

"So I defied them all. I danced elsewhere. Everywhere I could. I kept my ballerina body until fifty-four, by willpower, six-hour workouts. I kept up, refusing to crash. But eventually I was finally forced to retire. Ballet has a brutal youth obsession.

"But three years after retiring I started dancing again, by myself, for myself. It was like coming back to life after having been far away, somewhere else. I came to realize that of course the beauty of youth is amazing and wonderful, but there is beauty in life, beauty in being a human being; there's a beauty in just following joy."

"So you're here"—John found himself appreciating her thoughts, her trying to make sense of life—"following joy?"

"I never wanted to make money with ballet," she answered openly. "I only wanted to be wonderful. And I was. I still am, even when now dancing alone. There's a greater depth to my dancing now. It's like in life, you can always take in another person more deeply when you're existing on your own two feet. Like a very fulfilling sexual relationship, because you're very much existing on your own and yet you're totally able to enjoy and take in what the other person offers. It's strange and mysterious."

John nodded.

"Mysterious like you," she added.

"Like me?" John heard himself react pleasantly, although he found himself once again a bit uncomfortable, even intimidated by her directness, her maturity, although unusually stimulated by her thoughts, her mystique.

"Tall, dark, and handsome," she explained, looking up to his height of six foot three. "And more... There's an unusual intelligence, a quiet dignity to you. Virtue, conviction, inner strength, thoughtfulness, you wear them all on your sleeve, John."

"Thank you..." John responded softly, humbly, shyly, unaccustomed to such compliments, to such directness.

It was then that their eyes met and fell into deeper contact. And as John momentarily lost himself in her eyes, he found that her age dissolved and he suddenly perceived before himself only an interesting, attractive woman. In reaction, he found himself at once, by unthinking reflex, reminding himself of her age, sixty-two, and of his own age, twenty-nine, and of the great gulf of time separating them.

"It was nice meeting you, Sirkka," he heard himself say, serious, restrained. "But I have to go now, drive up to the summit. Document chromospheric observations."

"I enjoyed talking with you, John," she responded sincerely, leaning back relaxed, retreating into the dimness, where the echoes of her past Garboesque beauty called out to him.

Oddly, John found himself hesitating to leave.

Sirkka gracefully pointed in the direction of the summit of Gerlitzen. "The stars await you, John."

John nodded, smiled politely, and walked off, feeling a bit bewildered, as if he had just had a life-changing experience. Only he did not understand what it was.

~6~

John completed the last of his solar corona observations before sunset, as was necessary. As he gathered together his work materials, he found himself wondering about other solar phenomena, namely sunspots, which were presently few in number, the sun at the solar minimum of its cycle. If these black spots were really the surface of the sun made visible by the star's magnetic field welling up to the photosphere, why then were sunspots dark instead of bright? If heat were truly escaping from within? And the sun's corona is millions of degrees hotter than its photosphere. *This all points to the energy source of the sun as being external…*

Could the sun somehow be powered externally and not by nuclear fusion—or by both? Could certain changes in the sun be explained by an external, galactic… electrical supply?

"That's nonsense," John lectured himself aloud. "Flies in the face of everything we know."

Or think we know…

And John recalled something attributed to the brilliant scientist J. B. S. Haldane:

"The universe is not only queerer than we suppose, but queerer than we can suppose."

The thought focused John to consider that science had its built-in self-correcting mechanism for a reason: it allowed man's understanding to change, to correct itself over time. The concept of continental drift, proposed by geophysicist Alfred Wegener in 1912, had initially been dismissed and ridiculed by the entire scientific establishment, as at that time there was no known mechanism that could explain wandering continents. The idea had to wait decades for the explanatory and validating theory of plate tectonics. Then man's perception of the world suddenly changed—continents did move, sea floors spread and contracted.

Can we be wrong about the sun?

John smiled as he recalled the ancient Greek Herodotus and how the historian had answered the question of why the Nile flooded annually. It had previously been proposed by others that the Nile flooded because of melting snow or receding winds.

Herodotus had offered something quite different: that the normal state of the Nile was a flooded state. And that in the winter the sun in the sky was blown by the wind to the north, where it evaporated water, reducing the naturally flooded condition that would prevail in the summer when the sun was positioned differently in the sky and the Nile was in its normal state.

Herodotus had believed that the sun was an object in the sky like a cloud, and that it could be moved by the winds. He was absolutely certain of it.

Herodotus's explanation had been widely accepted at the time, for it fit the perception shared by his contemporaries. Yet Herodotus had been absolutely wrong. The sun was not what he had thought. The Nile had in fact flooded in the past due to seasonal rains and melting snow in the Ethiopian Highlands.

Can modern man be under as gross a misunderstanding about the sun?

John shook his weary head, realizing that perhaps his wild speculations about sunspots were due entirely to a tired mind. To spend the day studiously observing the sun while simultaneously continuing to ponder on man's place in the scheme of things proved mentally fatiguing. *Tiny, tiny man, less than a speck on a speck, and yet he might very well be the counterweight to the vast and empty infinitude of outer space? Solely because meaning holds some importance to him? But life without purpose…*

Floating in from the past, the astronomer poet Omar Khayyam visited John's mind again:

"After you and I fall behind the veil,

Oh, the long, long while the world will last.

And what of our coming and leaving?

A pebble cast into the sea."

And John decided to let it go, at least for today. It was time to leave. Besides, although the naturalist within him enjoyed the contemplative solitude offered to an astronomer, by the end of the day, he did find the loneliness that descended from the weight of that great dim dome above him growing rather disturbing.

So John left the tower, needing to assuage his loneliness. He wondered if Sirkka might still be at the observatory.

~7~

It was dark by the time John returned to the Kanzelhöhe Observatory, the sun having set. As John entered the facility, he found himself pleasantly surprised to hear classical ballet music coming from somewhere down the long, dark hall of the building's ground floor.

As he passed what had been the library, he saw that its doors were now closed, the art studio within dark. He remembered how slender and attractive Sirkka had first appeared to him, before she had moved into the light and her true age had been revealed. Still, he found himself hunting down the source of the music.

Ah, the old optical laboratory.

John stepped into the room's open doorway. The laboratory had been transformed into a ballet studio, complete with balancing rails, mirrors, and wall-to-wall vinyl slip-resistant flooring.

Sirkka was within, alone, dancing gracefully to the music.

So intent was she on her movements she did not notice John. Slowly, quietly, John leaned into the doorframe, making himself comfortable as he watched on in silence.

He found himself amazed at how light-footed Sirkka's jumping appeared—it almost seemed as if she were defying gravity. And her stepping was so elegantly elaborate. As were her pirouetting turns on one leg, rotating, rotating, and then dancing away on the tips of her fully extended feet—weightless, eminently graceful. It was magical to watch.

Sirkka danced on to the music as if in a trance, bending a knee outward while holding her torso upright, her head, shoulders, and hips so beautifully aligned. Next came a long horizontal jump: a leaping off one leg and landing on the other. Then more lissome jumps, but landing on both feet. Eye catching, quick pivots—so agile, so nimble. *Incredible.*

The music intensified, and her arms began to move smoothly, flowing effortlessly into different positions, her wrists and hands showing incredible elegance and beauty of form, mirroring the changing tempo of the music. John found it hypnotic to watch.

Suddenly Sirkka supplely bent forward at the waist, and then backward, before returning to the center. Raising and holding one leg out horizontally behind herself, she fluidly turned and turned, finishing with her legs rotating outward, her petite, willowy body radiating strength, poise, and dignity.

It was then that she noticed John and her eyes lit up.

"John!" She sprang toward him, lively, her toes flexed, dancing to him on the tips of her feet, fully playing out the visage of an iconic ballerina, her body completely supported, seemingly weightless, defying gravity. She laughed as she agilely stopped right in front of him, extraordinarily light in her movements.

"Wow," was all John could think of saying. It seemed right, so he said it again. "Wow."

"Dance with me." She smiled, allowing her head to unconsciously fall back, in a take-me-I'm-yours manner. Vibrant, fully alive, she took and placed his folder on the floor and pulled him several steps into her world.

"But…"

"Your shoes," she said, stopping abruptly, kneeling to pull down on his heels, assisting him in stepping onto the vinyl floor in his stockinged feet.

"But… I've never danced before."

She went to change the music, selecting something slow. Romantic.

"John," she said as she returned to him smiling, aglow, her untended mature beauty shining, "when is the last time you did something for the first time?"

Before he could answer, she placed her body against his, positioning one of his hands around her small waist, holding and raising his other in a waltz fashion. And she began to move him, dancing slowly, rhythmically turning the two of them leisurely around and around as they moved across the floor. John eyed her slippered feet shyly, uncomfortably doing his best to mirror her movements.

"No, John," she said softly, fully embracing the music. "Don't look, feel. Feel the music. Let yourself go, completely. Just enjoy the immediate experience, the moment, the beauty of life."

She closed her eyes as she danced him. "Forget all the hauntings of yesterday… Let go all your worries of today and tomorrow… And dance."

Instead, John found himself taking advantage of the opportunity offered by her closed eyes, and he secretly looked at her closely, examining her carefully. There was a slight tightening around her eyes, around her mouth, due to her pleasant smile. Elsewhere, fine lines of worry crisscrossed those born of joy; the story of her life was there to read. She was significantly older than he. Yet close up, her time-dimmed glamor and sensuality still shone through, casting forth an exotic attractiveness. Experience danced delightfully on her lips.

As they moved rhythmically, turning and turning, John noticed the sudden lovely contraction of her brows, as if passing thoughts were delightfully floating through her mind. And suddenly it was as if the world were turning instead of them, and John slowly closed his own eyes. In the darkness there was only the music, and he felt himself relax.

"That's it," he heard her whisper in her deeply accented voice. "That's it."

Eventually, he felt himself turning again, with Sirkka, to the music, which went on and on, beautifully. Finally, when it ended, he opened his eyes to find himself in the middle of the room, holding the retired, mesmerizing ballerina closely, looking down into her soft, come-to-bed eyes. As they gazed into each other, John felt something very pleasing sweep him away, and he sensed his soul hearing something from her soul. He felt the experience utterly confusing. It had never occurred to him, not ever, that he might—or even could—find a woman twice his age so... alluring.

"Ms. Torsten?" a voice interrupted their moment. It was a young girl, in her late teens, dressed similarly to Sirkka.

"Oh," Sirkka explained, "John, it's a student of mine. I give private lessons in the evenings."

"Oh." John nodded. "Lessons. Right. Well, I'll get my shoes, my folder, stop in my office. Thank you... for the lesson..."

John smiled politely and walked off in a bit of a daze. He now understood what had earlier escaped him. But he did not know what to make of it.

~8~

John spent the next several days engaged in early-morning hikes up to his mountain pool to visit his frogs and later, prolonged observations of the sun due to an unprecedented absence of sunspot activity. The energy output of the sun had diminished; ultraviolet radiation had decreased rather dramatically. Sol was acting oddly and John wanted to understand why. But whenever he attempted to apply analysis to his observations, he found images of the ballerina Sirkka dancing into and haunting his mind.

In response, John found himself renting the small lens-grinding shop directly across the hall from Sirkka's ballet studio. After taking a drive out to Graz to purchase a number of acrylic fish tanks, filters, air pumps, hoses, and other assorted equipment, he spent the next two days transforming the small room into an aquatic lab, complete with an assortment of frogs collected from the Nockberge mountains.

And then one evening John encountered Sirkka again, bumping into her in the hall between her studio and his lab.

Like his first encounter with the retired ballerina, John enjoyed the immediate pleasantness of their interaction, especially the underlying stimulation that was present due to the chemistry that existed between them.

He gave Sirkka a tour of his new lab, introducing her to how he was attempting to use science to save the world's frogs. Describing how amphibians were a keystone species to many ecosystems, without which the environment would change dramatically, driving other species into extinction.

"In many ecosystems," he revealed to her, "the population of amphibians actually outweighs all the other animal inhabitants combined."

John was surprised and impressed at how she actually listened with genuine interest to his science talk. Later, when she offered him additional complimentary dance lessons, he found that he could not refuse.

And so, over the days that followed, John allowed himself to fall into a pleasant routine of visiting and dancing with Sirkka at the end of the day, after the sun had set, after her other private lessons were finished. Each evening he found himself satisfyingly surprised at how much he was enjoying the lessons, dancing with her, being with her, in the privacy of that studio. He often stayed with her late into the night talking over tea.

"I keep a secret in myself," Sirkka confessed to John over late-night tea, "something that doesn't really exist. Is it good or bad, I don't know."

"I imagine it depends on what the secret is," John replied with a curious smile, focusing on her.

Sirkka smiled back but then grew serious. "When I was a young girl, my parents took me to Thailand. When there, I witnessed a young elephant being tamed for domestication. They called it elephant crushing. It was the saddest thing I've ever seen.

"The elephant was forced into a tight cage and tied with ropes so that it couldn't move. The men then barked commands at the young elephant—that it didn't understand—beating the animal with sticks and chains, stabbing nails into its ears and feet. They let the elephant go hungry, thirsty, refusing it sleep. It's how they crush the spirit of an elephant—break its will. To make it submissive to its masters."

John felt the remembered sadness in her heart as he watched her pause to wipe away a tear, after which she forced half a smile, resiliently.

"I was horrified," she went on. "So I invented in my mind an imaginary country, one with a constitution that forbade the enslavement of elephants. It was the only thing I could do. But then my country grew with me as I grew. And now it has a way of life, a population, and difficulties. I don't talk about my country but it's absolutely real to me. It has no geographic position, I know, but when anything happens in the real world my first reaction is, how are we going to react to that?"

"Are you the queen of this country?" John smiled, appreciating her mind, her imagination.

"No, I'm not, I'm sure it's a democracy. But for some extraordinary reason I'm always elected."

And they laughed together.

"More tea, John?" she asked him pleasantly.

"No, I don't think so. I was thinking about another dance?"

"To this music?"

He nodded. And they rose, embraced, and began to dance, slowly, focused on one another, surrendering to the moment.

The secret turning in them soon seemed to John to be the force making the very galaxy turn. He felt his mind unaware of his feet, his feet of his mind. Neither cared. He only kept turning, with Sirkka.

Sirkka parted from John and circled him, around and around, her movements silently whispering *I circle you.*

She circled him like a helpless, fragile planet in love with its star, the planet the lover of its sun. So elegantly did she orbit John that he forgot to breathe. When he finally did, his breath of air said *now*, and she rejoined him, surrendering completely to his embrace.

It was then that Sirkka looked so deeply into his eyes that John felt himself gently pull away, uncomfortable, ending the dance.

"Forgive me," she said almost with shyness, a wonderful dignity emanating from her countenance. "It's been years since I've given away sexual love with my eyes. I didn't mean to make you feel uncomfortable."

And she went to turn off the music.

John found himself walking up behind her, pursuing her by impulse, although he knew not what to say or do.

As she bent forward to switch off the recording, her floaty wrap skirt lifted above her hips and derrière and John felt a completely unexpected primal sexual urge rush through him with an almost unbearable power, commanding him to take her from behind. He was absolutely shocked by the corporal authority of the sensation. His mind reeled. Intellectually, a flash of insight informed him that the neocortex did not really control the deeper and older limbic and reptilian evolutionary layers of the human mind, of the tri-union brain, but was there instead to satisfy the base needs of that deeper anatomy. It was why he had rented the former lens-grinding shop: to be near her. Surely he must have realized that their dancing and interacting would lead to this moment?

But his mind was only vaguely listening to his intellect, so equally surprised was he that the barrier of physical age between them was apparently unrecognized by his body. He wanted her. Badly. *It's all in my mind? This barrier of age? Some gross misunderstanding imposed on me by social norms? By societal inculcation?*

Sirkka turned about to face him. And around them was born a great, waiting silence.

John stood there motionless, his will in abeyance to the deafening stillness, his heart and mind and soul feeling the tug of that great moment, the power it held over him. It was hypnotic.

In that silence he felt that if he knew Sirkka's touch, if he met her in that particular second, it would be then that he would truly be born a man, and she a woman. Yet he simultaneously felt terribly confused.

But… John's mind desperately struggled to make sense of the situation. *She's too old. I'm too young. Imagine the two of us out together in Villach or Graz or anywhere—the stares we'd draw. We missed each other in time. It's as simple as that. This is pleasant, but…*

It was Sirkka who finally ended the mounting tension, with a gentle and honest smile. "I feel I should hold on to you, John. That if I don't, you'll vanish. And I don't want that to happen. I'd like very much to remain your friend."

John was unsure how to respond.

"I'll see you again?" she asked. "To continue our lessons."

"Yes." John nodded, uncertain. "To continue our lessons… Goodnight, Sirkka."

"Goodnight, John…"

~9~

The next day John drove out to Graz to purchase a few additional items for his aquatic laboratory. The sheer act of driving felt good to him as it allowed his mind to temporarily disconnect, granting him reprieve from his troubled thoughts.

By the time he reached Graz, however, he found himself thinking of that first day he had seen Sirkka, in her cream leotard, her naked back exposed to him, standing there in the shadows appearing so slim and shapely, wearing those elegant ballet slippers.

He then saw her in his mind's eye as she really was: older, silver-haired, mature… but with a mesmerizing presence, still sensual—her eyes so full of life, her lips so inviting.

He wondered what it would have been like to meet a young Sirkka Torsten, to encounter Sirkka at his own age. In his mind he wished away time and its effects and he imagined himself and Sirkka dancing together, face to face, turning and turning, both of them at his age now. Slowly, he came to realize that in his fantasy he had fallen so completely into the depths of her eyes, into her soul, that twenty-nine or sixty-two, it was the same to him. And he felt quite confused again.

As John slowly came out of his imaginings, he found himself walking into the aquarium supply store that was his destination. It was there, past the empty tanks, pumps, and hoses, lost amongst all the splendidly colorful living tropical fish, that John experienced his mind wandering off once more, this time thinking again about the rise of life on Earth.

He thought for a second time about the origin of single-celled life, multicellular life, and how it had taken 3.8 billion years for civilization to appear on Earth. And how it had only appeared because Earth had experienced such a rare, unbroken line of life that was granted the time to evolve toward complexity for almost one-third the age of the universe.

John asked himself how many other Earth-like planets might be stable for life for nearly four billion years. *Perhaps one in the entire Milky Way?*

If so, Earth would indeed be the only place with clever, technology-generating intelligence in this entire empty galaxy. Meaning would indeed exist only here, only on Earth, only because it means something to us.

John nodded soberly to himself, finally convinced of his conclusion.

We're a local, temporary phenomenon. Highly unusual. A very, very rare configuration of atoms... A finite organism, with a brief existence, like my frogs, like these tropical fish... Yet we really seem to be it in the Milky Way. The only island of meaning in the galaxy.

And John shrugged as he surrendered to his mind delving still deeper, musing philosophically.

Our thoughts exist only within us and will only exist for such an infinitesimally short period of time... We need to take responsibility for everything we do and think...

And he thought again of Sirkka. Of the age displayed on her face. The fact that she had to age irritated him. *Isn't a brief, pointless existence enough to bear? Must we age too?*

John stood there still, for a long silent moment, composing himself. It was so very rare for him to ever experience such negative emotions. He normally existed in a state of enthralled fascination with life and the cosmos.

Nothing, John concluded, *is quite so disruptive to oneself as the discovery of an overpowering attraction to someone one can't have...*

And John dimly recalled the words of poet and playwright Oscar Wilde:

"The only way to get rid of a temptation is to yield to it. Resist it, and your soul grows sick with longing for the things it has forbidden to itself, with desire for what its monstrous laws have made monstrous and unlawful."

Will aging one day be cured?

John nodded to himself, feeling certain that the biological sciences would eventually unlock the secrets of life and stop physical aging, even reverse it, in essence gifting the world agelessness. In the future people would still die of diseases, accidents, but they would not age.

A man might approach a woman on the street and neither would be capable of determining their respective ages, both having the appearance and vigor of youth. The man might only be in his late twenties, like himself, while the woman might be well over a hundred, or even two hundred years old, by the calendar.

In such an ageless world, such a young man might become the lover of someone who was older than his great-grandmother.

And it would not matter. They would differ vastly in terms of the extent of their life experiences, accumulated knowledge, wisdom, but in the final analysis they would simply be viewed by society as two consenting, ageless adults.

But this future world did not yet exist. And John believed that it would not likely come to be in his lifetime.

~10~

John continued his duties at the Kanzelhöhe Observatory, diligently documenting his chromospheric studies of the sun, intensely probing the mystery of the complete absence of sunspots. But he was careful to leave the observatory each evening in a manner that allowed him to depart unnoticed. He needed time alone, to think about existence, the universe... and the unexpected ballerina who had tiptoed into his life.

But then, finally, after many evenings had gone by, John, alone in the second observation tower high atop Gerlitzen, feeling the weight of the loneliness that descended from that great dome above, heard in his mind Sirkka's pleasantly accented voice:

"I came to realize that of course the beauty of youth is amazing and wonderful, but there is beauty in life, beauty in being a human being; there's a beauty in just following joy."

And he longed to feel joy. He longed to be in the company of the mesmerizing speaker of those insightful words.

It was those remembered words that exerted their alluring power over him and tipped the scale. He could no longer deny his longings. It would be like trying to stop the dawn from coming. He only wanted to be close to her, breathing the same air. And so he went to her.

~11~

The lights were off in the ballet studio across from John's aquatic laboratory. No Sirkka. All was dark.

John stood there silently for several moments and then entered his lab. He had not been in there long—he had just lifted the cover off the main tank—when he noticed that the light was now on across the hall. But all was still silent; there was no sound of music.

He crossed the corridor and stepped into the dance studio's open doorway. Sirkka was seated within, on the floor, in a classic lotus yoga posture. She looked up at him, her casually battered, untended attractiveness aglow. Her eyes exuding echoes of her glamorous past, her lips revealing an erotic sensuality that magically still lingered on.

"It's been three weeks, John."

"Meditating?" he asked cautiously, motioning to her legs, which were folded inward like the petals of a flower.

"Looking for the real me inside the center of me," she answered with a dignified loveliness. "It seems I have to really look to see the original lines on the old canvas that I've become."

"Pentimento?" John asked.

"Pentimento." She nodded. "Life is a search, I think. In my youth I wanted to taste all life's pleasures. I still do. Dostoevsky once said that everyone must grow in his own crooked way. I'm contemplating what I need to shed. Do you have compassion for people growing in their own crooked way?"

John did not fully understand.

"Why are you here, John?" she asked.

"When I'm with you"—John struggled with it—"we stay up all night, talking. When I'm not with you, I can't sleep."

Sirkka rose and walked over to him, standing before him so delicately, looking up into his sensitive eyes.

"I feel like an empty wine glass," he went on. "You dance inside my chest, where no one sees you... But I do."

And John fell silent for the longest moment, just looking at Sirkka, entranced by her alluring mystique. He wanted to hold her close, so that they could cry out together with loving.

"I tried to keep quiet," he continued. "But I couldn't. I had to come see you."

It was then that John learned that the words of a thousand poets could not touch the heart like a single tear wept by a woman.

"Never try to understand," Sirkka whispered as the teardrop slowly rolled down her cheek, "what those lost inside love will do next."

John felt as if the sound of drums suddenly rose upon the air, but it was the throbbing of his own heart. A voice inside the beating said to him: *This is the way. In her beauty make poems. In her light learn how to love.*

But then his intellect gained sway, and he heard himself saying ever so gently: "But... the difference in our ages..." And he felt his heart ache with each word he uttered.

"There's a poem..." Sirkka responded hesitantly, reciting it almost shyly: "Never ignore a person who cares for you, who loves you, who misses you. Because one day you may wake up to realize you lost the moon while counting the stars."

And John heard the voice of Oscar Wilde again, this time the poet's words crying out so loudly in his mind:

"Live! Live the wonderful life that is in you! Let nothing be lost upon you! Be always searching for new sensations. Be afraid of nothing."

But he was afraid, afraid of social standards, of hurting Sirkka, of hurting himself. The great difference in their ages had consequences that he could not ignore. *In ten years, when she's in her seventies, will I still find her attractive? Or see her as an old woman? And then what?*

253

Despite his apprehensions, John found himself taking Sirkka's hand and silently leading her outdoors, into the evening sunset. As they walked, he sensed the generosity of her heart, and of his own. And he asked himself why he should be so responsible, so unselfish to refuse to give such joy to himself. If he denied himself, he would suffer. If he allowed himself, he would still suffer. Whether it lasted for a day or a year or her lifetime, in the end he could not keep her. No one can hold on to anything forever. No amount of pretending could ever alter that stark reality.

"I feel as if we've been walking in the surf," John confessed to her, unable to contain himself any longer. "Holding up our pant legs not to get wet. When we should be diving under, naked, deeper and deeper…"

It was at that moment that something extraordinary happened. The entire world suddenly went black, pitch black. The darkest, most unnatural black John had ever experienced— the sky above immediately filling with stars twinkling brilliantly in the blackness.

What just happened? How can this be?

John then felt a sudden foretelling chill fill the air and he saw the lighted full moon, in the east, go dark and disappear.

Oh…

He searched the night sky for Mars. He found it, bright and red.

"One thousand one, one thousand two, one thousand three," he started and continued counting aloud.

"What is it?" Sirkka asked, frightened. "What's happened?"

John motioned for her to be patient. When his counting neared 180 seconds, the equivalent of three minutes, he saw the light of Mars go out and the red planet disappear within the blackness of space. This could only mean one thing.

'The sun has gone out," John uttered, astonished.

It was the only reasonable conclusion he could draw. The sunlight brightening the moon had gone out a moment after darkness fell upon Earth. Mars, 30 million miles distant from Earth, suffered the same effect three minutes later—light from the sun traveling at 186,000 miles per second. But he had to be absolutely certain.

"Jupiter," he whispered, and he searched the night sky. He found the planet easily; it was bright white and an obvious sight to a trained astronomer.

"John?" Sirkka prompted.

John nodded to himself, looking at his lighted wristwatch. "We have an hour. We have to wait an hour. To know for sure."

And he explained to her that the sunlight that had stopped shining on Earth, and on the moon, and then on Mars, would stop shining on Jupiter in slightly under an hour, if the sun had truly gone out. It would take that long for the final photons of light sent from the sun to reach distant Jupiter.

John felt Sirkka hold him closely. "How could this happen?" she asked in a tone so close to a whisper he barely heard her.

"I don't know." He shrugged, hearing a rising trembling in his own voice. This was a danger that was supposed to be five billion years into the future. Yet it seemed to be happening now. *The missing sunspots?*

Suddenly the mountain's different birds began to cry out for the absent sun to shine. Their cries were the saddest, most evocative sounds John had ever heard. It was as if the sun were their lost lover and they were pleading with all their hearts for it to return. Their star's offered light of life had vanished too quickly…

And the words of John's old university professor crept through his mind. *There is my god.*

"There must be things about the sun and stars that we simply don't understand…" John concluded aloud. *We've been wrong, like Herodotus… The sun's not like a cloud, but neither is it what we think it is…*

John felt the sudden chill growing and he heard more birds crying out, as if announcing the end of the world.

So, we've had our day in the sun? And now suddenly it's all over for us?

He responded to the gravity of the situation by unexpectedly quoting aloud Omar Khayyam, slightly modifying the verse:

"It was a drop of water merged with the sea,
It was a speck of dust, united with the earth,
What about our entering and leaving this world?
A butterfly appeared and disappeared."

He then turned to Sirkka and focused completely on her, appreciating her more fully than ever before.

"What will happen, John?" she asked him. "If the sun has gone out."

John thought about it, calling upon what he knew. "Without sunlight," he reasoned it out, "photosynthesis will stop completely. Oxygen will soon no longer be produced."

And John shivered, suddenly feeling for the first time in his life the panic of being a completely helpless, mortal human being. For Sirkka's sake he tried to calm himself, although he could do so only to a degree.

"The temperature will continue to drop," he went on, "as Earth's surface cools. Falling maybe to… thirty degrees Fahrenheit, over the next twenty-four hours… Plants and microorganisms will begin to die.

"In a week… the global temperature will likely drop to zero. Earth's molten core, its internal geothermal energy, will prevent the planet's surface from freezing over, but the surface of the oceans will begin to turn to ice. Most plants will have died by this time, due to the cold, the complete absence of sunlight. Among animals, herbivores will die first..."

It took a great effort of will and concentration for John to go on, but he did. He needed to know what was to come. He was looking at a situation never before faced by any men of any earlier time.

"In a month... the temperature might drop as low as perhaps minus twenty. Ice will cover most of the world... Conifers might still be alive, some bacteria... But all other plants and cyanobacteria will be dead. Some life might survive near geothermal springs, or deep in the ocean, where geothermal activity keeps the sea warm. But there will be continuing global mass extinctions at a level never before seen. All of Earth will be dying..."

John needed to pause yet again to gather himself. The prophetic glimpse of the coming apocalyptic end of the world was draining the life out of him.

"In a year... world temperature might be as low as minus forty... Earth will be completely covered by ice... The only life left will be deep in the sea. Maybe some clever humans might survive, fighting a freezing battle in areas of geothermal activity, like in Iceland... But Earth will continue cooling... In a thousand years the surface temperature will eventually fall close to absolute zero, minus two hundred seventy-three point fifteen degrees Fahrenheit, and life everywhere will be impossible..."

"And we won't know for certain for an hour?" came Sirkka's numb response.

John nodded. He then looked to the western horizon, to where the lightless, now invisible setting sun must have still sat in the black sky. He imagined Sol in its former glory, as the tremendous roaring inferno that it had been until mere minutes ago. All seemed utterly lost. He and Sirkka would far too soon be reduced to specks of dust under dim starlight. *What was the point to existence?*

"John?" Sirkka pointed to something low on the ground moving toward them in the oddest manner.

John squinted in the blackness. It was not until he heard the croaking that he knew what it was. Frogs. His frogs. They had apparently escaped from the tank he had left uncovered, hopped out through his lab's open door, down the hall, and out of the observatory.

The frogs appeared to glance at John protestingly as they hopped past him, departing into the darkness.

What? Where are they going?

But then John realized that his frogs had no idea the sun had gone out. Nature was calling them, beckoning them back to their pleasant mountain stream, their hidden mountain pool. Through millions of years of evolution, the fight waged by their ancestors had gifted them a kind of raw courage, and a kind of purpose. To seize any moment offered, to live as if there were no tomorrow to entertain. It was the journey that was important.

Their escape would amount to nothing, their flight from captivity was hopeless, but they hopped on, thrilled by their freedom. Thrilled to simply be alive. *The happiness of a frog is to exist. For man, it is to know this, and to wonder at it.*

John smiled cathartically. Complexity had emerged naturally on Earth and would exist only for a brief period of time. *Our existence is necessarily finite, time limited. But we can think and feel and wonder and explore the universe.*

We're part of the universe, we've been gifted existence. And even if only for a short, temporary stretch of time, the fact that we exist at all is worth celebrating. We don't need anything else. We can think about the stars, is this not enough? Why devalue the remarkable. There isn't a point to our existence but it's worth celebrating!

"John?" Sirkka's voice interrupted his epiphany. "You're smiling…"

John nodded. "I know my place in the universe."

And he looked so lovingly into her eyes.

"John, I want to be your last of everything. Please hold me."

John embraced her, by habit placing an arm about her small waistline. And she smiled too, her eyes full of life despite the apocalyptic circumstance. She had, for the moment, all she desired.

"Shall we dance, John?" she laughed softly, nervously, allowing her head to characteristically fall back, in her take-me-I'm-yours manner.

And he took her, and they began to dance. They needed no music, only each other's eyes to become lost in. There was no longer any barrier of age. They were two ephemeral human beings dancing together under the stars, surrendering to the moment. Celebrating their existence.

They danced over to the grounds' old well, circling it as the moon does Earth. Wider and wider their circles grew, until they were back before the observatory. There, under the dim, high starlight, John paused to look upon Sirkka, to truly know the face that he so loved. As his eyes fell upon her, a single huge snowflake of exquisite crystalline perfection landed ever so gently upon her cheek, where it rested, melting so imperceptibly slowly. John thought about water, the magic of life, and of the beauty of life, the beauty in being a human being, the marvel of simply existing.

And he danced onward with Sirkka, until very miraculously he witnessed Mars reappearing in the heavens. And three minutes later the moon, its welcome brightness bathing them with reflected sunlight until the sky ignited and brightened, its billowing, heavenly clouds painted by the setting sun the most magnificent hues of red, pomegranate pink, and purple, as daylight suddenly lingered there on the horizon once more.

The sun, the heart of life, had somehow reignited. Its going out had been a temporary phenomenon, cause unknown.

Yes, there are things we still don't understand about the sun.

A celebratory chorus of birdsong rose, lovely dulcet notes aiming to the sky, singing to the sweet, beautiful sunlight: *We're alive! We're alive! We're alive!*

Life is to be lived and celebrated.

"Forever let there be the sun."

Recommendations

• *Loren Eiseley: Collected Essays on Evolution, Nature, and the Cosmos*, volumes one and two, edited by William Cronon, published 2016 by the Library of America, distributed by Penguin Random House, Inc.

Acknowledgements and Identifying Notations

• Sirkka dancing at a mature age was based on Italian prima ballerina assoluta Alessandra Ferri. Mrs. Ferri had temporarily retired in 2007, at the age of forty-four, before returning from retirement to dance in 2013. At her present age of fifty-four, Mrs. Ferri continues to dance. Certain comments made by Sirkka on ballet were drawn from a 2019 interview with Mrs. Ferri.

• Certain statements made by Sirkka about life were based on comments made by actress Viveca Lindfors, in an interview she once gave.

• Sirkka's talk of her imaginary country is based on a similar imagining as described by actor Peter Ustinov during an interview he once gave.

• When Sirkka quotes a poem without identifying the author:

"Never ignore a person who loves you, cares for you, misses you. Because one day, you might wake up from your sleep and realize that you lost the moon while counting the stars."—John O'Callaghan

• The author of "Dancing with Sirkka" believes the fictional character of Sirkka would have been intimately familiar with the description of pentimento given by playwright Lillian Hellman, given Sirkka's attraction to paintings, coupled with the influence her parents had on her, her father being a publisher of books on art, her mother a painter. This supposed familiarity was presented in Sirkka's dialogue.

• Certain poems by the thirteenth-century Persian poet Rumi were drawn upon for this story.

• The unmodified original version of Omar Khayyam:

"It was a drop of water merged with the sea,
It was a speck of dust, united with the earth,
What about your entering and leaving this world?
A fly appeared and disappeared."
In "Dancing with Sirkka," the protagonist, John, modified the last sentence to:
"A butterfly appeared and disappeared."
This author made this modification, changing "fly" to "butterfly," to reflect John's sense of optimism and his enthrallment with the beauty and fascination of life and the cosmos.

• John's thoughts on science-based philosophy were based on:
"Philosophy and the subjects known as 'humanities' are still taught almost as if Darwin had never lived."
The above sentence appears in Chapter One of *The Selfish Gene* by evolutionary biologist Richard Dawkins, a work that the author of "Dancing with Sirkka" believes the fictional protagonist John would have been intimately familiar with.

• Some of John's thoughts were based on:
"If you don't get what you want, you suffer; if you get what you don't want, you suffer; even when you get exactly what you want, you still suffer because you can't hold on to it forever."—Socrates

• One of the ending conclusions made by the protagonist was based on:
"The happiness of the bee and the dolphin is to exist. For man, it is to know that, and to wonder at it."—Jacques Cousteau

• "Dancing with Sirkka" presents certain philosophical conclusions by English physicist Brian Cox, as voiced during Dr. Cox's interviews on the *Joe Rogan Experience*, podcast episodes #610 and #1,233.

• The sun going out in this story is purely imaginative, based only loosely on the nonmainstream electronic sun theory that proposes that sunspots, flares, coronal heating, and coronal mass ejections are due to changes in the sun's galactic electrical supply. The contention is that the sun is powered externally and is not a fusion reactor. This author is not advocating this theory but rather utilizing it as a story-telling tool to make the point that science is self-correcting over time, always adjusting toward a more correct understanding of reality.

A Note from the Author

This author hopes the reader appreciated this story of love and a search for meaning, sprinkled with science. The story was written in homage to the late anthropologist, philosopher, and poet Loren Eiseley, celebrating and paying tribute to Eiseley's fictional and autobiographical writings. The story also presents and salutes certain philosophical conclusions by English physicist Brian Cox.

It may be interesting to note that the romance element of this story, "Dancing with Sirkka," is the mirror image of this author's previous story, "Down, Down, Down," in which the protagonist, Alec, was sixty-five and his love interest a woman in her early twenties. In this story it is John who is younger than Sirkka, John being twenty-nine, Sirkka sixty-two.

A small part of the inspiration for this story was the fact that Emmanuel Macron, when elected president of France in 2017, was thirty-nine years old while his wife was sixty-four.

This author long ago, as an undergraduate student, experienced his professor of botany one day entering the classroom, pointing out the window at the rising sun, and proclaiming, "There is my god."

This author would like to end by thanking his brother, Taylor, for providing the thought "Forever let there be the sun."

Niko Zinovii
Santa Monica, California
27 April 2019

Niko Zinovii

Ending Note from the Author

I hope readers enjoyed or appreciated these tales in some way. I wrote the stories employing informed imagination, philosophical thought, and a bit of daydreaming. I consider my writing to be nonstandard, sci-fi.

My personal favorites from this collection are:

"Down, Down, Down"
"The Butterfly Hunter and the King"
"To Rise Again"

In that order.

Niko Zinovii
Santa Monica, California
30 April 2019

niko@zinoviiartstudio.com

www.zinoviiartstudio.com